RAYMOND MITCHELL-HEGGS

A Peculiarly ENGLISH *Education*

A Peculiarly

ENGLISH

Education

MEREO
Cirencester

Published by Mereo

Mereo is an imprint of Memoirs Publishing

1A The Wool Market Cirencester Gloucestershire, GL7 2PR
info@memoirsbooks.co.uk   www.memoirspublishing.com

A peculiarly English education

ISBN: 978-1-86151-097-6

ONE

The winter of 1946/47 was proving to be particularly severe. Little joy prevailed anywhere in Britain as the New Year opened. London was still wrecked by the war, coal supplies were erratic and food rationing showed little sign of being relieved, even for the most basic of essentials. Monday, the first in January, was no exception; the day broke with snow still falling and a very cold north-east wind howling round the houses.

This particular Monday had a darker, more apocalyptic resonance, for this was the day the family had all been dreading and whose advent had hung like a dark cloud over the Christmas holidays. Now it had finally dawned, and no one was happy. This was the day when fate had decided that a small, rather nervous little boy was to go away for the first time in his life to embark on the long road to manhood; to be prised from the comfort of his mother's arms and thrust into the brutal, unknown world of a private boarding school miles from

London, set deep in the cold heart of one of the bleakest parts of the English countryside.

George Henry Hingham, just eight years old with blond curly hair, blue eyes and an open, rather innocent face, had been well looked after by his young and adoring mother, for he was her only child. He had been protected from the hardship, rigours and horrors of wartime London and had led a cosseted life, well fed and kept warm at all times. He was accordingly quite unprepared for any change in his daily schooling, particularly for becoming a boarder in a new establishment called Saint Eusebius Abbey. There, though he had not yet been told this, he would be trained in the art of leadership. He would acquire self-confidence and learn the art of survival. Little did he know, in his innocence, how long the journey was that lay ahead of him.

As the hour of departure drew near an air of nervous anticipation permeated the little house in Kensington as Henry's mother Veronica and her sister-in-law, his Aunt Elizabeth, worked one last time through the checklist of what was required of them by the school. Henry sat silently on his bed watching the two women as they carefully packed his trunk. It was new and shiny brown with the initials GHH boldly painted in black on the front, and had been delivered by Messrs Billings & Edmonds of Hanover Square the previous day. His mother, carefully following the instructions she had received from Miss Tremble, the Matron of St Eusebius, had placed clothes in neat little piles on the floor. There were socks, blue and grey, and shirts, uniforms, blue, five of each; shoes, smart shoes for class; football boots, soft shoes for gym, pyjamas, vests and underpants. A smart new blue blazer hung precariously from a door knob.

"We must ensure he's warm enough. It's dreadfully cold in the Fen country at this time of year" whispered Aunt Elizabeth as she squeezed in another vest. "The Llewellyn-Watson's little boy got pneumonia, I'm told."

The two women knelt on the floor, grabbing items as they worked down the list. They had had no say in where or how their children were to be educated. Such decisions were made strictly by the men of the family, based upon tradition and their own experience. Their choices were not to be challenged nor questioned, even in their absence. The requirements of the school, its rules and its regulations, were to be observed and obeyed to the letter.

"Ssh Elizabeth!" hissed Veronica, looking up with tear-filled eyes. "It's what his father always wanted, he and Gilbert." Gilbert was her husband's brother. "They revelled in their prep school days at Saint Eusebius and at Hawtreys in Kent but times have changed I fear, especially after the war."

"Rum lot of teachers too, from what I've heard" declared Aunt Elizabeth under her breath. "With the war over they say all sorts of riffraff and chancers are scrambling to get a job, no matter what or where it is."

"I'm told St Eusebius is still pretty sound," said Veronica, trying to be positive. "Lots of loyal old monks who know their business, get the boys into the right public schools and so on."

"New headmaster though! No one quite knows who he is, but they say he bought the school from old Taylor Bradfield, the ancient abbot who had been running the place for years. Most of the monks went off to war in 1939, or soon after. They kept the place running with walking wounded so to speak, but I expect they'll have had some of the old guard coming back, maybe new blood. Who knows? It'll be interesting to see. No perverts, no child molesters I hope!"

"The letter from the matron sounded nice enough" declared Veronica, endeavouring to inject a further note of optimism. "She said that despite rationing the school went out of its way to make sure all the boys were properly fed and well looked after. That's a comfort, after some of the stories I've heard."

"Hairbrush?" queried Aunt Elizabeth.

"I've already put one in."

"Toothbrush? Toothpaste?"

"I've put a brush in. The school's supposed to provide toothpaste and soap."

"Towels?"

"Oh my God. That's on the list. I'd quite forgotten." Veronica ran over to a cupboard and pulled one out.

"You'd better make that two. Most schools want two."

Henry watched nervously as the two women flitted round the room grabbing little things and items of clothing. Much as he adored his mother, he wished his father could have been available to see him off. He'd seen so little of his father during the war years and now he craved the confidence he always exuded; his calm, comforting voice, his tall figure, his neat moustache, his hair always neatly cut and parted slightly to one side. He knew his father was someone very senior in the army, a most distinguished soldier.

Quietly he clutched Royston, the new teddy bear which had replaced the one he had lost when the old house had been bombed. He had been given him by his mother for Christmas. "He will look after you, darling", she had said as they snuggled up in bed to open their Christmas presents. Now the Christmas decorations had gone and everyone was depressed. Everyone that is apart from Mr Binks, the cat, who sat at his customary place on the kitchen window, cleaning his whiskers, one eye fixed on the refrigerator door. In front of the house an elderly driver, called to take them to the station, was sitting in his taxi smoking a pipe and reading the *Daily Herald*.

Veronica, who was still only in her late twenties, did not share the enthusiasm of the male members of her husband's family for sending Henry away to be educated. She harboured deep fears that neither of them had any idea what their former so called 'glorious' school might be like now, especially in the aftermath of war. This winter was turning out to be particularly cold; it did not augur well for life out in some remote part of the Fen country.

Bags were finally packed just before eleven and the sad trio boarded the taxi for the journey to the station. They did not allow much time for traffic and on arrival went to the wrong platform, where the train had been incorrectly shown. Veronica, clutching her son's little hand, scuttled round the station concourse, followed by Aunt Elizabeth and a burly porter who humped along the trunk.

The train was late starting and when at last it slowly pulled out, filthy carriages were enveloped in clouds of escaping steam. Through the window Henry waved sadly as he watched his mother run alongside, tears rolling down her cheeks, giving him a final farewell. The train entered a long tunnel, and all was smoke and darkness.

* * * * *

Slightly over one hundred and ten miles north of London, Charles William Upton was also making his way to Saint Eusebius Abbey. Aged just twenty-four, he was single and had recently been discharged from his compulsory military service. He too was nervous, but for very different reasons. He had decided to try his hand at teaching geography and maths, subjects in which he himself had done quite well as a boy. He had never taught anyone before. Upton's ulterior motive, the real purpose that had attracted him to this vocation, was that he would be guaranteed to have a roof over his head, be given meals three times a day and a fair amount of leave during which he might be able to supplement his income.

He was not alone among the many young men endeavouring to capture such a lifestyle in England in 1947. There was still considerable unemployment, so he was grateful to have landed the job, despite the unspoken misgivings of the agents, Messrs Margolis & Tring, through whom the advertisement had been placed. They did not appear enthusiastic about Saint Eusebius, for some unknown reason, but, after his acceptance of the offer the school had made him through them, they had passed on the relevant contract and letters of engagement for him to sign.

The terms and conditions sounded innocuous enough, though the wearing of a monk's habit at all times, even while supervising sports, seemed to him to be rather ridiculous. There was a sizeable compendium about the holy figure after whom the school had been named, a man of whom Upton had never heard but about whom he was expected to know in detail. He was required to attend chapel twice a day, three times on Sundays, which he thought might be something of a challenge, particularly as he was not of any religious persuasion.

Margolis & Tring had in fact sent him details of a number of teaching opportunities in preparatory schools in East Kent, Sussex and the Home counties. All, they had trilled, were near to London and within easy access of centres of culture and learning. The message coming through was that whatever else was wrong about the school, St Eusebius was a very long way away from anywhere, there was little to do and only someone seeking isolation or active participation in a religious retreat would find the work attractive.

The former was, in fact, precisely why the job appealed. Upton was in something of a mess, emotionally at any rate, though he was reluctant to admit it. His father had been killed on active service, his mother had been the victim of bombing, which had left her mentally damaged, and his sisters had emigrated as soon as they had been able to with assisted passages, one to Canada, the other to Australia. He had no family to speak of and few friends. He was suffering a period of anguish and going through considerable self doubt as to his sexuality; in particular he was not sure how he felt about a man called Lance Corporal Jack Parker, of the Royal Corps of Signals, with whom he had had a brief sexual relationship when they had served together during the war. Parker, now a political activist, had pestered him for cash and sexual favours for which he had neither money nor appetite, and Upton was keen to be as far away from him as possible. With only his loopy mother left in the country, he had taken great care to ensure that no one should discover where he was.

A bitter wind howled along the platform as he disembarked from the main line train at Peterborough to await the cross-country service that would take him to somewhere called Horkinge over on the east coast. Upton sought warmth in the waiting room, but it was just as cold in there, since the fire had long gone out for lack of coal. Sitting down on a hard wooden bench, he opened an envelope which had come to him via his bank. It was the revised terms of his employment, sent to him by a Miss Tremble, secretary and assistant to the headmaster, Abbot Primus. He would be known, it declared, as Brother Upton. First names or Christian names were not to be used. He would wear a monk's habit at all times and attend choir practice. He would abstain from alcohol and smoking and at no time was he permitted to touch the boys, nor show any affection or administer punishment by way of physical contact. The school pursued a policy of enlightened education, the directive continued, and he would be charged with the supervision of junior sports in addition to his teaching duties. A list of the ninety-seven boys beginning the Lent term was attached.

Delving further into the brown buff envelope from the agents, Upton discovered a small typed note on plain paper. It read:

An incident has been reported to us of a case of physical assault by a member of the staff of this school upon another member of staff. We understand that this person, the assaultee, has now left the employment of the school. We believe that legal action may have been initiated on the part of the assaultee against the Abbot and other members of the teaching staff.

Upton folded the note and put it with the other papers. The revised contract told him that he would be given a room in a house called Herga, which was in the grounds of the Abbey, for which he would be charged seventeen and sixpence a week plus a further deduction for food which was considerably more than this. He was allowed one day off after two months' work but was required to stay at the school during holidays, when he would help with the redecoration and maintenance of the grounds. He was allowed two weeks' leave, not to be taken under any circumstances during term time. As a junior master he would report to Brother Secundus, the under master, who was in turn backed by Brother Tertius. Other members of the teaching staff were Brothers Quartus, Campbell and Jenkins. He was expected to know the names of all the boys within two weeks of arrival.

Upton sighed and folded the papers back into the envelope. It was not exactly remunerative work and he probably wouldn't stay for long, though anonymity was what he wanted and here it seemed assured. The terms of employment were far inferior to those offered by the schools in the south of England, and he wondered what on earth had attracted the other masters to the school, why the senior ones all had funny Latin names, and what, if anything, lay behind this strange façade of a school, masquerading as a Catholic abbey while declaring itself Protestant in its literature. To a non believer it seemed a strange arrangement.

Upton cursed. The connecting train was now running late. He would not only miss supper on arrival but would forfeit his interview with the Abbot which had been scheduled for that afternoon. It was an inauspicious start.

TWO

Three hours and forty minutes out of London, Henry Hingham stared out of the dirty, grime-covered carriage window with wide, tearstained eyes. The journey seemed interminable. Endless vistas of bleak, featureless snow-covered fields rolled past the train. At some remote station they had all been forced to change, slithering on ice-covered platforms to another train. Two senior boys seemed to be in charge. All five new boys were crammed into one compartment. Now the second train, a decrepit affair and even less comfortable than the first, struggled to meet some long-abandoned timetable as it rattled and clanked its way slowly across the Fen country against the backdrop of a flat cold winter landscape. The bleak afternoon light was fading fast. Henry had never seen countryside like this, so charmless, so inhospitable, so sinister.

He shivered, and the cramps came back again inside his stomach. He had never spent much time outside London except during the worst periods of the war, and the countryside was an alien environment to him; he liked big red buses, traffic, fire engines, especially fire engines racing to a bomb site, but most of all home; cosy, with a coal fire, lots of toys and Mr Binks to keep him company. Miserably he reflected on what his uncles had always told him; that he would love Saint Eusebius. He harboured a sense of foreboding, a dark feeling he had never had before. He wondered if he would ever see his parents again. He tried to fight back tears, but the memory of his mother, waving sadly from the platform as the train pulled out, remained etched heavily on his mind.

Another new boy, someone called Larkin, stared expressionless at the floor of the carriage; three others, equally mute and lost in thought, shared the bench seat of the battered third-class carriage. Opposite sat five seniors, beefy, confident, fit and as restless as springer spaniels on a shoot. They pounded and punched each other, laughing, shouting, full of merriment. School clearly held no fear for them. Indeed it came across as glorious relief from the tedium of Christmas holidays. The boys were in their early teens and the Lent Term was to be their last at Saint Eusebius. They chatted excitedly, full of enthusiasm for the challenges ahead.

"Who do you think will get swished first?"

"Well it won't be Ward. He's much too clever."

The questioner was a thickset, muscular chap called

Williams-Jones; the respondent was a boy called Bentley.

"Harding! Money on Harding! He always gets swished."

One of the other boys, Finlay, joined in. "Mum saw my marks this hols. She was horrified. Dad said I probably deserved it." He stood up, grinning from ear to ear, and pulled down his shorts, revealing a white bottom on which a dozen or so dull brown marks bore testimony of his thrashing the previous term. The older boy seemed delighted with his wounds, veritable battle scars and proudly won. He turned to show everyone the dull brown lines that crisscrossed his buttocks. The others laughed. "You'll soon get new ones, Finlay, don't you worry! Once Secundus gets to work!"

The big boys laughed and began to argue among themselves as to who was most likely to be the first recipient of the headmaster's birch. Vigorous corporal punishment by way of both birch and cane seemed to be something of an obsession to them. They recalled past punishments much as peasants might have discussed public executions in mediaeval times. They also seemed obsessed about food, or rather the lack of it, at the school, and how and where extra supplies might be smuggled in.

One of the new boys, at the far end of the bench from Henry, summoned up enough courage to ask what "swishing" was. This provoked howls of mirth from the older boys.

"Swishing is when you are beaten by the Abbot, the headmaster, or by Brother Secundus. They whip you on your bare bottom with either a birch or a cane, depending upon their mood." The speaker was a portly fellow, with a round face and mischievous eyes. His name was Elmden.

"And what he thinks your punishment should be" added Bentley.

"Yes" continued Elmden, "if you don't sing properly in chapel or someone says you haven't tried hard enough at games you get three or four."

"But if you do something seriously bad…" interjected Williams-Jones.

"Like trying to run away!" said Bentley.

"Yes, like trying to run away, then you will get six at least, maybe eight or ten."

"Watkins got twelve once."

The others laughed. "Watkins made a smell while he was being swished. Primus went crazy, took it as a personal insult!"

"Is Primus the headmaster?" continued the inquisitive new boy.

"The Abbot calls himself Primus because it's Latin for first. The other teachers are called Secundus, Tertius and Quartus. It means second, third and fourth.

Secundus is really evil, he beats us all the time. You see Saint Eusebius, the patron saint of the school, was put to death in Rome in 385 AD by being flogged till he conked out. It's drummed into all of us that we may expect to be swished. We all scream. Sometimes it's very painful, it's really terrible."

"If you're not swished by the time you get to fourth form then there's something wrong with you. My father says it's called a rite of passage, whatever that means" added Bentley.

The engine belched smoke out across the brown and wintry landscape and let out a mournful whistle. They rattled over a level crossing and continued to clank over endless iron bridges above long, straight, dark canals.

"D'you think they'll have a new monk this term to replace the one who ran away last term?" The questioner was one of the seniors called Mowbray; he was tall and thin, with curly flaxen hair. "You've heard the rumour?"

The older boys huddled together.

"He was said to have done something rude to Rosie."

"Who? Everett?"

"Yes. Everett."

"She's got big ones. I saw my sister undressing once. Hers weren't nearly so big as Rosie's."

"Ward said his father does rude things to people like

Rosie in Ireland all the time. Ward says everyone is expected to do it."

"What? Even the monks?"

"They're mostly priests in Ireland. They're some of the busiest, Ward said."

Henry remained lost in thought. In his mind he could see his mother, still waving, with her handkerchief held to her face. He tightened his grip on Royston, his beloved bear. "Royston will keep you company, You look after him now" she had said as he opened the wrapping paper. He was a lovely teddy, soft and gentle.

The hug was noticed by one of the senior boys.

"Hey, you there, new boy. Teddies aren't allowed at school you know!" He leaned across the carriage and kicked at the bear. "Soft toys are girlish and wet. Matron will ensure he goes on the rubbish tip as soon as we arrive."

"We are sent to Saint Eusebius to become men!" added Bentley jovially. "To become leaders. He's right. Kite won't let you keep that stupid thing."

Williams-Jones joined in. "We are to become leaders of the British Empire and go out and live in strange parts of the world with all the natives. Being half starved and in constant pain, that's what we are to be prepared for. Well anyway that's what they keep telling us at school."

"Plenty of that at Saint Eusebius" enjoined Elmden. "Just you wait and see!"

Henry felt sick. He was horrified that this horrible boy had kicked his special teddy. It was an act of unwarranted aggression, an insult. Tears rolled down his cheeks as his mind raced, considering what he might do to get away from this dreadful fate. He had come too far now to ever think of running back to London, to his mother, to their warm home. They had passed through five long tunnels, crossed interminable bridges spanning dark and gloomy rivers. Running back up the railway line to London was no longer an option.

Maybe if his mother came to see him as she said she would, he could hide in her car and go back secretly with her to London? This thought cheered him a little.

The train rounded a bend, giving the boys their first brief glimpse of the sea, a cold, grey, menacing expanse. Surf was breaking on a vast and empty beach.

"Look, the sea!" cried Finlay. Do you think we'll be allowed to go and swim naked again like we did last summer?"

"Doubt it" sighed Bentley sadly. "Not if Primus and Secundus go on swishing everyone. Someone saw our bottoms and reported Primus to the authorities. My father said his aunt had sent him something from the *Horwich Herald* asking whether the school should be allowed to remain open. Typically Primus told them all a pack of lies, saying it was all to do with games, so we're still here."

"Bennett's planning to burn the school down. I saw him in the hols. He wants to make sure Kite gets burnt too."

"Terrific. How's he going to do it?"

"Didn't say, just said he was planning it. He was reading all about escaping from Colditz at the time."

The train began to slow, the brakes making a grinding, screeching noise. It crossed noisily over a pair of points before entering a small, sad, run-down little station. A signboard, with peeling paint, announced HORKINGE NEXT THE SEA. It was late afternoon. Sleet, icy cold, was blowing in gusts from the sea. Two monks, middle-aged men in brown cassocks, were shouting through megaphones, even before the train had come to a halt.

"Out, out, out! Put all your luggage on the platform!"

"It's those pigs Jenkins and Campbell!" shouted Bentley. "Filthy scum! They should have been sacked last term! Particularly Jenkins. Yuk."

The boys in the compartment began to fumble for their luggage, climbing up onto the seats to pull down pathetic little parcels and small cases from the luggage racks above them. Henry thought he was going to faint from fear.

"Out, all of you. At once!" continued the monk called Campbell. "Anyone who tarries will be reported to the Abbot. You've got three minutes to get into the buses for the school. Anyone left behind will have to walk."

The two monks ran up and down the platform beside the train, shouting, waving their arms and threatening dire punishment for disobedience. It was not exactly the warmest of welcomes, but it was obviously quite normal to the senior boys, who now barged passed the terrified newcomers and jumped onto the platform. Henry, clutching Royston and his small brown cardboard suitcase, clambered down from the train onto the platform. He nearly fell, as it was a long way down. He shivered as the wind and icy rain blew along the platform. It was much, much colder than it had ever been in London.

"New boys to the back coach!" snapped one of the monks, as the resident station porter struggled to pull trunks and suitcases out of the guard's van in the last carriage. "Keep moving, all of you. Quick, quick, quick."

"Cattle get treated better than this!" shouted Bentley against the wind.

"And prisoners of war!" added Williams-Jones.

One of the new boys who had been in the compartment with Henry was trying desperately to climb down from the platform to reach something he had dropped beneath the wheels of the train. The monk called Jenkins raced up to him and seized him by the hair.

"What the hell do you think you are doing, boy, climbing under the train, you moronic idiot?"

"I've dropped my rabbit. He goes everywhere with me!" the little boy wailed as the monk dragged him, sobbing, away from the carriage, his hand in a steely grip on the little boy's scalp. He screamed with pain.

"All toys are forbidden at the Abbey" barked Jenkins. "Get into the second bus and await my arrival." He turned away and rushed off up the platform to where some of the older boys were sharing jokes. "Into the buses, all of you" he bellowed. He knew them all well and distrusted them. He regretted that he had found he had a good many of them in his classes for the new term.

"Mowbray, I will see you when we get to school. Andrews, Watkins, Bentley - I want all of you in my study when we arrive!" he roared.

"He hasn't changed. What a little shit" hissed Mowbray as he lugged his case to the waiting buses. "Worse than Hitler!"

"Perhaps we can really get him this term. You know what he and Quartus do in the gym? We'll send a secret note to Primus!"

"He might get an ecclesiastical chastisement like Secundus gave that other monk last term," beamed

Bentley, with undisguised enthusiasm.

"Goody!"

"D'you think he's been replaced? They can't get by with only six masters." "Primus, Secundus, Tertius, Quartus, Jenkins and Campbell. Yuk!"

"Two sadists, two perverts, an alcoholic and a thief."

"Haven't you forgotten Kite?"

"Kite! The Angel of Death! Of course not."

There were two buses for the boys from the London train, decrepit old wrecks which had clearly been worked hard during war service. They were parked in the small yard just outside the station. The seats were filthy and torn, the tyres were bald and the paintwork faded. The words "Great Eastern County Traction Company" had recently been painted on the sides. The two old drivers were smoking and pointing at the wheels as the boys embarked. Engines were started, blue smoke was everywhere and with frightful jolts the buses began to pull out of the station yard.

The convoy passed over the bridge above the railway. Henry looked down; he could see a small, limp, white object lying sadly beside the track. The buses growled and wound slowly through the bleak wintry rain-soaked country.

Henry found himself beside the boy who had lost his rabbit. He was sobbing uncontrollably. Between sobs, Henry elicited that the boy's name was Turnbull.

Henry clutched Royston more tightly than ever.

At the front of the bus the monk Jenkins stood up counting heads as the bus swayed and lurched along the narrow, pot-holed road. "There it is!" An older boy began pointing to a distant, dark grey group of buildings. It looked to Henry like a ruined castle or church of some kind, with two tall, dark, black towers that dominated the surrounding buildings.

"Is that where we are going?" he asked nervously, as the older boys began laughing and jostling among themselves. "Shut up, the lot of you!" snapped Jenkins. "I won't have ragging on the bus. You'll have plenty to do to temper your energies once we reach the Abbey." The bus dropped into a small culvert, temporarily leaving the Abbey out of sight, and, after much crashing of gears, turned slowly into a long private drive. There was a strong smell of oil and burning rubber. A faded blue sign announced "Saint Eusebius Abbey Preparatory School." The buses spluttered their way through the portals of a Victorian gateway, guarded by a small cottage from which smoke wafted from a single chimney.

"Hope Mrs Carps has some treats in store," whispered a boy two rows in front of Henry. It was one of the seniors from his carriage. "If it wasn't for her game pie I'd die of starvation, I tell you."

"Me too."

"And me."

Henry had no idea who Carps and Mrs Carps were, but they clearly offered some sort of beacon of hope, if only by way of sustenance, to the boys he was going to join at the school. Momentarily he forgot his mother and her tear-filled face and began to listen to the others chattering around him. Turnbull continued to sob miserably. Henry listened with growing interest. Carps, it seemed, was some sort of worker or handyman at the school, who stood out as a normal human being in stark contrast to the sadistic monks. The monks, the teaching staff, apparently thrived on a diet of pious religious euphoria mixed with the near starvation and ceaseless chastisement of the boys unfortunate enough to be in their charge. Carps looked after the grounds and taught carpentry, from which he had earned his name. No one knew what he was really called, nor how he came to be in the school's employ.

The buses, now reduced to a crawl, made their way along the rutted drive passed football and rugger posts in the rapidly failing winter's evening light. Henry found it all hard to take in. There seemed to be a huge ruin of an ancient church and, attached to it, other buildings towards which the buses were heading. These he guessed were the main school. The buses pulled up in an outer yard and Jenkins and Campbell were out in a trice. Like sheepdogs they started to marshal the boys into a crocodile line, with the older boys at the front and the new ones bringing up the rear. The boys who had come down on the London train were then ordered to march through another arch into a much smaller, inner courtyard where cars were parked and more boys were milling around. A large Lagonda, a 1938 model, dark green, was parked conspicuously against a door marked "Headmaster". A swarthy man was unloading cases from the boot.

"Hey, Ward's back, there's his dad's car! Look, Leno is taking the drink up to Primus' study." The boy in question, Ward, tall, with blonde curly hair, mature for his thirteen years, was leaning against the wall engaged in earnest conversation with another boy of about the same age.

"It's Willington Rushton!" whispered a boy called Roberts. "I wonder what those two are up to?"

A similar train of thought must have struck Brother Campbell as he directed the newly-arrived column through the boys' entrance and into the memorial hall. Campbell and Jenkins hated all the senior boys with equal measure, particularly Ward, whom Campbell had never yet managed to get beaten, though he felt he richly deserved it. Silently he vowed that this term he would make amends. He knew it was a matter of open warfare; either them or him. Humiliation and embarrassment were the principal weapons in their armament, with a slow attrition of minor abuses to weaken his authority. It was, he deemed, enough to drive anyone to drink.

The memorial hall, smelling of a vile concoction of disinfectant, varnish and new paint, constituted the reception centre for all the boys returning to the school. Those already at the school were siphoned off to the left while new boys were lined up on the right to be allocated their dormitories and their lockers in the central washroom.

At the point where the two columns came together again sat the matron, Miss Tremble, a square, grim figure of indeterminate late middle age. Dressed in an old-fashioned nurse's white uniform with a blue cardigan and thick brown stockings, she had upon her head a large white triangular headpiece which made her resemble some gaunt figure from a mediaeval painting. Her angular countenance, unsmiling and austere, gave nothing away as she eyed the returning boys with scornful indifference. This was not the countenance of a woman who bore any affection for her job, or indeed any affection for anyone at all. This was Kite, to whom the boys had referred on the train in less than complimentary terms. She did nothing to hide the portrait that they had painted of her.

In front of Miss Tremble lay a large oaken table on which an ever-growing pile of delicious-looking foods was growing. These were the so-called 'voluntary contributions' made by the parents to support and supplement their children's rations. There were jams, cakes of many sorts, pies, sweets, chocolates, even fruit, which was particularly hard to come by.

Miss Tremble watched, cat-like, as the long line of returning boys shuffled forward and dumped their contributions before her. One boy refused to hand over his parcel.

"Give that to me!" she snapped as the boy tried to smuggle a small Christmas cake past her table.

"My mummy made it. She said it was only for me and that I was to eat it as soon as possible before it went stale."

"Give it to me! You know perfectly well, Melchett, that food is not allowed to be consumed outside the boys' dining room."

Her large, muscular hand grabbed the offending cake and seized it. Melchett surrendered meekly.

"Food? Where's your food, Dexter?" the interrogation by the matron went on as the line moved forward. "Why have you not brought the contribution that is required of you?"

The boy being questioned was small and plump with a friendly, freckled face. "Didn't bring any!" he answered jovially.

"It is a requirement of the school. Your parents should have known."

"Oh they do. They know all right."

"Then why have you brought nothing for us, for us

all, to be shared among the community of the Abbey?"

"Because you know, and we all know, that we boys never ever get to see the food again. Look what happened last term when you and the monks ate all our food in one go."

"How dare you! The celebration of the Feast of Saint Eusebius is a matter of great importance to all the members of the staff. It is a tradition going back to the foundation of the school! For failing to bring sustenance to the Abbey I shall add three shillings and sixpence to your father's bill. I expect better of you."

Williams-Jones, following immediately behind, handed over a large dry-looking plum cake. He smiled as the matron snatched it from him and placed it on her pile. Nudging Harding behind him as they exited through a side door to the changing rooms, he whispered "My aunt got this frightful cake from a little man in Midhurst. I got the local farmer to let me have some poison which he uses to keep the vermin down. I've injected it, all over. It should give them quite a fright."

"That's murder, if you kill one of them!" Harding looked horrified.

"After the way they treat us they deserve it, especially Kite. Do you realise this place is worse than a German prisoner-of-war camp? At least they were allowed food parcels."

"And things to help them escape, like maps and so

on" added another voice.

"You planning on escaping then, Ellerby?"

"No, but Bentley is. He told me on the train. Bentley, Mowbray and Ambrose. They want a bit of excitement before they leave."

"Poison! Golly. Suppose you get the Abbot?"

"Primus? The bastard deserves it more than anyone. Him and that brute Secundus. Let's see if anyone comes to save them after all the praying we have to do on their behalf."

The boys all made their way to their various dormitories to leave their possessions. There were five, north, east south and west, plus a special, in a warmer part of the school, for the seniors and the prefects. Boys who wet their beds were placed in north, the coldest and bleakest, where a constant draught wafted away the smell of urine. Henry, forewarned on the train and pleased at having evaded the search in the memorial hall, hid Royston as best he could, under his pillow. Turnbull, given the bed next to him, was still sobbing and mourning the loss of his fluffy rabbit.

After storing their washing things and clothes, the two red-eyed little boys made their way down the stairs to where supper was being served. It consisted of fried bread with a thin layer of dripping, smeared on by a buxom young woman who seemed to be the matron's assistant. Lukewarm tea completed the meal. Prayers followed, and all the boys were then despatched to their various dormitories. All lights were out by eight thirty.

THREE

Charles Upton climbed down from the train at Horkinge and winced as the freezing North Sea air hit him in the face. The station was deserted. There were no taxis and there was nothing open in the high street. The whole town gave the appearance of having shut up for the night, if not for the season; there was no sign of life anywhere. Even the pub by the station had closed early, no doubt for lack of custom. Only a stray cat followed him, mewing pitifully for food.

Upton had overlooked the fact that Saint Eusebius was some distance from the town and he would have to find some way of getting there from the station. The thought of walking five miles in the dark and cold was not an option he favoured, but it might be the only one he had.

Just then a very old Austin taxi pulled up alongside him. "You lookin' for transport, sir?" The driver was elderly and fat and smelt of cigarettes.

"I was hoping for a taxi at the station, but everyone seems to have gone home" said Upton.

"Nothing happens in Horkinge except in the summer when they come for the beach. Where yer goin?"

"Saint Eusebius School."

"Thought as much, since you're smartly dressed and like. Bit late aren't ya? They opened this afternoon?" .

"Trains all running late, all the way from Newcastle."

"Bless me, you've had one hell of a journey. Jump in, I'll run you up there. It'll be five bob."

"Thanks."

Upton climbed into the back of the venerable old taxi. The driver was clearly keen to talk.

"Hope you don't mind my saying, sir, but there's an odd feeling about that place. Them monks have got something of a reputation round these parts and their matron is a right old hag."

"What sort of reputation?"

"Hard to be precise, sir. One of em's a bit light fingered when he comes into the town, but there's more to it than that. They're sort of fanatics. Ever heard of the Christian Brothers in Dublin?" Upton shook his head.

"Terrible lot they were. My sister's married to an Irishman who was brought up in the Industrial School. He said they were obsessed with the sin of impurity, by that of course they meant sex, because as priests they weren't supposed to be getting any. Any boys who looked at another boy's private parts were flogged till the blood flowed down their thighs. Used to tie them down across a vaulting horse in the gym and make the others watch. Terrible, quite terrible."

"You mean they're doing the same sort of thing at Saint Eusebius?"

"Worse. They had a suicide last term. Bet you didn't know that."

"What happened?"

"I had to take the relatives up to the school. Ever so nice and humble they were. The little boy's parents had been killed in the war, he was their only child. I felt so sorry for them. No sense of remorse or even an apology from the people at the school. Almost the opposite in fact. Sort of arrogance, as if the little boy wasn't good enough for them."

"What happened?"

"Hanged himself in the latrines, poor little fellow. Rumour has it that he just couldn't take any more of it."

"That's horrendous. Thank you for the warning."

"Sorry to be the harbinger of bad news, sir. I thought you might have known."

"No. I don't know anything about the place at all. It'll be my first job after coming out of the army. But I'm very grateful for your having told me now."

"You'll soon wish you were back in it, sir, if what we hear is true. They run it like a prison."

They passed through several villages and hamlets, all silent and dark. The driver gave Upton a summary of what went on in that part of England, the tourist trade, how they had all suffered in the war, the lack of hope for the future. Then he came back to the school.

"You goin' to be teaching then?" The taxi slowed and passed the gatehouse into the drive. He clearly knew his way.

"Yes. I'm the new junior master."

"Last bloke came a cropper. Left in a hurry. Watch out for the big South African bloke. Sorry to be so depressing sir."

"Not at all. Thanks again for the warning."

The taxi slowed down and pulled up in the inner yard before the main school building, where a light shone over a doorway. The driver passed over a card.

"Call me if you need to get away at any time. You won't be the first. Good luck sir, and, if I may say so, I think you'll need it!"

He gave Upton a wry smile, tinged with pity. Upton watched, wistfully and not without a twinge of regret, as he drove off into the dark, changing gear as he passed into the outer grounds.

It was becoming clearer by the minute why Margolis & Tring had been less than enthusiastic about the school. For the first time he felt distinctly nervous; he wondered what on earth lay ahead and, indeed what he had now let himself in for.

The school was shrouded in darkness as Upton rang the front doorbell, save for a small light which shone from a room on the top floor. He heard footsteps approaching, bolts being run back. The door was opened abruptly and a tall, fierce-looking woman in a dressing gown stood before him.

"Yes?" she snapped, wrapping the dressing gown around herself to keep out the cold.

"I'm Mr Upton, the new master."

"Brother Upton? You should have been here hours ago. You were expected for evensong and to supervise the boys on their arrival. Did no one tell you this? What do you think you are doing arriving at this hour?"

"The train was late. The connection was cancelled. There were no taxis at Horkinge station."

"We don't accept excuses at Saint Eusebius, Brother Upton" she sneered. "You will soon discover that our standards here are higher than at other schools, or indeed among the riffraff in the street. Wait there!"

She disappeared into the passageway and returned almost at once with an envelope and a key.

"The Abbot wishes to see you at five thirty tomorrow morning. He's very annoyed, as he had expected you to be here this afternoon at three for your introductory interview. This letter will tell you when and where your duties as junior master are to begin. Your habit will be found in your room at Herga and this is the key. Your room is the small one on the top floor." She handed over the key and the envelope. "Herga is the masters' residence and you will find it a short way up the track along the side of the playing fields."

She was about to slam the door, but Upton put his foot against it.

"I would be grateful if you could point me in the right direction, since there doesn't seem to be any light anywhere to show me where to go" he said. She scowled at him, clearly irritated by his challenge.

"Up there" she snapped, pointing into the darkness. "It's about three hundred yards. I expect Miss Tapscott will have left you a note." She gave him a withering look and slammed the door in his face.

Upton picked up his suitcase and started to walk in the direction she had indicated. It was a muddy track which passed beneath an arch before leading out onto what he could just discern as playing fields. The rain had eased off temporarily, but there was still a lot of cloud and only the intermittent light of a waning moon to guide him. A light shone from behind the curtains of the little lodge that stood by the gate, and he could hear a girl's laughter.

He walked on, wondering how on earth he was expected to find the Abbot's rooms in the darkness, when he came upon Herga. It was an Edwardian house, somewhat out of keeping with the rest of the school buildings, but a light was over the door and there were lights within the house. He let himself in and opened the letter the woman had given him. It was warm inside.

"Oh, you must be Mr Upton. I am so glad you have finally found us!" A kindly-looking lady emerged from behind a curtain which protected the drawing room door. She was an attractive woman probably in her early thirties thought Upton but she had about her the air of someone who had suffered some terrible personal tragedy, presumably in the war.

"Do come in" she said. Cup of tea? Biscuits? I don't suppose you have had anything to eat for hours." She offered her hand. "I'm Melanie Tapscott. I look after the housekeeping side of the school. I do hope you can cope with the cold of this place. I've put an extra blanket on your bed. You are in the little room at the top of the stairs, opposite the bathroom. The boys, poor souls, suffer in terrible silence at the cold and damp but there is little I can do. The Abbot insists upon a Spartan way of life. I try to look after you masters as best I can."

She poured out a cup of tea from a silver teapot; it had obviously been ready for some time. She opened a packet of digestive biscuits. "Have you had to travel far?"

"Newcastle. And all the trains were running late. That's why it had taken me so long to get here."

"Oh, you poor man, you must be starving. Here, do have a biscuit."

They moved over to a small one-bar electric fire and sat in aged chairs. Upton held his hands in the glow and told her about his trials and tribulations on the railways.

"Who are the others staying here, Miss Tapscott?" he asked. "Oh, and before I forget, the lady who gave me the key said I had to have an interview with the Abbot at five thirty tomorrow morning."

"Ah, you will have seen Miss Tremble. She's our matron. She is never very friendly to the masters, nor indeed to anyone. Let me fill you in with the details." She got up and reached for a map of the school showing where everything was, including Herga, the chapel, the memorial hall, the schoolrooms and the dormitories. "First, this is where you have to go to reach the Abbot's rooms." She marked the route in pencil and the door that would give entry to the tower where he had his quarters. "I have had some difficulty in finding a habit that will fit you but I do have two other sizes in the store room. Mr Everett, your predecessor, was a short, rather fat man; I don't think his size would have fitted very easily. Do you take sugar?"

"Thanks. One lump."

"We are terribly constrained by the rationing here at the school but we are lucky with some of the surrounding farmers and landowners, who let us have extra cuts of pork, chicken and of course rabbits, which are very plentiful."

"How many other masters are there?"

"Six besides yourself. There is the Abbot, our headmaster, who is known as Primus – first, you understand - and the three senior masters, Brothers Secundus, Tertius and Quartus. Secundus lives in the little lodge by the arch you came through and Tertius lives here, in the best room on the first floor." She handed Upton a cup of tea. "It's all rather silly really, everyone being called Brother all the time, since none of you have any religious or clerical qualifications. Still, that's tradition for you I suppose. Brother Tertius, George Holby is his real name by the way, feels the cold dreadfully and suffers from chilblains and awful colds. He likes to have a good soak in a hot bath. You must be patient with him."

"And the others?" Upton was warming to Miss Tapscott. She seemed a sad, rather lonely figure who could be a useful ally in a dangerous world.

"The other three masters living here are Brother Quartus, who is considered to be a senior and has his own front door to this house round the side, and Brother Jenkins and Brother Campbell, both very different sorts of people. Brother Campbell I fear has some sort of money problem, and Brother Jenkins has a terrible temper." She lowered her voice. "He also likes to drink. They are both terribly cruel to the boys."

She refilled their cups. The biscuits were delicious.

"Tell me a little about yourself, Mr Upton?"

"Charles, please. May I call you Melanie?"

"Privately, but not in front of the others. The Abbot hates informality." She smiled. "It's one of his foibles."

"He has others?"

She continued smiling. "I think I'd better let you find that out, Charles. They run this school as if it were an adjunct to Canterbury Cathedral, but proper services are conducted by dear Mr Natterjack, the curate at Horkinge, who comes up on Sundays for Sung Communion. Now what about you?"

Upton gave a brief description of his war service, his family, and gave her a somewhat untruthful account of why he had taken the job at Saint Eusebius. Miss Tapscott looked suddenly at the clock over the mantelpiece.

"Oh dear it's terribly late. You've got an early start. I'd better show you where your room is." She led the way up the stairs to a rather austere little room with an iron bed which must have come from the army at some time. Upton noted that she had fine attractive legs. There was a towel and some soap, and hanging on a nail behind the door was the habit Upton was going to have to wear throughout his stay at the school.

"I am sure you will be comfortable" she smiled. "But if there is anything more you need, please don't hesitate to ask me in the morning."

Upton listened to her descending the stairs and turning off all the lights as she did so. The sound of raucous snoring was coming from one of the other rooms. He unpacked his case and tried the habit. It fitted his shoulders but was rough and coarse. He wondered how he would cope. He also wondered who the others were, what secrets they were all concealing and most of all who the South African was that the taxi driver had warned him to be careful of.

In the North Dormitory, the coldest in the school with the windows opened not less than six inches, Henry and Turnbull were sobbing themselves to sleep. Their damp, clammy, hard and lumpy beds were a new and dreadful experience. In the West Dorm, by way of contrast, Ward, Mowbray and Bennett were already hatching plans over a bottle of communion wine just stolen from the chapel. The first term of 1947 had begun.

FOUR

Snow had replaced the rain during the night. The wind had gone round from south-east to north and a light dusting of white now covered the roof and the grounds of the Abbey. It reflected eerily in the pre-dawn light. In the distance the great bell of the Abbey clock boomed out the quarter hour across the still and sleeping countryside. It was five fifteen in the morning and bitterly cold.

Upton adjusted his garb and pulled up his long woollen stockings as far as they would go in an endeavour to keep warm. Apprehensively, he made his way quietly down the stairs of Herga and slipped out of the door towards the main body of the school. He had had a nervous, unsettled few hours sleep, mulling over both what Miss Tapscott had imparted and the conversation he had had earlier with the taxi driver.

The first meeting with the Abbot had obviously been chosen to test his stamina, and his aptitude and suitability for the monastic life that he was expected to lead. He felt both an idiot and something of a fraud dressed in his ill-fitting and abrasive monastic garb, for he had never taken holy orders and had not the slightest interest in matters ecclesiastical.

He walked quickly across the quadrangle of the inner courtyard, his footprints leaving marks in the pristine snow. Silently he opened the door that led to the stairs to the headmaster's study. A faint light shone above him, coming from the first floor. Clutching his reference papers in his hand, he climbed the stairs, nervously anticipating what sort of reception he was going to get. It was just five twenty five. He wondered what hours the Abbot was used to keeping. Was this routine, or was it a one-off to test his mettle?

As the clock struck the half hour he tapped lightly on the door.

"Come!" Brother Primus was seated in a large high-backed chair. He rose to welcome Upton and extended a hand; the grip was firm but the skin calloused, more like that of a labourer than a man of the cloth. He was a large man, about six foot, with a sizeable girth and broad across the shoulders, and bald save for a thin tonsure of white fluffy hair around the temples. Large bushy eyebrows conveyed an air of the gravitas of academia, but the eyes, light blue and rather cold, gave a hint of another, possibly darker, side to his personality. It was hard to determine his age, for his baldness might have disguised a much younger man. He could have been anything from early fifties to late sixties.

"I'm glad that you have chosen to come and join us, Brother Upton. We welcome you to our team at Saint Eusebius. We have much work to do and great duties to perform!"

The opening remarks sounded genuine enough. There was no mention of his late arrival the night before, nor any hint of the displeasure to which Miss Tremble had alluded. The Abbot pointed to one of the chairs before his desk.

"Make yourself comfortable, Brother Upton."

The room, while Spartan in its furnishings, was lined with antique leather bound books; it was essentially a private library. The floor was covered with a series of Persian rugs, worn but still attractive and far from threadbare. A small electric fire, with only one bar in operation, provided lukewarm heat. A large fat cat, a tabby of no noticeable distinction, lay before it, paws outstretched.

"They have made you comfortable I trust? Tea? I find it clears the mind at this time of the morning." He had a deep, sonorous voice.

"Thank you, sir."

The Abbot reached over to a small brown teapot which stood to one side of his desk. Someone had provided two cups and a small bottle of milk. He poured the tea and passed a cup to Upton. Sipping silently, he then shuffled a pile of papers from a portfolio and laid them out upon his desk. Upton guessed that he had prepared all this in advance and was only doing it for theatrical effect. The Abbot put on a pair of round metal framed spectacles

"Margolis & Tring have given you a good report" he said. "Tell me a little bit about your background, and perhaps most importantly, what motivates you, Brother Upton? What made you choose to come to Saint Eusebius? I am sure there must have been more attractive opportunities for a man of your capabilities, especially in the south of England. You are not trying to hide away from the world, or from anything or anybody in particular I trust?"

The light blue eyes stared unnervingly through the steel-framed spectacles. It was of course the one question Upton was keen to avoid, but he knew the Abbot would soon flush out any prevarication.

"I am seeking solace, sir, a place for meditation after what has happened to my family during the war" he said. "I harbour doubts that I would have been able to find such quiet or time for meditation were I to have joined one of the other schools that the agency had told me of." He gave a brief account of the fate that had befallen his parents. He hoped this would explain his choice and reasons for coming to the school.

"Don't be disillusioned, Brother Upton, when I tell you what I expect of my teaching staff." The Abbot stirred his tea slowly, as if to let the message sink in. There was a long and pregnant pause. The inquisition still had far to run. Upton began to sweat.

"What did you do before electing to enter the world of academia, the teaching profession and, in our case as I always stress to newcomers, the imparting of religious knowledge to young and receptive minds?"

"I was in the Royal Corps of Signals, sir."

"Your rank? You were commissioned I assume?"

"No sir. Lance Corporal. I was only conscripted at the very end, in 1945."

"Not commissioned, though? Tut tut. That's sad. I always try to attract the officer class. It's so important – especially given the background of our pupils."

"I'm sorry, sir. I'll try to do my best."

"Of course you will. Another cup?"

Upton shook his head. The Abbot helped himself.

"Well, well. Where should we begin? You know us, though of course we don't yet know you." He smiled beneath the bushy eyebrows. "You have the papers from Margolis & Tring. You will have seen our record for academic excellence; our boys rarely fail to reach entrance to the top schools, to Eton, Radley, Rugby and Oundle, to name but a few. At sports we also excel, though I have to admit that sometimes we have to exert a little pressure on our boys to overcome their protagonists. You are not against corporal punishment, I trust, Brother Upton?"

"No, sir. Not at all."

"You've been beaten in your time, I trust?"

"No sir. They were lenient with the cane where I went to school."

"That school being?"

"St Mildreds, sir. In Kent."

"Never heard of it. Never mind."

The cat, woken from its slumbers, stretched and then jumped up onto the Abbot's chair. It sat upon his lap, purring and digging its claws into his apparel. The Abbot continued, his voice slightly more authoritarian and severe in tone, maybe as a result of this admission.

"You may find it a little strange that we dress here as monks, given that we are not participants in the Roman faith, but it is part of our tradition. I assume you have no problem with this, Brother Upton?"

"No, sir. None at all. I knew the school had always had deep religious roots. I had assumed, given the small number of Catholic boys that I was told would be coming to a school like this, that you would be practising the Anglican Communion. It was what inspired me." Upton was lying, helped by the quickness of his wit under such stressful circumstances.

"I was myself brought up as a Catholic," declared

the Abbot. "Part of my childhood was spent in Spain. I was trained, and beaten, I might add, by Jesuit priests. I still pride myself on my ability to speak their language fluently." He paused briefly to put the cat down from his lap. "What I admired of the Jesuits was their dedication and commitment to the spreading of the Christian message through order and discipline. You know of course of the Jesuit doctrine that by taking the child to seven they would give back the man. Discipline, Brother Upton, as you will shortly be seeing, is an integral part of our educational process, the process of creating the whole man."

The Abbot replenished his tea. There was another pregnant pause, the atmosphere turning a little frostier.

"Do you have any questions, any points, any misunderstandings, and doubts about which I should make myself clearer perhaps?"

Upton paused before replying. His thoughts returned to what the taxi driver had disclosed.

"No sir" he replied, "not now at any rate."

"At any rate!" the Abbot's voice took a distinctly frostier tone. "At any rate? What do you mean by that, may I ask?"

"Well, sir, when I have been here for a few weeks there might be something..."

The Abbot interjected "A few weeks? Might be? I sincerely hope not. Once you have joined us you are part of the fraternity. Do you harbour doubts?"

Upton shook his head. He thought quickly, not wishing to provoke any form of confrontation. So far he had not pressed him further as to why Saint Eusebius had been his choice. The interview was clearly still full of danger.

"I was thinking along ecclesiastical lines of authority, sir, given, shall I say, that you are all dressed more in a Roman tradition."

This seemed to defuse the tension, certainly from Upton's standpoint. "A sensible question, Brother Upton, and most perspicacious if I may say so. We report to the Bishop of Branchester, whom no doubt you will meet in due course." The Abbot quickly returned to his more sinister obsession, their philosophy in respect of discipline and punishment at the school; the vital need for the boys to conform at all times to the standards of those they wished to emulate, to crush eccentricity, sentiment and non conformity. It sounded ominously like views brought across from the creed of the Waffen SS. Himmler would have been proud.

"I maintain absolute discipline at Saint Eusebius" he continued. "Without which we would all be lost. Boys, as I see it Brother Upton, are akin to wild animals; they are full of spirit but they must be broken and trained, like horses and dogs, if we are to bring out the best in them." The Abbot sipped his tea, not once taking his eyes off his new master. "What influences behaviour is not so much the home or the family, nor genetic make up for that matter, but the peer group in which the boys grow up. The survival instinct, which teaches the young either to conform with their contemporaries or to become their leader, starts at an early age, before puberty in fact. What you have to remember is that unless trained and disciplined properly, huge variations in behaviour can result. That is why we adhere to the Jesuit tradition. We take our boys at seven or eight and make them into men in the five years we have. This term we have an excellent head boy in Timothy Thompson-Brown, to whom all the juniors aspire. He has matured into a true leader, a great athlete, and will, I am sure, become a fine leader of men. He is down for Wellington. His father had a distinguished war career with the 60th, the Green Jackets. I am most encouraged."

Upton shifted uneasily in the high-backed chair. Something in his garb was grating harshly on his thighs. He wanted to scratch, but thought the better of it. Maybe he had been bitten by fleas.

"Discipline" continued the Abbot, "is therefore vital for all of us. Behind you, you will see what I use to impose order in this school." He flicked a switch which illuminated one wall of his study. Upton turned. On the far wall lay a fiendish looking line of canes and whips suspended from a line of hooks. They ranged from a large knobbly cane at the extreme right through various smaller weapons of chastisement to split reeds, and a sort of birch or switch on the left. "It is important, in my lexicon at least," continued the Abbot, "that boys should see the results a flogging has upon their peers. I therefore prefer to use the birch, for while it may not bring as much pain as the cane, it draws more blood and leaves greater marks upon the flesh as a warning for the others to eschew. My Chief Disciplinarian, whom you have yet to meet, has other thoughts!"

He grimaced, rather unnervingly, as the cat jumped back onto his lap. This must be one of the foibles to which Miss Tapscott had alluded; probably more of a fetish to judge by the sudden change of tone. Upton's thoughts went back to what the taxi driver had imparted about the little boy who had committed suicide the previous term.

"You agree with this, I trust?" asked the Abbot.

"Certainly, I agree that discipline is important sir" Upton nodded, his mouth dry with apprehension as to what might be coming next. "I learnt that in the army."

"Last year" continued the Abbot, placing his elbows on the desk and putting his fingertips together, "I had the most distasteful task of having to expel a monk for the most heinous of offences." He looked up questioningly, fixing Upton with an unnerving steely gaze. "One of the seven deadly sins of which you are doubtless aware." He paused for effect. "Lust! If there is one thing that I cannot abide, Brother Upton, it is sexual impropriety. This monk, whose name I shall not divulge to you, was reported to me as having had an association with one of our young female staff. A matter of gross indecency."

He sighed and stroked the cat in silence for a few moments.

"You see, Brother Upton, I am not in any way opposed to the natural urge for reproduction, but it must be followed within the sacred confines of marriage. Those who do so outside it are guilty of great sin."

"He didn't wish to marry the girl, sir?"

"Oh, no. Oh dear me no. As you will know from your contract with us, sexual activity of any sort is one of the most serious misdemeanours that any monk could possibly commit. We monks are not allowed to marry, ergo we must forsake and fight against all urges of the flesh and the devil."

Picking up a silk handkerchief, the Abbot slowly wiped his spectacles. "The other, in many ways worse sin, one proscribed in the Bible, is that of a man lying with a man."

Upton felt a cold sweat in the palm of his hands and the dryness in his mouth worsened. He struggled to control his emotions, for the interview seemed to be moving onto potentially very dangerous ground. The Abbot fixed Upton with an unnerving stare that penetrated to his very soul, as if to expose his real reason for coming to Saint Eusebius. He continued with his questioning.

"You have yourself never had any leanings in that direction I hope? You have a girlfriend?"

"No sir. On both counts. I lost my girlfriend during my term of military service. We moved around a lot in signals. I have never had anything to do with a man."

"Good. For buggery, or any activity of a sexual nature between men, or men and boys, is something that is simply not tolerated at this school. I have in the past had my suspicions about some of your predecessors, especially paedophilia, the depravation of youth, but I am happy to say that, at this very moment, there is not a single homosexual among the teaching staff."

He stopped, and, as if to make sure that his message had indeed truly sunk in, he declared, "We do in fact have a special licence, dating from when the school was founded in 1877, a licence revived from the Abbey of the sixteenth century, that the Abbot, or his appointed officer, has the right to administer corporal punishment, should he deem this fit and appropriate, to any monk so caught in such disgraceful acts of impropriety. Perhaps you are not aware of this?"

Upton shook his head "No, sir. I was not."

"It is engrained in our constitution, Brother Upton. It is enshrined in the vows that are taken by all the monks at this Abbey. You knew this not?"

"I came, sir, to teach, as junior master. No one mentioned or drew my attention to this."

"How very unfortunate for you then!"

"I have not taken any vows, sir. I am not a monk; I am merely dressed as one to comply with the school's regulations."

"They told you that?"

"Not specifically. There is no mention of taking vows in the letters I have received from the agency."

The Abbot slowly shook his head. "No, there wouldn't be, Brother Upton, for by joining us you have already committed yourself to be bound by our rules. The very wearing of the monk's habit is in itself a commitment to the Brotherhood."

Upton had not seen anything about this in the two-page letter he had received from the agents, nor in the thick memorandum of code accompanying his contract of employment. It sounded a dangerous omission, and one that could lead him to being the victim of a personal vendetta. Was this something to do with the warning about the South African? He resolved to return to his room to review all the paperwork very carefully again, quickly, as soon as the interview was over.

"You will not have had the pleasure of meeting any of your fellow masters yet, but we shall all be together before chapel, which will begin after breakfast" said the Abbot. He shifted in his chair as if in pain, throwing the cat off his lap again.

"But I will summarise. The monks I employ at this school are men with the highest standards of probity and honesty, devoid of the vices of alcohol and tobacco, deeply religious and utterly committed to the imparting of knowledge to keen and receptive minds." He put Upton's papers to one side of the desk. "My deputy here is Brother Secundus. I am of course Primus, but I like to think of myself as primus inter pares. Each of the monks is capable of undertaking the duties of the others. Secundus is a fine man, a great sportsman and like me, a strong disciplinarian. Then we have Tertius, a dear man, a classics scholar and a tower of strength to our teaching abilities, and Brother Quartus, a Cambridge Blue, who is in charge of physical education. I manage the school with three junior masters, Brothers Campbell and Jenkins; you are the newest.

"I would like to have increased my staff to seven, but the governors would not allow this. I am afraid you will find the workload, including sports and supervision of games, somewhat onerous, but I am sure you will cope and be quite capable in meeting our exacting standards."

"I hope so, sir."

"There are other non-stipendiary members of the staff; the Reverend Natterjack, who conducts our services mostly on Sundays and Mr Ainsley, the organist. There are back-up staff; some kitchen workers and a man who looks after the grounds. None of these are of any importance to you." The Abbot took off his thin steel-rimmed spectacles and put Upton's papers into a folder. He was however not yet done.

"I'm not quite clear what previous qualifications you have, Brother Upton, in the teaching profession?"

"Well, not a lot sir. I trained as an electrician and I specialised in electrical engineering in the army. I became quite adept at transmission technology during my time with the Royal Corps of Signals."

"But no front-line teaching?"

"No sir, except to the platoon."

"Ah. That's acceptable. That's what I wanted to hear." He put down the papers. "It means at least that you have commanded attention, passed on your education so to speak. Let me tell you about the female members of our staff. There is our matron, Miss Tremble, who is adored by the boys. She handles their physical wellbeing with great aplomb and gives sympathy when it is due, but broadly follows the policy of this school that the pupils must learn the art of survival. I don't need to remind you, Brother Upton, that as one who has fought the enemy and seen what horror war is, the world is a harsh and bitter place. Matron Tremble ensures that the next generation will be ready to carry on the great burden of civic responsibility and duty to our King and Country. And then there is Miss Tapscott."

"I met Miss Tapscott when I arrived last night. She seemed very kind."

"Ah, yes, dear me. Poor Miss Tapscott. Something dreadful happened to her family, they were bombed I believe, and she lost her fiancé at the beginning of the war, in 1940. She came to us, rather like the cat here, as a refugee from the storm of life. You know about the school of course?"

"Certainly sir. It was founded in 1877, but the Abbey goes back much further. The Brotherhood, founded in 1090, was destroyed by Henry VIII but then ruined buildings were restored and Saint Eusebius reopened as a place of religious retreat in the eighteenth century."

"You have done your homework well, Brother Upton! Broadly we were completely rebuilt, in the gothic style so beloved of the Victorians. Only the masters' house, Herga, was built later, in 1910."

The Abbot rose from his chair, strode across his study and reached for a package on a table. Upton noticed that he had a slight limp. He wondered if it was a war wound, and if the Abbot had indeed been in the conflict.

"These are your instructions and your duties, Brother Upton. I regret that I have immersed you somewhat at the deep end. I would like you to take Geography for the lower boys, immediately after morning prayers, French at eleven, supervise the junior tables at lunch, and take the new boys for a run round our grounds at two thirty pm. You will then supervise common entrance revision for the seniors at five before we all meet for evening prayers at seven."

"A busy day indeed, sir!"

"Don't say I didn't warn you, Brother Upton" he smiled thinly. "We expect our teaching staff to be committed in, how shall I put it, body and soul at all times."

He handed Upton the papers, indicating that his interview was over and assuring him that his door was always open should he have any questions about the workings of Saint Eusebius. Thankfully the Abbot had not pursued the questioning of his reasons for coming to Saint Eusebius, and Upton realised that he had thus been spared having to obfuscate his association with Parker and give any details of his past.

FIVE

Six melancholy strokes chimed from the school clock as Upton left the headmaster's rooms. In the dormitories bells rang loudly and relentlessly, rousing the boys from their slumbers. The new boys, wide-eyed and shocked at the harshness of the morning bells, were marshalled like sheep by their dormitory monitors. They stripped off their pyjamas and put their towels around their bodies. Hurriedly they followed the monitors to the changing rooms on the ground floor where they would have their cold showers, clean their teeth and be inspected by the matron. It was bitterly cold, but nervous energy drove them on.

Miss Tremble sat on a hard wooden chair at the end of the line of basins to inspect the boys before they were required to run through the line of six cold showers. She knew some boys by name but shouted at the new ones, clearly unaware of who they were. All boys were required to stand before her, turn slowly so that she could see any skin disease or blemish on their bodies, and submit to her forceful examination of their backsides, where coarse and calloused fingers were thrust into rectums for crude examination of potential constipation. Older boys such as Ward, Bennett, Mowbray and Harding were allowed an extra fifteen minutes in bed and came down to showers after the others; a small amount of warm water was added to the showers as a sort of concession to their seniority, but this was a privilege that could be withdrawn at any time for the slightest misdemeanour, or indeed simply incurring the displeasure of the matron. All were examined by her in the same crude manner, her fingers probing genitalia and feeling the testicles of those boys who displayed signs of puberty. There was a quick return to the dormitories, where beds were made and clothes put on. Dressed in uniform, all boys assembled in the dining room for breakfast; lukewarm porridge was served along with powdered egg and a thin piece of bread.

Henry had taken great care to hide Royston, not under his pillow but at the foot of the bed, where he hoped no one would probe should there be an examination of the dormitories while they were in class. He was tense and nervous, not sure where the next threat was coming from. He had still to collect his books and pencils from the office. He was comforted to some extent at seeing the look of bewilderment on the faces of the other new boys; he knew he was not alone in this climate of enforced anxiety and stress into which he had been so abruptly thrown.

★ ★ ★ ★ ★ ★

Upton walked briskly to Herga, aghast at what he had been told was now required of him. No wonder there had been such a high turnover of staff. The agents had never said that such a workload was imposed upon the masters at this school, nor had they made any mention of corporal punishment being applied to the teaching staff if they broke the so called Rules of the Brotherhood of the Abbey. He resolved to take a day's leave as soon as he could and confront them in London. This however could not be done for at least two months, according to his contract of employment, and he wondered how he would fare in the interim.

The clock now chimed the half hour, a mournful two bells. Upton glanced at his watch and gasped. Time was running out; staff breakfast was scheduled for six thirty. He quickened his pace, leaving his papers in his room, and ran back to the room in the main body of the school where the kindly Miss Tapscott had shown him breakfast would be served. Opening the door nervously, he advanced towards where four other monks were eating.

"You must be Brother…?"

"Upton."

The questioner was the oldest of the four. He sat slightly apart from the other three, who were at the long refectory table in the masters' dining room. "I'm Brother Tertius" he said. He held out a warm hand; it was soft and gentle. "It's not my real name of course, as we all have to take these strange Latin titles once we reach seniority. These are my colleagues, Brothers Quartus, Campbell and Jenkins."

He pointed to the others, who looked up briefly, stared without interest and continued their eating in silence. A strong smell of fried bacon and eggs wafted in from the kitchen, where a buxom young woman and a foreign-looking man could be seen engaged in cooking. Upton looked round, somewhat bewildered. He didn't know what to expect; the Abbot's interview still lay heavily upon his mind.

"I hope you will be happy here" continued Brother Tertius. "It is something of a shock for those not accustomed to living the monastic style. The food is quite good except for the luncheons which we are required to have with the boys. Have you taken holy orders?"

"No. I didn't think it was a prerequisite for the job."

"It isn't. But we try to live in prayer all the same."

He looked at Upton with sad, weary eyes. Campbell and Jenkins rose noisily from the far end of the table and shuffled out of the room. Quartus belched, wiped his mouth with his cassock and prepared to go. "Nature calls!" he declared in a vulgar tone. He pushed back his chair and winked. "See you lot in chapel then!"

The buxom, nubile girl Upton had seen in the kitchen banged down two plates of cooked breakfast and returned with a large tin teapot. She poured the tea messily into their mugs so that it splattered onto their cassocks and threw Upton a leering, lustful smile, flashing brilliant blue eyes. As she walked away she rolled her hips and gave them both an inviting look.

Brother Tertius leaned forward. He whispered in a quiet voice "Take great care, Brother Upton, for that woman is a strumpet, a harlot, a Jezebel, a woman of evil. She has caused nothing but trouble since she came to work here. She is the incarnation of the devil and of all his evil works in this holy and divine establishment..." he stopped as the girl flounced back and noisily put a rack of toast on the table.

"Anythin' else then?" She eyed them inquisitively, hands on hips, her large breasts wobbling beneath a thin brown shirt which left little to the imagination.

"No thank you, Rosie. That will be all."

"And you?" she was addressing Upton.

"No thank you."

She stopped and looked Upton up and down. "You're new aren't you? Expect you're runnin' away from the world like all the other losers in this place. Tell yer somethin', all this monastic stuff you 'ave to wear doesn't half scratch your arse. I watched you when you came in. Bet you've already got itchy legs!"

She turned on her heel and strolled saucily back to the kitchen. "Don't say I didn't warn you" whispered Brother Tertius, helping himself to toast. "She is a very bad influence, but staff are hard to get in a place like this and we have to put up with what we have. There are two Italian prisoners of war, well they are free men now but they seem quite happy here, Leno and Romano. They are very helpful in keeping the place going. Leno by the way acts as school chef, as our last one ran away last term. The police came looking for him."

"You've been here long, Brother Tertius?"

"Since before the war. The Abbot bought the school in 1939, so it's his, though he's always pretending there is a board of governors. It's just a ruse for his stinginess and to squeeze more out of us masters."

"There's a master called Secundus isn't there? Doesn't he eat with us?"

Brother Tertius lowered his eyes and squeezed his hands together. Upton sensed he had touched upon a sensitive subject.

"I should be Secundus, in terms of seniority" he declared, almost in a whisper, "but the Abbot was persuaded by this man to take him on as his deputy. We were very short staffed in 1940 with so many being called up for the war. I don't know what the agreement was."

"There was an agreement?" Upton looked up questioningly.

"I am not sure. Brother Secundus just turned up one day and said he was prepared to work here so long as he could be deputy headmaster."

"And you didn't want that? To be deputy headmaster?"

"It would have meant having to beat the boys. I find that most distasteful. As the term progresses you will begin to see all sorts of sad little red-lined bottoms in the changing room. Brother Secundus, unlike me, veritably relishes in meting out chastisement."

He continued to talk about the school, the previous term, which had been most unfortunate for them all in a number of ways, and his hopes that perhaps the New Year would yield something better. He did not elaborate upon what had gone before and Upton restrained himself from asking him about the suicide. He was housed in Herga and that might prove a good place to ask him more about the school in the course of time.

"Goodness me" declared Tertius, staring at his watch "we must get ourselves ready for chapel!" They rose from the table and walked towards the door.

"I hope you last longer than the bloke what was 'ere before you!" sneered Rosie as they left the room "Take care you don't get your arse tanned too!" she added, flicking the crumbs left by Campbell and Jenkins onto the floor.

"Ignore her, dear brother" muttered Tertius as they walked to assemble for morning prayers, "but don't ever lower your guard!"

★ ★ ★ ★ ★

In the boys' dining room, unsupervised save by Miss Tremble and Miss Tapscott, Ward outlined his plans for the coming term. He exuded the confidence of a battle commander on the eve of engagement; Mowbray, Ambrose, Bennett and Williams-Jones listened in rapturous silence.

"All great victories are won" began Ward, "by the removal of those who are in ultimate command. You have only to look at the last war to see what I mean."

"Those whom the Gods wish to destroy they must first make mad, or something like that" added Williams-Jones. "Tertius taught us that in history last term!" The others, not so well briefed as Ward on military history, nodded in agreement though not quite aware of what the implication was. They would follow him whatever he suggested. Rebellion was in the air.

"Removal of Primus and Secundus?"

"Absolutely. Cut off the head of the beast, in this case of the organisation, and you will ensure instant collapse."

"Explain, Ward?"

"Eliminate the commanders, the generals in charge, and what will you have? Old Tertius, the school pussycat? Quartus - We all know what he wants! The artful dodgers, Campbell and Jenkins? None of them could run this place."

"What about the new monk? The fellow who's replacing Everett?"

"Not a threat."

"So what do we do then, Ward? Tell us your plans!"

"The first thing is to get rid of the enemy. I've been giving this a lot of thought over the Christmas holidays. We've got to get them where they are vulnerable."

"No problems with Jenkins and Campbell, but Secundus will be difficult. He doesn't steal anything or try to bugger any of us. Where's his weakness?"

"Rosie" replied Ward without hesitation.

"Rosie? In what way?"

"He's fugging her! I'm sure of it."

"What's fugging, Ward? What do you mean?"

"It's what animals do. My father showed me in Ireland."

"And Primus?"

"He'll be more difficult. I haven't worked it out yet."

"And there's Kite. You've got to get rid of her!"

"You bet we will. There's a lot of planning ahead" declared Ward, eating the last scrap of his tasteless white bread. "I want ideas. Quickly and from all of you."

SIX

Melanie Tapscott sighed wistfully as she took up her customary place in the back row of the chapel. It was the first Morning Prayers of the term and she waited with a sense of sadness for the daily, dreary ritual to begin. Mr Ainsley, the school organist, was warming his arthritic fingers on the keyboard of the organ with his usual repertoire of psalms. Everything was so predictable, if not repetitious, and in many ways so completely out of touch with reality. Monks? An abbot? The school wore the mantle of a Catholic institution, though it was far from being one. It was a kind of Anglo Catholic mix, High Church but without allegiance to the Pope. Indeed the founding father of the school had laid down specific rules that forbade any association with Rome or with Popish *pronunciamenti*.

She rubbed her hands to try to keep warm in the extreme cold of this freezing, unheated place of worship. How she hated the place! It was a distant relative in Branchester who had suggested that she apply for the job of housekeeper as she had nowhere to live in the south of England and, like Upton, she needed a roof over her head. The new term, in the winter of 1947 seemed to be one of the worst ever. Not only was the snowfall exceptional but food rationing was, if anything getting worse, despite the country supposedly having won the war.

The chapel, a Victorian structure built next to the ruins of the old Abbey, accommodated the entire school of ninety-seven boys. Four blocks each of six pews stood on either side of the knave. At the entrance of the chapel, through the west door, lay two pews at right angles to the others, higher than the rest, carved carefully in walnut and reminiscent of those to be found in the choirs of great cathedrals. From this vantage point the headmaster, the Abbot and his staff could keep a watchful eye on the entire school. Lower boys and new boys were placed in the front pews, the newest directly below the steely gaze of the Abbot, where they had to reverse themselves at times of prayer, kneeling on the hard stone floor of the knave, heads in hands, directly facing the older boys in middle school who were given the luxury of proper pews. Opposite Miss Tapscott, on the rear pew, sat Miss Tremble, the matron, charmless as always, whose attitude engendered so much of the cruelty in the school.

Miss Tapscott wondered what horrors lay ahead in

the long dark months until the next holiday. Suicides? Escapes? Only one thing was certain; there would be no let up in the harsh and brutal school regime.

Miss Tapscott waited for the procession to begin. She was a small woman of medium height with rather sad grey eyes, her dark hair raked back into a bun and a face which once, in happier times, must have been quite pretty. Now just over thirty one , she had no home and nowhere to go other than to see her elderly mother who was incarcerated in a nursing home near Carlisle. Christmas had been a miserable time. Her mother was becoming senile, their finances were fragile and the warmth of her little room at Herga was the only home she knew.

Miss Tapscott had a sister, Lottie, widowed too after her husband Geoffrey had been lost at sea. Lottie however was bouncy, always full of self-confidence and the zest of life. It was a characteristic she must have inherited from their father, who had been lost so cruelly on the one bombing raid on their town after all that he had been through in escaping from Dunquerque.

Lottie had been a Wren in the war and had now landed a very good job in Whitehall, something to do with the navy. She had somehow overcome the shock of widowhood. Miss Tapscott had seen Lottie over the Christmas holiday; Lottie had plans to remarry, she told her, though she did not elaborate. It only depressed poor Miss Tapscott further; she hated her incarceration at Saint Eusebius and despised herself for not being ambitious enough to look around for something better.

As Mr Ainsley broke into the opening hymn, a huge bronze cross was carried into the chapel by the precentor. Tradition had it that the head boy was precentor and this term, Lent, that boy was Timothy Thompson-Brown. It was a great honour. Tall, blond, blue eyed and beaming with pride, his place at public school already assured, he headed the procession, followed by the Reverend Natterjack, the elderly retired parson from Horkinge, who usually conducted the Sunday services. Mr Natterjack, his scrawny head emerging from an oversize dog collar, reminded Miss Tapscott of a giant turtle she had once seen in a zoo.

Behind him came the so-called monks, the most junior to the fore. She saw poor Mr Upton walking beside Brother Jenkins, awkward and clearly in considerable discomfort in his new monk's habit; he evidently had no knowledge of the English Hymnal and no idea what he was supposed to be singing. Behind them strode Brothers Campbell and Quartus, the former thick-set and beefy, singing lustily.

Beside him, Quartus, whom she had never liked, sang with a fine baritone voice. He was short and stocky. He had a small toothbrush moustache and a beard, was ginger blond and slightly bald; he wore wire-framed spectacles. His round face exuded an air of arrogance bordering on conceit. Poor, sad, Brother Tertius came next, trying to make himself heard beside the huge overbearing figure of Brother Secundus, lean and muscular, tall and thin, with fierce and challenging pale blue eyes.

Miss Tapscott distrusted Quartus, for there was something sinister in the way he handled the boys, and she had never taken to Secundus, for he was an out-and-out sadist with a fearsome lust for cruelty and punishment. His eyes were abnormally close together and he exuded an air of menace wherever he went. She couldn't stand his clipped South African accent.

The monks moved into their assigned places as the boys filed in. Miss Tapscott recognised the villains, the habitual troublemakers among the seniors; Ward, Oldham, Carmichael, Reed, Bentley, Williams-Jones, Mowbray and Fairchild. Bennett seemed to be grinning about something secret. There were the scruffy occupants of the middle school. Her eyes focused on the little boys, some looking hardly even seven, the entry age for Saint Eusebius. There were seven new boys this term and three little ones who particularly caught her attention; two had short curly fair hair, the other neatly trimmed brown hair. They looked like sheep being driven into the abattoir, their faces betraying hopeless, helpless bewilderment and misery. Miss Tapscott wondered how they would fare in the environment into which their parents had now unwittingly condemned them. Her mind flashed back to the previous term and she shuddered at the thought.

At the back of the procession came the Abbot, Primus, limping slightly, tall and austere, singing louder than the rest of them together. Miss Tapscott winced, Matron Tremble scowled, as she always did, and Brother Upton looked on somewhat bemused at the extraordinary position he had now found himself landed in. He wondered what on earth was coming next.

Mr Natterjack intoned the prayers in a squeaky voice, seeking pardon and absolution for the sins of all those present. Then, on a signal from the Abbot, Mr Ainsley blasted out the second hymn, giving all present a chance at last to get warm from singing, if nothing else.

And so the service of Morning Prayers went on for twenty minutes or so before everyone filed out again, the boys, desperate for their books and pencils, running to the office, pushing and jostling to be first in the queue. Henry had no idea what to do next; he just followed everyone else and stayed close to his fellow new boys, although he knew they would be just as confused as he was.

SEVEN

It was after lunch on that first day when one of the senior boys detached himself and came up to Henry as they were trooping out of the dining room.

"Hello, I'm Anthony Ambrose" he declared, extending a hand. "You must call me just Ambrose I'm afraid, as we aren't allowed to use our Christian names at school."

He was an athletic, mature boy, quite tall, with fair hair and red, ruddy cheeks. "It's my duty as a senior to look after you for the first months you are with us and to make sure you understand how Saint Eusebius works" he began. "I know it's all a terrible shock and I can remember only too well when I first arrived here as a new boy. Let's go and sit over there and I'll tell you what you should do to get the best out of being here."

Henry found himself completely taken aback that anyone should have shown any interest in him at all. He had been thrown out of bed by the dormitory monitor, who had mocked him for having Royston in bed. It

confirmed what the other boys had said on the train;
Royston would be confiscated. He didn't feel however
that this was a worry he could impart to Ambrose, so
he just listened in silence as Ambrose spelt out the basic
rules and regulations, the need to be keen at games,
enjoy a team spirit and not be a loner. Ambrose was in
his fifth and final year.

They went over to a bench by the window, where
Ambrose pulled out a tatty-looking set of rules which
they all had to get to know by heart. Ambrose warned
him of the pitfalls of being a new boy, of the peculiarities
of the monks, how bad-tempered most of them were
and how he should deal with Matron, whom everyone
hated. They all called her Kite because of the shape of
the ridiculous white thing she wore on her head.

"Follow all the others, don't pick a fight, do what
they say and try not to get noticed" was the broad
advice he gave, then quite unexpectedly he referred to
Royston. "I bet you've brought a teddy bear or a fluffy
toy with you? All new boys do, and Matron hates it. I
heard that one of the new boys lost his rabbit at the
station and Jenkins pulled him by the hair. I hope it
wasn't you!"

Henry shook his head. "It was Turnbull. He's in the
bed next to me."

"But do you have a toy?"

"My teddy's called Royston. He was given to me by

my mummy for Christmas. She said he was to look after me."

Ambrose scratched his head and stopped for a moment in thought. "Royston is in great danger. Have you hidden him?"

"Yes."

"Where?"

"Under the bed, the mattress I mean."

"Kite will find him. She's always skulking around trying to catch boys breaking school rules."

"If she finds him, will she give him back at the end of term?"

Ambrose shook his head. "Afraid not. She destroys all the fluffy toys. It upsets the new boys, and she knows it. It is part of her horrible nature. She seems to have a particular hatred of teddies. No one knows why."

Henry saw that the other new boys were also being counselled by senior boys. Turnbull was looking very mournful in another corner of the room, as were the others who had been on the train with him.

"Tell me, will I get swished?"

Ambrose looked up, startled by such an unexpected question.

"What?"

"Will I be swished?" Henry repeated.

"Who told you about swishing?"

"The big boys who were in our carriage on the train.

They seemed to think it was funny, but it sounds horrible to me."

"Don't you worry, Henry. No one's going to swish you."

"Matron pushed her fingers up my bottom before morning showers. Does she do it every day?"

"It's a health thing. I know it's horrible but they have to supervise our well being."

"I hate it!"

"Yes. I agree. It's not nice."

"The boys on the train said she did other nasty things, but I don't know what they meant."

"Don't you worry. She'll leave you alone." Ambrose was at a loss as to what to say. Clearly some seniors had been boasting. He wondered who they were; this was just the sort of thing that gave the school a bad name." Matron's job is to look after our health, especially in the winter when we catch colds and things. She only does what she thinks is right. She does occasionally examine us, but only if she thinks we might be ill or getting ill."

"She doesn't do it for fun then?"

"Of course not! She looks at our feet as well. Do you like football?"

"I don't know. I have never had the chance to play it. Not at my other school in London."

"You'll find it great fun. It also keeps you warm in this terrible climate."

"Will I have classes with the man who pulls

everybody by their hair? The one who dragged Turnbull by his hair at the station?"

Ambrose guessed he must have been referring to either Jenkins or Campbell, since Tertius never hurt anyone and the Abbot and Secundus were above such attacks, confining their energies to application of the birch or the cane.

"No, I don't think so. There's a new master, a new monk, called Brother Upton, who has joined this term. He will be taking the new boys; the junior masters always do."

Bells started to ring stridently throughout the school. "Oh dear, that's the call for games" said Ambrose. "Look, Henry, about the bear. I've got an idea. I'll tell you the next time we meet to chat."

They got up from the bench and went their separate ways. Henry followed Turnbull and the other new boys to get ready for sports. He was pleased he had met Ambrose. Maybe he could confide in him; he needed someone desperately to hold his hand at this frightening time.

★ ★ ★ ★ ★

For the senior boys who had been overlooked or refused promotion to prefect, the new term presented the start of a regular campaign, one almost military in its planning, to humiliate, embarrass and hopefully to destroy the morale of the teaching staff as quickly and as brutally as possible without going so far as to be the recipients of a thrashing from either the Abbot or his deputy. No one messed with those two. Poor old Brother Tertius, however, Brother Quartus with his physical obsessions and Brothers Jenkins and Campbell were fair game. They would be watching for the new man, Brother Upton, but as he took only the juniors and the new boys, disruption of his class would have to wait a term or two.

Mowbray watched as Brother Jenkins began writing on the board. How they all hated the man with his skills at near-decapitation with an airborne copy of the Latin Primer, his bad temper and his sharp cracks to the head with an open palm; he also smelt, of smoke, mothballs and drink. Rolling up his piece of blotting paper and wetting it with spittle, he aimed the ball at Jenkins' head and let fly with a ruler. The effect was electric, instant and so, so gratifying. Hit behind the ear and almost simultaneously on the back of the head by a well placed shot by Carmichael, he spun round in rage, bellowing abuse and emitting a stream of threats which all present knew he could not carry out.

"This term, this year indeed, will be different. If any of you think you will escape a sound thrashing, you'll be in for a big shock. The Abbot has asked me specifically to report any misbehaviour to him and by God I shall. As I know who threw something at me I shall be giving their names to the Abbot immediately after class. Don't think I don't know who it was! Mowbray, Watkins, Fairchild – I know you did I!"

"But sir we didn't, how could we?" cried Watkins. "We shall tell the Abbot you just make these things up."

"Silence!" roared Jenkins, but the disturbance only grew in intensity, and feet began to be stamped. All attempts to teach Latin foundered. Quietly the classroom door opened. The austere figure of the Abbot stood within the portal. There was instant silence.

"Everything in order I trust, Brother Jenkins? I heard rather a lot of noise emanating from this room, more than I would usually expect."

"Everything is in order sir" stammered the embarrassed monk, his face purple with rage, his competence once again challenged, his continued employment once again in question, as if the previous term had not been bad enough.

"Good!" hissed the Abbot. "Good, Brother Jenkins." After a pause loaded with menace he went on, "Good. I shall expect a little less exuberance, if I may, in subsequent classroom behaviour!"

The Abbot ran his eyes round the room, noting the silent, servile attendees and knowing full well what had happened, and indeed would happen again.

"Of course sir" coughed Jenkins "of course sir. There will be no repetition."

"You can assure me of that, Brother Jenkins?"

"Of course sir."

The Abbot turned on his heel and disappeared as silently as he had come. The boys gave the monk ten minutes' grace while Jenkins, infuriated by what he had allowed to happen, scribbled out the prep required for the next class. Then, very slowly at first, they began to stamp on the floor and bang the books on their desks.

It was going to be a difficult term, a battle of wits, for the irascible Welshman. By the time the bell brought relief Brother Jenkins knew he would have a tough time handling the sixth; he cursed Secundus for giving him the class.

Such sentiments were also felt by Brother Campbell two classes down the corridor. His pupils were middle school but, with subtlety and cunning, they too had reduced his class to a meaningless shambles. His hands were shaking, his cheeks were blotched. His humour was not improved by someone having written in large letters *Whisky makes the world go round* on the back of the revolving blackboard. Twelve pairs of eager eyes counted the minutes until he reached the bottom of the first board and swung it over the moment it was complete.

Brother Upton by contrast escaped such a baptism of fire; he found his charges wide-eyed and receptive to whatever he said. Charged with teaching geography, he really had no syllabus, nor anything to go on by way of directive. He elected to talk about the Earth and decided to speak about oceans, tides and how they worked. Among his pupils, Henry listened with enthusiasm; it quite took his mind off his bear. Brother Tertius, evoking the glories of mediaeval England in his opening history lesson, also had a quiet class; that was to be expected. He was, after all, really the only master in the school who knew how to do his job professionally.

In the gym, Brother Quartus set up the vaulting horse for his first class after break. He was taking the seniors, and Secundus had specifically told him that he expected the boys to be fit for football, for they had an exacting series of matches ahead of them if they were to retain the Inter-Schools Championship Cup.

The Abbot continued to prowl. Secundus, having no class that morning, inspected the playing fields.

★ ★ ★ ★ ★

Upton returned to his room at Herga after lunch to get ready for games at two thirty. He was determined to re read the terms of his employment and to take the whole matter of staff discipline up with the agents on the next trip to London. He found the papers he wanted but realised to his surprise that someone had been into his room, either while he had been teaching or during lunch, and had searched through his possessions. A five-pound note, a substantial sum, which he had hidden, he thought, rather skilfully in a pocket in his dressing gown, had been removed. Other things had been tampered with and a new tube of toothpaste had also disappeared.

It was while worrying about this that he encountered Brother Tertius climbing breathlessly up the stairs.

"I'm terribly sorry to trouble you, Brother Tertius, but someone has been into my room and has searched through all my possessions. I am missing a five-pound note as well. Do you think this could be one of the support staff? Outside robbers perhaps?"

The older monk shook his head. "Leno and Romano are very well looked after. They would never do such a thing and we are far too isolated from anywhere for there to be burglars about. Are you sure you have been robbed and not mislaid the money?"

"Absolutely. Whoever came into my room turned it over completely."

"How distressing, how very distressing. And on your first day with us."

"Should I report this to the Abbot? To the matron or Miss Tapscott?"

"It's a little premature, in my opinion, and, besides, everyone is so frightfully busy getting the school going again after the holidays. I don't quite know what to suggest."

"It scares me. We teaching monks are so vulnerable."

"The war has brought upon us many bad habits and a breakdown in self-discipline. Leave it with me, Brother Upton. In the meantime, if you do have any things of value Miss Tapscott does have a small safe in her storage room. I believe Miss Tremble has one too, but she has never volunteered to allow anyone to use it."

"I'll try Miss Tapscott! Thank you so much for your help."

* * * * *

It was just after tea the next day when Ambrose found Henry again. "Look, I've done an inspection of the dorm, your dorm, and I've found a loose floorboard where you could hide your teddy bear. The problem is that it is under Turnbull's bed so you will have to leave him there once it's done. Come with me, we've got ten minutes. We'll hide him now."

Sadly, but with at least the threat of Kite removed, Henry gave Ambrose his bear and together they managed to squeeze him into a tight gap under the floorboards directly below the bed.

A week later, Ambrose took Henry under his wing again. He thought his charge was settling in as well as anyone, given the harsh conditions of the school. He seemed to be enjoying games.

"You've managed to keep your teddy hidden?"

"No one suspects. I miss him, but I think he's quite safe there."

"Good. Kite spends her entire life skulking round the dormitory trying to find us doing something wrong, hiding food we don't like or something that we have been given extra by Leno or Romano."

"When do we get letters from our parents, Ambrose? My mummy promised that she would write to me after a few days."

"They won't give us our letters until we have been here for two weeks or more as Primus thinks it is bad for us to be thinking of our homes when we should be concentrating on what we must do at school. Besides, all our letters are looked at by Kite before they're given to us. It's the same the other way when we write home on Sundays. If she sees anything rude about the school or the staff she shows the letter to Primus and they tear it up. Your parents just get a brief typed note saying you are enjoying being at the school and that you are settling down well and so on."

"But that's not true!"

"I know. Carnforth and Williams-Jones say it's just like what happened to their fathers when they were prisoners in Germany. Everything was censored."

"So we can't tell our parents what's happening to us. That's horrible. Is there no way…?"

Ambrose paused and rubbed his chin. He was on difficult ground. His responsibility was to help his new charge to settle in, not to discourage him nor exacerbate what he knew was one of the crueller acts of the Abbot and his staff.

"There is, but I can't tell you about it just yet" he whispered.

"Why not?

"Because I need to get to know you better. What I do myself is I have a sort of secret code with my parents. If I say for example that I am having a "really super duper time" my father looks up the code which we have agreed upon. Then he knows I have either been beaten, the food is worse than ever or Brother Campbell has had too much to drink. It works quite well. "Primus is in a sunny mood" means he has been particularly bad tempered again. Someone dreamed this up after his father had told him that prisoners of war did this sort of thing to get past the Germans. It works well here. Kite hasn't a clue!"

"My father's still away" sighed Henry. "I couldn't do that. When will you tell me the secret Ambrose? I mean how to overcome Miss Tremble stopping all our letters?"

"As soon as I can. Don't worry!"

The dreaded bells began to ring again, this time for evening prayers.

★ ★ ★ ★ ★

For compulsory sports the school was divided into teams by age. Senior boys were made to go on a long run organised by Secundus, followed by intensive football training. In the gym each afternoon Brother Quartus trained the athletics squad, his firm hands helping the seniors to get over the parallel bars and achieve spectacular feats on the vaulting horse. They had a good squad this term and Quartus, like Secundus, was determined to achieve success with his charges. Thompson-Brown, Cottesmore, captain of games, and Phelps showed particular promise and Quartus was particularly keen to see them succeed; extra classes were arranged for the three most talented boys to secure the Victor Ludorum prize. He stood back to admire their physicality, their emerging pubescence, the advent of manhood.

Henry found himself, with the other new boys in junior school, being made to run round the field adjacent to the main school building, supervised by Brother Upton, whom he rather liked. Every night he slept soundly, hardly thinking of home, safe in the knowledge that Royston was secretly hidden under his neighbour's bed.

Two weeks later, when he thought it would be safe, he removed the bear from its hiding place, concealed it in his bed and slept soundly with it snuggled up against him. It had been a particularly exacting day with lots of sports to do in what had been, in terms of the weather, quite a nice day. He was really enjoying football, was good at it - so they kept telling him - and had great fun tackling and outwitting his opponents. He was utterly exhausted however, and fell asleep immediately.

When he awoke to the strident call of the bell on the following morning, however, Royston had disappeared.

EIGHT

Henry looked everywhere for the bear. He asked Turnbull if he had seen him and searched throughout the dormitory in case anyone had stolen him for fun. His endeavours exhausted, he confided his loss to Ambrose.

"Kite has taken him" replied his chum. "He couldn't possibly have been taken by anyone else. Exactly the same thing happened last term when Coleman lost his donkey. He adored his animal. It had lead hooves and was called Conxi. Ramsden lost a rabbit and Kingston a sort of mouse. Kite crept round the dormitory about midnight, according to Fielden, who was dormitory captain that term. She quietly stole all the animals from the boys as they were sleeping."

"Did they ever get them back?"

Ambrose shook his head

"Afraid not. Primus has ordered her specifically to destroy anything that might provide any thought of home or any form of comfort to us. That's why we're all marched into chapel twice a day, to make us think of the hardship of Jesus and all the saints, Saint Eusebius especially."

Ambrose could see that Henry was on the point of tears. He patted his shoulder. "Look, I will do what I can and have a word with Leno, who handles… that sort of thing." He nearly said 'rubbish', but realised that the word would upset Henry all the more. Silently he cursed Kite, indeed Primus and Secundus too, for making all their lives such misery, and longed for his coming release to his public school, where conditions just had to be better. He watched with anguish as his crestfallen little charge made his way sadly out of the room.

There was only one thing he could do. He ran down the back stairs, the shortcut to the kitchen, where he found Romano peeling some rather diseased-looking potatoes.

"Leno? 'e no 'ere. Can I 'elp?" said Romano. Ambrose explained what he thought might have happened to Hingham's teddy bear.

"I tell Leno, Mister Ambridge. Leno 'e always rescuing things from Missa Tremble's rubbish." He gave Ambrose a paternal pat on the back. "You no idea what 'e finds, your letters for one!"

Ambrose smiled "Do your best, Romano, we won't forget."

★ ★ ★ ★ ★

Upton found the work expected of him very demanding. He had not been in the best state of physical fitness on his arrival at the school, and the first few days of sports activities had taken its toll on him. Now, as the third week opened, he felt a lot fitter and indeed a lot more confident. His fellow staff members, with the exception of the kindly Miss Tapscott and the affable Brother Tertius, remained nevertheless distant, cold, aloof and haughty.

Upton wondered what secrets were harboured by his fellow juniors, Jenkins and Campbell, while the matron, Miss Tremble, remained dour and forbidding. No further searches had been made of his room at Herga, but he had placed what little money he had with Miss Tapscott. He didn't much care either for Brother Quartus, who reminded him of a captain he had once come across in the army; smarmy, obsequious and arrogant, not a character to be trusted.

Among the staff, Rosie continued to bait him with a stream of lewd and basic sexual suggestions, indicating a disturbing desire for sex with an older man, particularly one dressed up in holy garments.

St Eusebius School, Upton observed, had been built round two quadrangles; an inner small square, around which lay the heart of the establishment, the school rooms, the headmaster's rooms, the dining room and the memorial hall, and an outer, much larger quadrangle which contained the dormitories, the gym, the swimming pool and the classrooms. At the far end of the quadrangle lay the school chapel, a heavily restored section of what had once been part of the great Abbey of Saint Eusebius. Behind the chapel, at some distance, stood the two massive towers of the former abbey, amid the ruined walls of the great church that it had once been. A Victorian arch had been built where the larger quadrangle gave out onto the grounds of the school. Beside it stood a small self-contained two-storey house, heavily covered in ivy. It was a Victorian folly, constructed as a gate house, with small leaden windows. A door, badly peeling with black paint, peeped out from beneath the ivy.

Upton remembered that it was here he had heard a girl laughing on the night he had arrived. He had barely given it a second thought until, on this particular day returning from the playing fields, he saw the menacing figure of Brother Secundus standing in the doorway, beckoning him to join him. He sensed it was an order, not an invitation. His heart sank. He had taken considerable trouble to avoid any contact with this brutish thug with his domineering demeanour ever since he had come to the school.

"You there! Come in here, I want a word" Secundus barked. He turned and walked back into the little house.

Upton, nervous at this unexpected summons, did

as he was bidden. The deputy headmaster wasted no time in coming to the point. He walked across the room and leaned against the mantelpiece of the small drawing room.

"Take a seat. What's your name again?"

"Upton."

"Brother Upton sir! May I remind you, as I do your lazy colleagues Brother Jenkins and Brother Campbell, that in this school you will address me as sir at all times, including when we meet on the playing fields."

"Yes, sir. Of course sir." Upton had not previously appreciated what a big man he was physically. He also had a very strong accent. Clearly this was the man the taxi driver had warned him to look out for, not a person he would want to meet on a dark night. He wondered what had brought such a man to a remote school like Saint Eusebius, and recalled what Brother Tertius had said. Secundus was certainly fit. He was obsessed with sport and trained ceaselessly on the playing fields with the older boys.

He didn't mince his words. "I don't know whether you are a queer, Brother Upton, like most of them that come here, or whether like me you are a normal heterosexual male but observe chastity as part of the rules of taking orders at this Abbey" he declared, pacing up and down within the confines of the small room. Upton sat in silence; he knew he was now sweating nervously. "But let me tell you that I, as deputy headmaster and Chief Disciplinarian, have the mandate from the Abbot to administer whatever punishment I deem fit to any member of the staff who I consider has transgressed in matters sexual and moral. You heard about Everett, your predecessor?"

"Yes. Miss Tapscott told me he had had my room in Herga." Upton replied hesitantly.

"Nothing else? Nothing from those queens Tertius and Quartus?"

"No sir. Brother Tertius hasn't said anything and I never see Brother Quartus. But then I've only been here three weeks."

There was something very frightening about the man; he visibly exuded menace. It was not so much his close-cropped blond hair, slightly greying at the edges, nor his thick bull neck, as the way he stared with penetrating light blue eyes, set abnormally close together. His accent was strange too; South African, clearly, but with an unusual mixture of English slang.

"Well, my friend, let me tell you something about this Everett, this creature that came to us from somewhere in the darkness. You do not know the story?"

"No, sir. Not at all."

"We have here a young female, Miss Rosie Robinson. You may have seen her serving in your dining room?"

"Yes, yes I have sir. A very attractive young woman."

Upton had thought the ex-Italian prisoner of war, Leno, was probably teaching her the facts of life, but decided to keep quiet.

"Miss Robinson is of course still a virgin. She is deeply religious and has suffered greatly from the war."

What a load of crap, thought Upton, but he kept his peace. She was probably the local tart.

"How sad. I'm sorry to hear this."

"The Abbot and I have promised to ensure that she spends her time with us, when not working, in prayer and contemplation" he continued, expanding upon this, as if Rosie was herself thinking of becoming a nun or something. It seemed strange, given her constant vulgarity and rudeness at breakfast and dinner every day. Then, abruptly, his mood changed. He at once became threatening, almost as if the woman were his daughter and that Upton had some plan to seduce her. He walked across the room to a cupboard under the stairs that led to his bedroom and pulled out a vicious-looking instrument of punishment.

"Know what this is, Upton?"

"A whip, sir. A very big one."

"A South African sjambok. Made out of rhino hide." He waved the weapon of chastisement and began cutting the air viciously with great swishing strokes. "This, my friend, is one of the most effective and devastating weapons ever invented by the white man for keeping the natives under control in Africa."

He slashed at a cushion, which immediately emitted a great cloud of dust. He slashed at it again, as if to make his point.

"I gave Everett eight strokes of this! I had to tie him down. Groist man," he continued in his heavy South African accent, evidently with relish, "you should have heard him howl! Even the Abbot thought I had gone a little bit too far, but my mandate is my mandate and they can't take that away from me!"

"You beat Mr Everett, sir, because he had assaulted Miss Robinson?"

"She said so. He denied it of course, the lying bastard. He left the school that afternoon." He smiled thinly "I bet he's still got my marks on his arse!" He put the sjambok back in the cupboard. "We've business to discuss, Brother Upton. As you know this school must beat all others in sport, winter games and cricket; anything less than excellence from the boys is unacceptable. I look to you to report any boy to me who is not trying on the field, or who says he is not interested in sport. The headmaster and I decide the punishments; he usually gives them the birch, which makes a bloody mess of their backsides, while I prefer the cane. Four strokes of the cane from me is quite equal to eight of the birch." he smirked again. "I like to watch my victims squirm as they sit in class!"

Upton was wondering how long this interview would continue, since he had an afternoon class to prepare for, when there was a knock on the door. Miss Tremble walked in. She scowled at Upton.

"The Abbot wants to see both of us in his rooms this instant. We've some unforeseen problems."

Secundus picked up a small book that was lying on a table and threw it at Upton. "Take a good hard look at this my friend. It's *Techniques of Sports Improvement*, by Reiner Balzer, translated from the German. Study the last three chapters before we next meet. He was SS. No wonder they had such a bloody marvellous army!" Grabbing a cloak he stormed out of the room followed by the matron.

★ ★ ★ ★ ★

Upton shut the front door of the lodge, wiped his brow and walked slowly on to Herga. Clearly Secundus was a deranged, half-mad sadistic swine who would stop at nothing to satisfy his lust for violence and chastisement. Letting himself in with his key, he was surprised to find Campbell in his room again.

"What are you doing in here?" he challenged him. The Scotsman looked up without a hint of surprise.

"This was Everett's room. I lent him some medical equipment. I cannae find it."

"Well, have you asked Miss Tapscott?"

"She didn't know. She said Carps had cleaned the

whole place before you arrived. He might have them."

"Who's Carps?"

"Harry Marshall. He teaches carpentry, hence the name. Lives in the gatehouse."

"And has he?"

"Said he couldnae remember."

"Where did you get my key from?"

"Everett. He gave me a copy."

"I would like it back please."

Upton held out his hand. Campbell grudgingly surrendered the key. It explained one thing at least; he wondered if Jenkins had one too. As he stumped out of the room he growled "If you find three sets of scissors, some bandages and a thermometer would you please hand them back to me."

"Of course."

It was a few days after this incident that Upton realised he had lost nearly all his underwear, a pair of shoes and some socks.

"Ah" said Brother Tertius sadly, as they showered after sports, "I felt I couldn't warn you when you said your money had gone missing. Campbell is always doing this. He pawned poor Everett's suits and he's even taken the Abbot's whisky. I've seen him throw the empties in the hedge."

★ ★ ★ ★ ★

Abbot Primus took another tablet to alleviate the pain. He was suffering both physically and from nervous apprehension. He had been ill at ease ever since the first communication from the lawyers had arrived. His humour was not improved by the recurrence of his old war wound in his right leg, contracted at Teruel in the Spanish Civil War, in which he had fought, most valiantly he thought, for the Republic against the fascist forces. The cold damp climate of the Fens did nothing to improve his health.

Once again he picked up the letter that had been addressed to him personally and brought that morning by recorded delivery. It was from lawyers acting for Everett, who was seeking damages for assault and compensation as a result of his beating by Brother Secundus. The sum in question was more than two years' total income for the school and, if the action were successful, would bring about its closure and collapse. A tense atmosphere prevailed accordingly in the Abbot's study that afternoon.

Holding the letter open, the Abbot looked at Miss Tremble and Secundus with furious, accusing eyes. Secundus, denied his beloved sports training, was in a particularly belligerent and cantankerous mood.

"Look at this!" bellowed the Abbot. "Look what a fine mess you have got us into now! This could get us all closed down! You know the trouble we had last year with the suicide. I told you specifically that Everett was only to be given a notional punishment before his dismissal, not some barbaric flogging from the 16th century!"

"We were only following the practice of the Brotherhood, sir" snapped back Secundus. "It states quite categorically that any misbehaviour by a monk, particularly of a sexual nature, that brings the Abbey into disrepute must be punished in the most severe manner. I don't think that eight shots from a whip is anything out of the ordinary."

"And you?" the Abbot turned to Miss Tremble. "I believe you helped Secundus to hold the man down?"

"Absolutely. We did nothing out of the ordinary, at least as far as I am concerned. We did a similar thing to Parsons two years ago. We never had any complaints."

"Parsons ended up in a mental institution. His time here would not have helped."

"Parsons was caught in the act of sodomising the head boy" Miss Tremble replied icily, staring at her accuser. "In the showers. Wasn't that sufficient?"

The Abbot waved the letter in front of them. "This is from one of the most prestigious and well-regarded solicitors in London. In New Square, Lincolns Inn no less, if that means anything to you. I have been making enquiries; their clients rarely lose their cases."

"What is Everett claiming?" sniggered Secundus. "That I hurt him? Pah. If I'd known I'd have thrashed him even harder!"

"You won't think it so funny when they come to

arrest you for grievous bodily harm, I can assure you Brother Secundus. You might get away with chastising Africans this way in your country, but in Britain we do things differently."

"Let'em come! I've nothing to be ashamed of."

"Not only is there a charge of grievous bodily harm coming your way, but an action has been taken out by Everett to have this school sued for damages. You realise what this means? We will all lose our jobs! Once the parents get wind of this a number will be removed and we still have the scars of that suicide on our hands. Once we fall below the minimum fee income required to maintain the school, we will have to close. It's as simple as that."

"The boy was feeble. A bedwetter. No fibre. No leadership potential. Should never have come here!" interjected Miss Tremble, scowling at the Abbot. "Who's going to support Everett in testifying against us? That old poof Tertius? Quartus, Campbell, Jenkins? They wouldn't dare!"

"Campbell, and Jenkins, if I may interject, will do anything for money. I wouldn't count on it."

"I'd await the next move – call their bluff." The big South African stretched and yawned. "Never respond to threats. Build your defences."

"This isn't Rorke's Drift, Brother Secundus, in case you hadn't noticed."

"We have plenty of ammo to defend ourselves with."

"Good. In that case you will be the one to undertake our defence. Miss Tremble, you will assist Brother Secundus in his endeavours in this matter. I want a draft reply to this letter on my desk by prayers tomorrow morning. Now, get out, both of you and don't darken my door again today!"

The two visitors stumped out of the Abbot's study without a further word. Rage burning in their hearts, each vowed silently to make life even harder for those beneath their charge.

NINE

It was five weeks into the new term, and the smell of new paint and disinfectant had diminished. The food was, if anything, more revolting than ever. Grease was everywhere; on the edge of their bowls, all over their knives and forks, on the table, dribbling down the cheeks of the ravenous boys as they stabbed at the chunks of dark brown gristle and fat that constituted lunch. This was the main meal of the day, the break between the solid dry porridge of breakfast and the dripping on bread that passed for supper. Meals never changed at Saint Eusebius Abbey, at least not for the boys, and what had been served up during the wartime years continued unchanged into peace time; rationing and belt tightening during the years of national reconstruction were cited as the reason. Lunch came with boiled cabbage and diseased-looking potatoes which were served up with everything. Fish, boiled and tasteless, of indeterminate origin and species, was served up on Fridays. Boys who had spilt their food in their urge to suppress their pangs of hunger were forced to stand and watch while their colleagues ate before them.

One such boy, a timid ten-year-old called Bull, stood pitifully on a small stool, as punishment for this misdemeanour. At least a third of the boys now had bad colds; snot-covered wet handkerchiefs were wiped across little red noses as the noise of sneezing made conversation difficult. Ward pushed the last piece of gristle around his bowl. He stabbed several times to try and catch it, quickly wiping the spilt grease from the table before the eagle eye of Miss Tremble could notice his offence

"I'm going to get this dump closed down!" he declared loudly, looking at those around him and challenging Jenkins at the end of the table to comment. He guessed Carnforth would know what he had in mind. The others, forks poised in mid air, looked up in hopeful expectation. Snotty Symonds let out a fearsome nasal explosion, covering them all in fine spray.

"What, burn it down, Ward? I know others are thinking on similar lines. Bennett has a plan; he says it's foolproof" beamed Chatwin, a chubby chap still in the Fourth, wiping his mouth with a snot-stained handkerchief. "Bennett reckons a fire in the stationery cupboard would get the whole thing going."

"Yeah. We've thought of that too, Ward" added Brassington. "Trouble is we've found out there's an asbestos wall. It might contain the conflagration. Bennett's apparently searching for somewhere better."

Martin joined the debate "What about the oil tanks, the ones for the central heating? They'd go up with a terrific bang. Just like they did in the war. My dad was a commando. He loved blowing up the Eyeties." He grinned, looking at Leno and Romano, who were clearing plates away for pudding. He was always going on about the exploits of his father. His father had even written a book on how he had escaped from a prisoner-of-war camp. It was called *Farewell Campo Duce*. Several signed copies were in the school; they were well thumbed and studied very carefully.

"You need a big explosive to fire oil, Martin, otherwise you are on the right track" said Ward, who clearly had prodigious knowledge of the subject. "My father has access to dynamite. We use it to blow up the roots of rotten trees on our farm in Ireland. Is that what you'll use?"

Other boys now joined the debate. The eagle eye of Miss Tremble sensed trouble; she looked around for authority. Jenkins sat at his appointed place, reading a copy of *Racing News* which he had pulled from the pocket of his habit. His mind was miles away, focused on other much more interesting things.

"You should be taking care of your responsibilities, Brother Jenkins!" Miss Tremble hissed in his ear. "And watching what that scoundrel Ward and his little gang are up to!"

Jenkins jumped, woken out of his reverie. "Of course, Matron, of course."

Ward continued, unfazed. "No, the answer for getting rid of this lot is poison" said Martin. "Williams-Jones has it all planned. We are just waiting for the day. We think it could be the School Feast day when all the monks stuff themselves."

"What's Williams-Jones going to use?" asked Ward, raising an eyebrow with surprise. Williams-Jones always confided in him. He was surprised not to have been told.

"He said he'd put strychnine in his cake. Harding told us."

"I'd prefer cyanide. They use it to kill rooks and vermin on our farms. It works wonders. Saves the gamekeepers having to go round shooting them one by one. I'll try and get some for next term. Mustn't let my father know or he'll go mad."

"Ward!" barked Miss Tremble, bearing down on them like some monstrous galleon in full sail. "Why are you whispering?"

"I'm not Matron. I just didn't want to shout. In case you didn't know, it's considered rude."

Miss Tremble stumped across to where they were sitting and seized him by the hair. "You're lying to me, you disgusting little creep. You're plotting something. I know from the look in your eyes."

"No Matron. Honestly I'm not!"

"I've not had to put up with you for four and a half

years without knowing something about your deceit and cunning" she cried, letting go of his hair. "You Irish are all the same, liars, cheats and thieves. You'll probably be planning to murder us all next if I know your lot!"

Carnforth hid his face and pinched himself to stop from laughing. The eagle eye missed nothing

"You've got a problem, Carnforth?"

"No matron. Just a tickle in my throat. Pepper."

"We don't use pepper in this school. You know that quite well."

He was saved from further interrogation at that point by a bell. It was time to clear away and prepare for pudding, heavy stodge with custard.

"When will we know when they've taken it?" asked three eager voices.

"When you see them drop and writhe. Rats wriggle and squirm before they die."

"Can't wait to see her on the floor – and Secundus too!"

"You will in time, you mark my words, that is, if Williams-Jones had put enough in in the first place."

"But suppose he hasn't? That could be terrible."

"Risk we'll just have to take, won't we!" remarked Ward, as they lined up for pudding. Miss Tremble returned to her place in the dining room and scowled round at the array of disgusting faces with their grease-stained mouths. How she loathed the little brutes. Only their constant flogging gave her cause for happiness.

There was another group which caught her eye, this time under the supposed supervision of Brother Campbell, who was otherwise distracted searching through the back pages of the *Horkinge Daily News*. The group comprised a number of particularly aggressive boys from the Lower Fourth with years ahead of them at Saint Eusebius. Leading the pack was a scruffy tearaway called Oldham, who was backed up by Melbury, Constable, Steatham, Rockley and Linforth. Their plans were more mundane; escape was not on the menu, as the creation of havoc, abuse of anything held in high regard by the monks and an endless war of attrition against Kite were the prime objectives of their aggression. The liberation of the letters from their parents, suppressed or edited by the matron before distribution, was a matter of particular ire to them and indeed to all the boys. Plans were well advanced for a coordinated, multi-faceted attack upon this dreadful woman.

* * * * *

Classes did not improve as the term advanced, at least not in terms of master-pupil relations. The new monk, Upton, was watched warily, yet with a certain sense of anticipation, much as jackals encircle their intended victims. Terror continued to be exuded by both Primus and Secundus. There was grudging respect for the elderly Tertius, who at least had some idea how to teach and make his classes popular, and there was disdain for the overtly paedophilic Quartus whose muscular physicality was thrust upon all those who took his fancy. For Brothers Campbell and Jenkins there was no respite, yet each adopted a policy of outright confrontation, backed up inevitably by physical violence at the earliest opportunity. Oldham had never shown any remorse in the relentless baiting of this tetchy Scot; he was a sort of picador, charged with enraging the Campbell bull in the hope that one day the matador, the Abbot, would give him the final coup de grâce.

This particular day he had taken glue from the model aeroplane and hobbies class and poured it thinly on Campbell's chair. The effect had been spectacular, but Campbell had exploded. "Och, ya dimwit!" he screamed, scratching at his backside as he rose from the chair and walked among his pupils. He carried with him the hard-edged Hillard & Botting Shorter Latin Primer, which he brought down with a mighty crack on Steatham's head.

"I'll get ye to give me the right answer Steatham, before this term is over!" he roared. He strode slowly through the class glowering with rage and pent up fury. Middleton-Cheney was next. He received two blows and a clip round the ear. The rest of the class sat mute in fear as their teacher wandered past the desks, dishing out random punishment to all who caught his eye.

There were still another eight weeks to go to the distant Easter holidays. Parsing Latin was not getting any easier, not helped by the fact that Campbell had no idea how to teach. He had arrived mysteriously in the middle of the summer term of 1945. Everyone whispered that he had been let out of jail and that this was the first job he could find. It was evident to everyone that he had no money. It was also evident that he liked to drink; whisky, and lots of it. He had a fondness for cheap cigarettes. Oldham, Steatham, Middleton-Cheney and Linforth were not the only ones who harboured a deep loathing for this foul-mouthed thug with halitosis who passed for a classics master at the Abbey.

Attempts had already been made to get rid of him. In the previous term, Henriques, one of the school forwards in the First Eleven, had aimed a ball at the window of Campbell's room in Herga, but missed. He got the wrong window, hitting the monks' ground floor shower room, from which a naked Brother Quartus had fled covered with shards of glass and bleeding into the snow. This had been enormous fun for all the plotters, but Campbell's Christmas present had gone awry. Henriques, beefy and as fast with his brain as his feet, had skilfully persuaded the official enquiry, headed by the menacing Secundus, that the whole incident had been an accident. They were after all practising for the critical match against Magdalene's. Henriques had passed on to Winchester, on a scholarship. Herga's windows had been covered with steel mesh to avoid a repetition, and Brother Quartus nursed a sore back and buttocks until the end of term.

Campbell, however, knew that the so-called 'accident' had been a deliberate attempt upon his person. His dislike and disdain for his pupils had, if anything, grown worse during the Christmas holidays. He now took over some of Everett's classes for juniors and for those considered to be intellectually unworthy of the attention of the headmaster; they included maths, never an easy one, French, where he probably knew even less than the boys, and history.

"You've heard?" whispered Steatham, still rubbing his head, as they left class,

"Heard what?" Middleton-Cheney had a headache coming on and his ears were hurting.

"His days are numbered!"

"He's given in his notice, or the police are coming?"

"Williams-Jones is going to kill the lot of them with poison. He's already laid the bait."

"Wow! Poison in his whisky? That'd be brilliant."

"Can't say more. It's ultra secret. Won't tell anyone will you?"

"Course not. Can't wait though!"

They glanced back at Campbell, grinned and went their ways.

★ ★ ★ ★ ★

Upton made his way down the stairs to reach his class on the ground floor. He decided to take a short cut through the washrooms, despite the standing orders that no masters were to go there; the boys were not showering, so there would be no one around. But there was someone. A small boy, crouching in the corner, was being kicked and punched by three others. He was screaming for them to stop, but they carried on, laughing, goaded on by their victim's howls for mercy.

Upton paused, stood silent to try and work out who they were, for they were older boys, probably in third form, and not in any of his classes.

"This'll teach you for being wet!" cried one, kicking the victim in his stomach "and for being such a disgrace to our school."

"I tried, you know I tried!" bleated the crouching victim, between sobs, but his entreaties fell on deaf ears. More blows rained down on him.

"You let them score against us, you pathetic turd!" a bigger boy declared, whacking a shoe hard into the victim's backside.

"Stop this at once!" barked Upton, advancing on the trio and their victim.

"I want your names this instant. I shall be taking this overt act of cowardice and bullying to the Abbot, who I hope will chastise you in the way you most deserve."

There was a moment of silence, broken only by sobbing of the victim on the floor of the washroom.

"He deserved it, sir. He's wet and he's let the school down."

"Yes, he's really let us down. He must be punished. Brother Secundus says we must root all weak people in this school."

"Brother Secundus will not condone bullying, and nor will I. Who is this boy on the floor?"

"It's Watkins, sir. Wetty Watkins, because that's what he is. He's wet."

"Yes, he's wet, really wet" said one of the others "he deserved it."

Watkins, badly bruised and bleeding over one eye, rose to his feet and rushed from the washroom. Upton took their names. The bell for class began to ring.

Suddenly the accusing voice of Miss Tremble was at his back.

"What are you doing in the washrooms, Brother Upton? You know it is against school rules for masters to visit or pass through them at any time. Only the Abbot and I may enter the washrooms. I shall advise him of this. You have been warned!"

"There was a blatant case of bullying, Matron, and I went to investigate." He named the boys and their victim. Miss Tremble looked at him disdainfully.

"There is no such thing as bullying in this school, Brother Upton, and the sooner you realise that the better."

"Three boys kicking a weaker one in the washrooms! When they know that the teaching staff will not intervene? If that's not bullying what is? It is rampant in this school and you know it. And what about the wounds suffered by Watkins? To what do you attribute that?"

"Watkins fell down the stone stairs leading to chapel. He cut his head. I know because it happens so often."

"What, that boys fall down these stairs as a matter of course?"

"They are steep and quite well worn. We have warned boys to be careful."

"Boys are being beaten black and blue by their peers and you do nothing about it?"

"There's no bullying in this school, I repeat, and furthermore, if there was, it is none of your business to do anything about it!"

"So I'm to stand by meekly and watch all this going on?"

"Your words, not mine, Brother Upton. You might say that, but who am I to comment?" She gave him a look of withering scorn and turned on her heel.

Later Upton caught the Abbot as they were preparing for evening prayers and recounted what had happened. He looked surprised at Upton's evident distress.

"I appreciate your concern, Brother Upton, and bullying is indeed a most loathsome act. Rest assured that I shall of course administer a sound caning to the perpetrators. I must warn you however that softness among boys is not something that we accept at Saint Eusebius. Both Brother Secundus and I believe in the triumph of the strongest, as in the animal kingdom so among the human race, and that the weaker of the species will succumb to the stronger. Boys must be prepared here for the realities of life. This school is mandated to prepare the young to be the governing class, not clerks in a bank. Sometimes there are those who will not..."

"Surely, sir, these boys have not yet reached puberty!" interrupted Upton. "Their character, their manhood has yet to be formed. The boy Watkins could have a Field Marshall's baton in his knapsack, or whatever it is they say. He mustn't be damaged..."

"We know best, Brother Upton, in matters of this nature. Miss Tremble keeps a watchful eye for any misbehaviour. She puts the boys' welfare always to the forefront of her duties."

"But there is bullying, sir. I now realise how much more I would have seen if I had kept my eyes and ears open."

The Abbot gave a condescending smile and muttering something in Latin, dismissing Upton with a wave of his hand. No wonder they had had a suicide the previous term, he thought, with staff as insensitive as this.

* * * * *

It was just before evening prayers when Ambrose managed to get hold of Henry.

"Leno's just told me that he has found your bear, with a lot of other toys, waiting to be taken away by the dustmen tomorrow morning. I have asked him to rescue him and keep him hidden until we can think of a safer place to hide him. Thought you'd like to know!"

Henry was thrilled. "Thank you Ambrose, gosh that's an amazing bit of good news!" In truth he had almost given up hope of ever seeing Royston again. "Is he all right?"

"All the fluffy toys have been left out in the rain. Leno says they are all in a bad way."

"At least we have got him back!"

Ambrose was surprised at Henry's growing maturity in handling such an emotive subject as his lost teddy bear. Clearly the survival instinct, so beloved of Abbot Primus and his cohorts, was already having an effect on the little new boy for whom he had responsibility. He

wondered what else might have changed in the little
fellow's head.

TEN

That evening, down at the gatehouse at the foot of the school grounds, Mrs Marshall put down the soaking tea cloth with which she was wiping the plates for their supper and called out to Harry.

"It's ready, Harry" she cried, trying to make herself heard over the noise coming from the radio. Harry, turning it off, came into the little room they used for meals; it was an annexe off the kitchen and was adjacent to the boiler. It was cosy and very welcome in the depths of winter.

"His Lordship see you all right, then?"

"Twelve bottles this time! I'd say he did. Ireland's finest malt."

"There's a catch, must be somewhere, when they give you things like that."

"Not with 'im there ain't. You know how far we go back!"

"War's over now Harry. Everyone has to stand on their own two feet."

"Well he helped us get the job here. Don't look a gift horse in the mouth, as they say. There are people out there who are homeless, nearly starving, and we were the country what won the war. You wouldn't think it, what with all the rationing there still is."

"What about the boy? We looking after him and all his friends again this year? You want to be careful, Harry. Bloody Abbot's never taken kindly to you or what you do up at the school."

"He can't afford to annoy Lord Ward. By the way, I forgot to tell you his lordship asked me to look after the gun. The boy got a four-ten for Christmas. Wants me to teach him how to use it. Talk about how the other half live."

"You're not going to let a twelve year old boy walk round the grounds of this Abbey blasting everything in sight with a shotgun? You must have been barmy, Harry, to have let 'im talk you into it."

"Made it worth our while. I didn't promise the boy anything. Told him, and his lordship, that I'd keep, it locked up. It's in that cupboard under the stairs"

Mrs Marshall grunted a somewhat insincere approval. "I don't drink whisky, you forgotten?"

"I'll trade some bottles for some gin for you. Vicar in Horkinge's always ready to do a trade. Told his lordship I'd try and give the boy some practice round the grounds; rooks and things. May be up on the border with the Littlemore estate."

"Don't you go and get caught poaching! I've heard they've got a new monk come to join them at the Abbey."

"Poor sod. Hope he's not a poofter like the rest of them."

"Better if he was. After what they did to that poor Everett bloke!"

"Heard a rumour Everett's suing after what that Secundus fellow did to him."

"Right nutter."

"Who, him or the monk?" Mrs Marshall put two plates of hot, steaming stew on the table, then poured them out two large cups of tea. "There's something sinister about him, the monk I mean."

"Wouldn't want to meet him on a dark night, nor the Abbot for that matter. Not on a night like tonight."

"The Abbot has a drink problem. His lordship told me."

"The least of his vices, if you ask a simple soul like me. There's too much caning and flogging at that place. Not normal, not right it ain't."

Harry shrugged. "Parents pay. It's their choice. Kids could always complain if they wanted to."

"What up there? No way. It's what the upper class call upbringing. Make them fight wars and so on. Abbot's always rabbiting on about breaking horses and training dogs, doesn't sound too religious to me."

"I expect the boy will be over with his friends as soon as the food, or lack of it, hits them."

"And don't you go showing off your pistols to them neither. We could both end up in trouble if word gets around that you've got an arsenal of German guns in this house."

"I'll be careful. Only Ward and that friend of his."

"Ambrose?"

"Yeah, him. Maybe one or two others."

"Not Philips I hope. Didn't he strangle one of the cats?"

"No that was Maltby. He left in disgrace."

"Wasn't he thrashed by Secundus?"

"You bet he was. Saw that brute Secundus only yesterday picking willow for his whips down by the beck. Didn't even bother to look up when I passed. Even a pig would have grunted! "

"Poor little bastards. You know I've got a funny feeling we are going to see something unusual happen this term."

"Not another suicide I hope. School should have been closed after what they did to him. Certainly that Tremble woman should have been sent packing."

"He hanged himself. Ward told us the story. He wet the bed, parents both killed in the war. Some elderly relatives had to come down to take away his body."

Marshall poured himself a large whisky from one of the bottles Lord Ward had given him. "I'll keep the guns under lock and key. You're right; silly idea to look after the gun for the boy. I'll make sure he won't find it though."

"You mind how you go, Harry. As I've always said, they don't like you up at that place, see you as being on the side of the boys."

"Well I am aren't I? I'm hardly going to collaborate with a bunch of sadistic perverts if that's what you think. Did you hear about the Spaniard?"

"Spaniard? What Spaniard?"

"Some scruffy bloke sniffing around last week. Asked for someone with a fancy name but they sent 'im packing. Leno did. Could have been that so-called Brother Campbell. He's always using other names!"

★ ★ ★ ★ ★

That February of 1947, the Feast Day of Saint Eusebius fell upon a weekday. The Abbot accordingly declared that the preceding Sunday would be the occasion for his annual speech to the boys in the memorial hall which would follow Mass in the chapel at eleven. The great and the good from the Diocese of Branchester had been invited to attend. It was an unfortunate choice, for heavy snow fell again across the whole of the eastern counties, cutting off villages and rendering travel, even by train, almost impossible. The wind, having brought snow from the north, had now swung round to the east bringing a vicious, biting, cold wind from the Steppes of Russia.

Upton put on extra clothes, but the cold tore through him as he walked across from chapel to the memorial hall. This building was a Victorian adjunct, like the chapel, to the original ruined monastery, and it sat like an ugly carbuncle at right angles to the school itself. It was large, designed to contain the whole school when necessary, and had a raised platform at one end. The platform was used for ceremonial occasions, for invigilating exams and, when crimes of a particularly serious nature had been committed, for school floggings.

On the walls were memorials to the old boys who had given their lives in the service of their country. A tablet commemorating the seven who had fallen in the Zulu Wars had been moved to a side wall. Six huge spears, assegais, were placed on either side of it. Two long lists of those fallen in the First World War stood on either side of a memorial window, and work was under way to place another large one to the left of one of them recording the names of those who had perished in the Second World War; names of casualties from Burma and the Far East were still being added.

The memorial window itself was of a garish early twentieth century depiction of the execution and death of the patron saint of the school. It had been painted by one of the monks in the 1920s and plans were in hand to replace it with an even more powerful depiction of the flagellation and death of Saint Eusebius.

Williams-Jones yawned and nudged Alexander. They had heard it all before, dozens of times. The procession was about to begin. Mr Ainsley, already tired from playing Sung Mass, watched in the mirror of his windowless room for the signal from the Abbot. He had before him a repertoire of two patriotic tunes, *Rule Britannia* and *Land of Hope and Glory*. On the signal from the Abbot he would play the National Anthem.

"Look at Thompson-Brown!" hissed Knight from behind the other two. "What a creep!"

Thompson-Brown, his blonde hair greased down and parted impeccably, led the procession as he had done for Sung Mass and as he did for chapel every day. Instead of the golden cross, however, he now carried a carving of Saint Eusebius, which was to be placed with great ceremony beneath the window of his execution. Behind him trooped the monks, the most junior foremost, the older ones, Secundus and Tertius, bringing up the rear. Two archdeacons from the diocese, big beefy men clad in black with gaiters and wearing flat broad-brimmed hats, came next, having somehow overcome the weather. Finally the huge, intimidating figure of the Abbot brought up the rear. They spread out on reaching the platform, rather like vultures, each taking his designated seat in order of seniority, the two archdeacons either side of the Abbot. Thompson-Brown fussed around to ensure that the Abbot's seat was exactly in the right position for his speech. From one side Miss Tremble watched the boys for the slightest hint of irreverence at such an important ritual.

Upton, as the most junior monk, sat to the extreme right of the stage. He stared at the ranks of assembled boys, wondering what was going through their minds. He himself wondered how long all this elaborate formality was going to last. Rosie had been right in her warning; the habit did scratch his legs and he was developing a very sore behind.

As the National Anthem ended, a spotlight shone onto the huge, bald head of the Abbot as he rose to address the company. He proffered no words of welcome and stood without notes, to make his speech. To Upton it was all bizarrely theatrical.

"You boys have been sent to me to be made into men" he began, in a commanding bass voice resonant of his power and authority. "And into men we shall make you, like your fathers and your grandfathers before you." He turned and pointed to the war memorials. "They, like those mentioned here, gave up their lives for their King and Country."

There was a brief pause, a moment's silence to let the message sink in. He turned back to the assembled ranks and studied them, much as his cat might have looked upon ranks of mice assembled for slaughter.

"For the past few weeks, in the holidays, you have

been exposed to softness, warmth, possibly an excess of good food. This might have been enjoyable for you, but rest assured you have not been sent to this school for your comfort and indulgencies but to be trained and hardened for the realities of life as leaders of men, generals, admirals, colonial governors, custodians of our great Commonwealth and Empire..."

Upton recognised the philosophy and the creed from his first interview with the headmaster of the school. It confirmed his obsession with Jesuitical theocracy, their suffering in the conquest of Latin America and the spreading of the gospel of truth and light among the pagan hordes. Oldham had more worldly thoughts, especially of his last Christmas lunch, his tummy rumbled as a smell of cooking, possibly of braised beef, wafted into the hall from the nearby kitchens. The new boys watched in nervous anticipation.

"And so, as we prepare ourselves for Lent, we must be ready for sacrifice" he continued, outlining the pain and suffering that all of them, including his fellow monks, should be prepared to accept. He exhorted the school with a rousing challenge that Saint Eusebius would be the leader in its field, in sports and all matters academic. By this time however he had lost his general audience, with boredom if nothing else, all, that is, save Thompson-Brown, who beamed and nodded condescendingly with spaniel-like devotion.

Ward caught Miss Tremble's eye. He was Irish, and a distant renegade great uncle of his had fought against the hated British before the Republic was created. No king and country rubbish for him; he was a revolutionary, and by God he'd show them yet what he could do to them and the ghastly school. He smirked in defiance, knowing it would irritate and annoy her.

Others cast surreptitious glances at their watches. Chiswell, in middle school, eyed the assegais. He imagined himself spearing all the seated black-clad figures, helped by a gang of all his friends. Only the archdeacons, content in the knowledge that a good lunch washed down with fine claret was to follow, smiled benignly from the stage.

"Thus, we shall instil in you, while you are in our charge, a sense of not only duty to your Monarch and to your Fatherland but a spirit of adventure, of boldness, of daring, of undertaking risk, both commercially and in the field of battle, for those who dare shall win and those who do not shall forever be confounded." As the Abbot concluded, and at a signal from Thompson Brown, the entire school broke into its usual rendition of *Land of Hope and Glory*. Then everyone filed out of the memorial hall, the boys separated from the Abbot and his guests from Branchester, and made their way wistfully to the dining room, well aware from the smells that a much better lunch was being served up somewhere else.

★ ★ ★ ★ ★

The spirit of what the Abbot had promulgated had indeed already been taken up with relish by the boys, particularly by Ward and Oldham, long before they had had to listen to his dreary deposition. There would now be adventure from within their ranks, there would be risks undertaken and these would be met with courage and daring.

Little did the Abbot know what had lain in the minds of the cherubic rows of faces that stood to attention before him as he and his guests had made their way out of the hall. Two groups, or rather gangs, were in fact already at work. Ward's contingent had plans for escape to good living involving theft of the monks' food and the Abbot's whisky and the communion wine. Oldham's plan was to create chaos, sow discord among the monks, and hopefully see off Campbell and Jenkins. Both groups were united in their loathing of Matron, who was scheduled to be the first target. Ward furthermore had plans for Secundus, but achieving his demise was going to be extremely difficult; ideas were requested.

There was also the problem posed by the prefects. The six prefects, dapper and smug in their special seniors' clothes, provided the monks, especially the

Abbot and Secundus, with a stream of inside information. In a school where the boys thrived on prisoner-of-war escape stories, prefects earned the sobriquet of stoolpigeons. They were distrusted, disliked, and avoided as much as possible.

Ward was assisted by Carnforth, who had just turned twelve. He was a deceptively cherubic individual whose dexterity and deceit had been hugely successful, notwithstanding a few beatings, many as a result of trying to injure Miss Tremble and other masters who had reported badly of him. While bringing about the beating of a prefect was deemed a great success, more important things lay to hand, particularly the exposure of Campbell as a thief, of Quartus as a pervert and of Jenkins as a drunk. Not everyone had such drastic remedies as Williams-Jones, who had of course openly declared his intention of poisoning all the staff as they ate boys' rations, or Bennett, who quietly planned to burn the whole place down.

The heavy snowfall was in fact exactly what Bennett had been hoping for. To the dismay and fury of Secundus, all games were cancelled that afternoon and boys were instructed to do extra work, attend to their hobbies or find other pursuits. Only in the gym did Brother Quartus insist upon athletics being held as usual.

Bennett, knowing he had about twenty minutes to put his plan into action, slipped out of the kitchen door as Leno and Romano rushed in some confusion with more dishes for the Abbot and his guests, Secundus and Miss Tremble. Quickly he ran round to the back of the garage, where the Abbot's car, a venerable Rover saloon, lay under dust covers. Using a pump Carps had lent him, he began methodically to drain the tank, putting the petrol into milk bottles and concealing them in another outbuilding beneath a pile of rotting logs and old timber.

His mission completed, he held his pump carefully against his chest and sneaked back the way he had come. No one saw him enter or leave the building.

★ ★ ★ ★ ★

That night Miss Tremble lived up to her reputation as an avenging angel. With her thin, lined, foxy face tensed as if for a hunt, she opened the North Dormitory door and began to walk silently passed the sleeping boys. She wore rubber-soled flat shoes that hissed quietly on the linoleum as she made her way along the beds. It was nearly eleven o'clock and the wind, howling round the building and rattling the ill-fitting windows, helped to hide her footfalls. She paused carefully before the new boys, pulling back the blankets of those whom she suspected of harbouring toys, pleased that she had found and destroyed Henry's bear. No one eluded her;

a fluffy cat belonging to Seggins, another new boy, was quietly removed as he slept.

In Herga the monks too were preparing for bed. Upton made his way to the bathroom to clean his teeth. A light was on, but the door was not locked. Inside, to his surprise, he found Quartus towelling himself and examining his genitalia.

"Oh, I'm so sorry. I'll come back later" said Upton.

"Come in, old man, come in. Nothing to be afraid of!" joked Quartus in his cheeky-chappy voice. He continued to study his penis as if he were looking at some *objet d'art*.

"He's no threat to you old man. Much better things to be thinking about, haven't we!" he continued in his awful nasal accent, as if his penis was some sort of friend and they were planning a venture together.

"I'll be back later" said Upton, shutting the door.

"As you wish" replied Quartus, breaking wind. "I'll be out in a jiffy."

Upton had kept his distance from Quartus ever since the monk had admonished him for not singing loudly enough at morning prayers. "Got to do better than that, old man, or the Abbot will see you off!" he had said in a stage whisper, well within earshot of the Abbot. As Upton had never had any sort of religious upbringing, hymn tunes were quite unknown to him. It was the unctuous tone however, together with the accent, that had finally got to him. He loathed the man. He also suspected that Quartus, being very sporty and fit, might in some way be in league with Secundus; a spy, a quisling perhaps?

Down the passage, Brother Tertius prepared the work for the next day's classes; the history of military warfare in the Middle Ages. He took off his spectacles and sat back in thought. Brother Upton, he mused, might just be the figure he was looking for to help him complete his tableau of the martyrdom and death of Saint Eusebius.

★ ★ ★ ★ ★

The fire at the gatehouse cottage burnt low as Harry Marshall flicked through the pages of the *Horkinge Herald*. In his hand he held a half-empty glass of whisky. One of his spaniels lay asleep on the mat before the fire.

"Hey, Nellie, get a load of this!" he cried.

"Can't it wait till morning?" replied a voice from the small bedroom upstairs.

"Course it can, love, but I'd just thought you might be interested. Bears out what I was saying last term."

Harry got up suddenly, frightening the dog, which woke with a start and ran from the room.

"Just listen to this report here." He folded the paper to make it easier to read. He started to climb up the small staircase that led to the bedroom. "Report from the legal news at the back of our local rag. I nearly missed it. Listen. This is what it says: 'Robert Alexander Campbell, who gave his address as St Eusebius Abbey School, was yesterday acquitted on technical grounds of three charges of obtaining money by false pretences. Campbell furthermore asked that five similar cases be taken into consideration, saying that he was innocent of these for the reasons that had been stated. After reviewing the case the judge told Campbell that he was extremely lucky not to be facing a custodial sentence. Should he reoffend, warned the judge, he would be sent down without any hesitation.' Well, well. That's turn up for the books!"

Harry reached the top of the stairs, folded the paper and threw it on to the bed.

"Well I never!" said his wife. "You always did have your doubts, didn't you Harry? What with the way he goes on up at that school and all. D'you think the Abbot will find out?"

"He will if he reads this paper."

"Nasty man, that Campbell. Never did take a liking to him."

"You're not the only one. You should hear what the boys have to say about him."

"When did this happen? Recently?"

Harry looked at the date of the paper and at the date of the legal proceedings. "They'll not have seen it. It was five weeks ago, before term started. This must be an old copy, the one the butcher wrapped the meat in."

"No it's not. Look it's quite clean. It must have been one of the ones they left here while we were away in Plymouth."

"Makes sense. Explains why Campbell is running round the school being so bloody awful to everyone."

"What about Jenkins? I reckon he's a right rotten apple too. Didn't he have some one after him too?"

"Not as far I know. Not yet anyway."

"Heard rumours they're in trouble about that Everett bloke."

"Wouldn't be at all surprised after what they did to him. There's a new monk joined them this term. Met him?"

"Not really. Quiet bloke. Not like Everett. Seems OK."

"Someone had better warn him about that Rosie if he isn't to go the same way as the others!"

"Too true."

"Wait till I give a this report to the boys. That'll get Campbell worried true and all!"

"Ward will love to hear it, knowing how much he hates that man. Go and put the dogs out and hurry up to bed. I'm absolutely freezing."

"Not till I've finished his father's whisky!"

It was snowing lightly again outside. Harry wondered what jobs they would have for him up at the school in the morning. Before he went up to bed he looked again at the splendid collection of pistols he had liberated from the German officer corps in the last days of the war. He wondered how much he could get for them from a collector if he ever had to sell them. He was particularly fond of the Luger and its ammunition, which he kept in the left hand drawer of his desk in the little dining room. He had fired it once and was amazed at its handling and balance. No, he wouldn't shoot the Abbot's cat with it, but it could come in handy, he mused, for knocking off a rabbit or two from the neighbouring estate.

There was also a small, very light, pistol designed for use by a woman if attacked at close quarters. He had never paid much attention to it. He had liberated it from a house just after the regiment had crossed the Rhine, complete with ammunition and put it with the Luger for safekeeping. That was before the shell had exploded in the house beside them. He had been lucky, and so indeed had Lord Ward as he had pulled him and another officer out of the rubble.

ELEVEN

Veronica Hingham tore open the cheap-looking envelope with the Horkinge postmark, hoping and praying that it was a letter at last from her darling Henry, but her disappointment was immediate. It was yet another tacky, typed letter from the school, written by the matron. "Dear Mrs Hingham" it began. "I am writing to inform you that your son James" ('James' had been crossed out and 'Henry' written thinly above) "has now been with us for five weeks. He is settling satisfactorily into the workings of our school. He is doing well in his classes, gets on with the other boys and clearly enjoys games. He is in good health. Yours sincerely M. Tremble, Matron."

Veronica put the letter down on the table and took a handkerchief to dab her eyes. She knew, with her mother's instinct, that all was not well with Henry, but she felt there was nothing she could do. Richard was still on secret service, somewhere in Europe she guessed, and Giles, his brother, was less than sympathetic.

She wondered if Uncle Gilbert, her own brother, might have some useful suggestions. She picked up the telephone and dialled his number. As luck would have it he was in.

"They censor the letters, Veronica" he declared immediately. "It's quite common practice. These school johnnies don't want lonely little boys slagging off their institutions. I expect Henry has written every week and thinks you have received all his correspondence. He probably wonders why you have not replied to him."

"But I write to him every week, Gilbert!"

"They'll be withholding the letters if they think you are too sympathetic. I knew a case once where the matron actually wrote as if she was the mother. She was able to copy the handwriting pretty accurately. Her letters, not the originals, told the little boy to pull himself together, to be a man. To forget being a child."

"What happened?"

"I'd rather not say."

There was a long pause.

"You see Veronica, many little boys lost their fathers in both world wars. It was then, and is now, a dreadful time for the poor little things."

"Henry is very sensitive. He should never have gone away, so far, so young."

"It is the norm though, Veronica. Well, let's say for those from our sort of background."

"I'm worried he'll try and run away. In this weather. He could die unseen, unloved, in some ghastly snow-covered *ditch*!" Veronica sobbed uncontrollably into the telephone.

"I've an idea" said Gilbert. He well knew how emotional and irrational his sister could be and how she doted on her son. "Give it another week or so and see if he writes. Ring up this matron person, and if you don't get a satisfactory answer, we'll go down to the school unannounced and find out what's going on. There's a good rail service from London, or we could drive if I can get hold of some petrol coupons."

"Can't we go now? I'm so upset."

"Weather's dreadful and the roads are blocked with snow. No, now would not be a good time. But in a week's time perhaps it will be better."

"He could be dead by then!"

"No he won't, my dear. No he won't. We'll probably find him playing quite happily with the other boys."

"I doubt it!"

Still sobbing, Veronica hung up. She walked over to the kitchen cabinet, took out the bottle and poured herself a large gin. Then she sat back and contemplated the next move. Somehow they had to visit the school no matter how inclement the weather, and the sooner the better too.

★ ★ ★ ★ ★

By coincidence Ambrose sought out Henry that very

same morning. He said he had some suggestions about where to hide Royston, who was still being kept by Leno hidden on top of a cupboard in the school kitchen.

"Leno told me Romano has a hiding place in the garage where the Abbot's car is kept" explained Ambrose. "He's got a revolver there that he took off a Spaniard he found prowling in the grounds a few weeks ago."

"You think it's safe?"

"As much as anywhere. Royston will be out of the school building and the Abbot hardly ever uses his car. It's quite dry too."

"When can we put him there?"

"Too dangerous for you, or me, to go round the back of the school, it's out of bounds and Kite can see everything from her dispensary. I'll see if one of the Italians can do it. By the way have you got a letter for me to send to your parents?"

"I gave it in yesterday, to Kite."

Ambrose scratched his head. "Could you do me another one, Henry, really telling them how it is? I can't make promises, but we have found a way of getting letters posted from this place that neither Primus nor Kite know about."

"You bet, Ambrose. When?"

"As soon as you can. Certainly give it to me by Thursday if it is to go this week."

★ ★ ★ ★ ★

Brother Campbell was in a particularly bad mood, even worse than usual. He knew, or rather hoped, that he had got off lightly with the magistrates in Lincoln, but as he walked over to the red room to prepare for the afternoon Latin class which the Abbot had told him to take this term, he somehow felt that his past was going to catch up with him. Well, he for one did not molest the boys, he thought in self defence, and further more he was deemed by the Abbot to be quite a good teacher, despite having absolutely no qualifications whatsoever for the job.

He opened the door to the empty classroom by kicking it, as his hands were full of books, and stared in silent fury at what someone had written on the blackboard. It wasn't the first time either.

The Abbot's an absolute fool
To give Campbell a job in this school
He's a thief and a thug
A bum and a drunk
With the brains of a half-witted mule.

Furiously he started to erase the offending lines, wondering not only which of the boys had perpetrated the act but more importantly how the information had come to reach the school. In his heart he felt that it must be that bastard Carps, for he seemed to be the conduit for all information to and from the school. To his, frustration he had no way of proving it.

Then the door, which he had kicked to close behind him, opened quietly and the Abbot appeared silently behind him.

"Who wrote that?" boomed the Abbot.

"No idea, sir. No idea!" Campbell squawked, furiously scrubbing off the offending verse.

"There must be a reason behind this, Brother Campbell. I'm not going to be fobbed off with such a feeble response, particularly if I find that we are about to be charged with harbouring criminals in this school. Give me a sound reason why this should have been written in your classroom, in full cognition that you would be the first to see it?"

"I can't imagine sir. I'm in no trouble with the law."

"Things have been reported to me as having gone missing. We had two silver eighteenth century candlesticks stolen from the Abbey chapel over the Christmas holidays. I have asked the police to investigate. We are so isolated that it must have been an inside job. Dear Mr Marshall and his wife were away in Plymouth briefly, otherwise they would have reported any suspicious activity. You've no idea then?"

"No sir. None at all."

"Brother Secundus is a dab hand when it comes to punishment, let me remind you Brother Campbell. Brother Everett's expulsion should be a warning to all monks who serve in this Abbey. We are the purest of the pure. It is our standard of probity that must be imparted upon the boys. I may beat boys for disobedience from time to time, but the offence pales into insignificance if I were to find any misbehaviour, of any type, especially theft among my staff."

"I have not stolen anything, Brother Primus, sir. Do you want me to swear on the Bible for this?"

"I think perhaps, in the circumstances, that that would not be a bad idea at all, Brother Campbell. I will see you after Vespers in my study."

The Abbot turned and without further ado, left his junior master, now a nervous wreck, to prepare for class. Campbell, trying to control his shaking hand, reached into the recesses of his bag and pulled out what appeared to be a bottle of golden-coloured cough mixture. Looking around him furtively, he drained the bottle in one gulp, taking great care to replace it once again at the very bottom of his satchel.

★ ★ ★ ★ ★

Williams-Jones watched with growing apprehension, indeed with mounting dismay. The monks, along with

Kite, appeared to remain in excellent health. He had put enough poison in the cake to kill a dozen rats, but no one looked even slightly under the weather. The Feast of Saint Eusebius had been and gone.

"Any idea when they'll be eating our food? Their rations can't be that good and it's mid Feb. Lent's starting" declared Williams-Jones mournfully. "Carps did say he'd brought a brace of pheasants up for the Abbot."

"The Abbot won't share them with anyone" sighed Gladstone, "except possibly with Secundus. They'll get into the wine and the whisky. Ward's already managed to steal two bottles of communion wine and one of whisky. Natterjack never locks the cupboard up. Anything missing is blamed on Campbell."

"Gosh! How super."

"They're planning something on Kite, but Ward won't say what it is."

"Ambrose has plans. Are you going to lessons with Rosie?"

"Lessons with Rosie? That tart! What, in the kitchen?"

"You won't call her a tart when you've been on one of her classes."

"What class? What does she teach?"

"Lots of things."

"Well how do you get chosen for this?" asked Rice,

who had joined the conversation. "Does she teach cooking?"

Williams-Jones looked at him quizzically, not quite sure how much to give away. It was all still a big secret, a wholly new line of fun. Heavens knew what Primus would do if he found out. He chuckled to himself. "You really want to know?"

Both boys looked at him eagerly "Yes. Yes we do."

"She examines your willy! Only Ward and I have done it so far but she is looking for other students, as she calls them."

The others shook their heads. Kite normally did that. They had no idea what he was talking about.

* * * * *

"There's a ghost in the school" Formby declared to the eager and expectant faces. "I've seen it!"

It was breakfast, freezing cold as usual with tepid tea. It was the time of a full moon; more snow had fallen in the hours of darkness.

"Don't be so silly. It was probably Kite going out to have a cigarette or something. Everyone knows she wanders round at night." scoffed Knight.

"Kite's been doing it for years. You saw her silly headdress!" added Jackson

The others, in third form and in the same dormitory as Formby, mocked him at his gullibility.

"No, honestly, it wasn't Kite. I'm not stupid. This ghost was sort of grey, well a grey silhouette like you see depicted in spooky books. I couldn't see its face as it was going along the side wall towards the ruins of the old Abbey."

"He might be right, chaps" beamed Northcliffe. "After all there's quite a history attached to this place. What time did it appear?"

"Don't know. It was very late. I think the school clock struck two."

Formby shivered at the thought of his having seen this mysterious shape.

"Maybe Mr Natterjack can tell us about ghosts. After all, aren't priests supposed to be able to communicate with them?" he continued.

"Natterjack doesn't know anything about anything. He useless, absolutely useless." retorted Knight.

"Why doesn't someone ask the Abbot? He'd know!"

There was a stunned silence. No one would ever dare put such a trivial question to the Abbot, nor to Secundus for that matter.

"What about Tertius? He's been here for years" suggested Newton, cutting in on the conversation.

"He told one of the other forms something about the history of the Brotherhood of Saint Eusebius. He alluded to past spirits and spirits of the dead that were restless and had to be exorcised, at least I think that those were the words he used."

"Let's all watch out for the ghost" proposed Knight. " You say it can be seen from the last two windows of the West Dorm?"

"Think so" said Formby.

Braving the cold and the ever-watchful eye of Kite, the boys took it in turn to look out of the window. Nothing appeared. On the fourth night it was cloudy, with no moon. No one saw anything. Formby was ridiculed for his imagination.

TWELVE

Brother Tertius tapped lightly on Upton's door. It was just after ten o'clock at night and Brother Campbell was being arraigned in the Abbot's study. They were now half way into the Lent term.

"I have left the hot water for you, if you'd care to use my bath" said Tertius. "The water is not too dirty and it is very, very hot." He was wearing a short silk dressing gown that was slightly too small for him. "So nice to go to sleep after a really satisfying hot bath, I always think, don't you?"

"Thanks Tertius. I'll certainly take up your offer" Upton replied.

"George, please! We are thankfully in the privacy of our own home in Herga."

Upton accepted the invitation. He immersed himself deeply into the steaming hot water and started to reflect on the day's events. Tertius followed him into the bathroom and began to clean his teeth.

"Rumour has it that Brother Campbell's in a spot of bother I hear" he said. "Petty theft or something."

"I'm not at all surprised. You know I found him in my room the other day" declared Upton.

"Oh dear. Doing what, precisely?"

"He said Everett had left something in the room that he had lent him. Everett gave him the key, so he said."

"Miss Tapscott controls all of this most carefully" sighed Tertius. "She would have insisted that Everett hand back his keys before vacating his room."

"Apparently not. I asked for the key and Campbell handed it over. Without a murmur."

"But not an apology?"

"No. Not a word in that direction. Frankly I was rather shocked. He seems a most abrasive, charmless man. I can understand my predecessor Everett being deeply aggrieved at the humiliation, not to mention the pain, of being thrashed by Brother Secundus. I wouldn't have been surprised to have been told that he just walked out without a word."

"Brother Everett, dear Sebastian as I used to call him, was set up by that harlot Rosalind, who claimed that he had tried to sleep with her. Charles, I have to tell you that Sebastian was not that way inclined. He clearly liked working with the boys, but ran into some difficulty with Brother Quartus. It was over Thompson-Brown, the new head boy this term. Rosalind told endless lies because she wanted carnal relations with a man in holy orders. As I said to you at that first time we met at breakfast, be very careful about her. My advice would be to see the Abbot should she try making any accusations as she did with Sebastian."

Tertius watched intensely as Upton reached for the soap and stood up in the bath to wash himself. "I had a terrifying encounter with Brother Secundus, by the way" said Upton. "He started waving some frightful whip thing in my face, threatening to thrash me if I did anything wrong, well anything sexually abnormal for a monk, he was quick to emphasise." He laughed, sat down again and washed off the soap. "I suppose if I robbed the coffers, or sold off all the school's books, that would be all right." He reached forward to clean his toes "What I keep asking myself, George, is how a school like this, miles from anywhere and completely cut off from civilisation for lack of public transport, manages to attract a South African thug to come and teach? He's quite clearly a most sadistic brute."

"I'm deeply saddened too" replied Tertius. "As you know, I would hate to have to punish anyone physically. It's really a sign of weakness in a man that he has not the character, nor the wit for that matter, to win over the confidence of the boys under his supervision. I myself never have had any problem with those who come up to me. This Secundus fellow came to us in 1940 after apparently being wounded in the war, though I have yet to see any evidence of this."

"Mental rather than physical perhaps? Shell shock or something of that sort."

"I remember the day well" continued Tertius "The

old Secundus, dear Basil Hawtrey, had resigned after his son, desperately wounded, was rescued from Dunquerque. He was in a terrible state about this and felt that he had to be near to the nursing home down in Hampshire. Could see his point. The Abbot asked me to act, temporarily, as Secundus which I have to say I did rather well. Then suddenly this awful man appeared with glowing recommendations. A letter from the then Bishop of Branchester extolling his pastoral work and confirming that he had been a missionary in the Transvaal or somewhere like that."

"Does anyone check references?" Upton hoped that the answer would be in the negative, as his own credentials were distinctly thin.

"Good heavens no, dear boy. This was in the war. One was lucky to find any male who wasn't incapacitated. Secundus was good at games, much better than me, though academically he leaves much to be desired. The Abbot, though, thought he was magnificent."

Brother Tertius, his teeth cleaned, sat down facing Upton on the lavatory seat. "I'm rather hoping that Sebastian will bring charges. If not against the school then at least against Secundus, for grievous bodily harm if he has any sense."

"You want to see him out? Finally fulfil the role of deputy?"

"No. That's not fair, I'm probably too old anyway. I think he brings great unhappiness to this place."

"Oh, nonsense. About being too old I mean!" Upton rose from the bath and reached for his towel. "Won't the Abbot trot out this special clause about his right to punish his monks as being an intrinsic part of the terms of employment in this quasi ecclesiastical establishment? He stressed this most forcefully to me when I had my introductory interview, though truth to tell I can't find any mention of this in the papers I signed with Margolis & Tring."

"You won't, dear boy, you won't. It's a total fabrication. A ruse to keep the masters in their place."

Tertius coughed, as if suddenly overcome with acute embarrassment. He did not quite know how to take the conversation forward.

"George, if I may change the subject, the Saint Eusebius picture. I'm still looking for my model. You have a very fine physique. You could be just the person I require. I noticed your comportment from the very first time we took showers together after games. I'm sorry if I'm being personal or you think me impertinent."

"Not at all, Charles" said Upton. Tertius smiled awkwardly but benignly. "One of my hobbies, as I told you, is painting, and when time permits, sculpture. For some time I have been working on a painting I would love to leave to the school. It depicts Saint Eusebius after his martyrdom, on the way to heaven."

He stood up and started to move to the door. "Last year I had Robert Crampton, the head boy, as my model. I'm now rather bereft of suitable candidates, certainly from among the boys, but your body, strong, firm, athletic, would be absolutely ideal. Could this be of interest?"

Upton thought for a moment how he should handle what was obviously a subtle, albeit covert, pass from his fellow teacher. He had come to the school specifically to get away from his albeit brief homosexual past and it did not need the abusive language of Secundus to tell him that Tertius was of the same persuasion. It was a question of trying to resist anything like this in such a stressful environment and so isolated a place as Saint Eusebius.

"Let me think this one over." Upton answered as he bent down to dry between his toes. "It's all so hectic here George. I don't know how I will find the time."

"Wait till spring comes and the workload becomes easier!"

So Tertius wanted to use him for his new painting for the memorial hall. Upton thought for one awful moment that Tertius was going to come over and touch him or even kiss him, but he didn't. He slipped silently out of the room, giving him a sad and rather rueful smile.

★ ★ ★ ★ ★

Upton passed a sleepless, restless night. He churned everything over in his mind, for this was not going to be an easy. He had to resist Tertius but didn't want to alienate him. Homosexuality, while illegal, was nevertheless a natural human trait, he told himself. Yet the whole point of his self-exile had been to put distance, considerable distance, between himself and any relationship with another man.

It had all started one hot summer afternoon in late July 1944. The invasion of France had been successfully executed and less pressure now fell on the soldiers in the Royal Army Service Corps. Private Upton and his immediate superior, Lance Corporal Parker, were lying hidden in the bracken in a field about three miles inland from Beachy Head. The radio transmission mast for which they were responsible had been checked and found to be in order, and they had two hours to kill before returning to barracks.

Both men wore shorts and had taken off their shirts; Parker was drawing on a cigarette.

"Nothing's going to change, you know. Not when this bloody war is over" said Parker.

"What do you mean by that?"

"You know anything about mining? The life the miners lead in this country?"

"No. Afraid not. My father was a teacher in Shropshire."

"Well I'm telling you the bastards will treat us just

like they did after the First World War. Massive unemployment. All the working class forced to grovel to the likes of Lord Lambton for jobs. Ever heard of Lord Lambton, Private Upton?" He spat out the word "Lord" with a rough northern accent.

"No. Who's he?"

"Owner of one of the biggest coal mines in the country, in County Durham. My granddad died in one of them. The bastards made no effort to save the miners, said it was too dangerous. When the enquiry was held it was obvious they hadn't invested enough in safety. All they did was take take take. When the next election comes I'm voting to kick out Churchill and all this rotten lot. I don't hold out much for Labour, but at least they've promised to nationalise the mines."

At that point Parker laid his left hand very gently on Upton's thigh. "Hope you don't mind?"

"No. No not at all." Upton felt a frisson of excitement. There was an adrenalin rush, a sexual arousal such as he had not had before, certainly something far more exciting than anything he had felt when he had a brief coupling with a barmaid behind the lavatory in a pub in Lowestoft.

"Stalin's my hero" continued Parker, slowly caressing Upton's thigh while pulling on his cigarette. "Shot all the rich and the aristocrats in Russia and liberated the working class. I hoped the Russians would make it to Calais. They still might make it, you know.

The Yanks are a bunch of bloody wankers and the British officers about the same. Look at that incompetent arsehole Davies, Captain Davies!" As he poured forth this diatribe against the ruling class, Parker was very slowly working his hand up under Upton's shorts. "When we're demobbed I shall join the Labour Party and help them fight and kick the Tories out. I've got my eye on Middlesbrough and a seat in Tyneside."

"You want to be an MP?"

"Stepping stone. I want total revolution for the working class!"

Parker stubbed out his cigarette. Slowly he undid the fly buttons of Upton's shorts until he could slip them off entirely. Upton felt paralysed, a rabbit before a stoat. He should have stopped him, but the pleasure was intense, overwhelming.

Parker started to work on Upton's erection with the same manic intensity that he had moments before devoted to his political aspirations. After urging Upton to do the same for him, and they had each ejaculated, he pulled up his shorts, lit another cigarette and continued with his philosophising as if this sexual exchange had never taken place.

"It's essential that the voice of the working class be heard once the Germans have been defeated" he declared, almost as if addressing a political rally rather than a fellow common soldier in a hayfield. "It's vital that people like us take forward the struggle of the masses, hopefully with the support of the Soviets." He stubbed out a half-smoked cigarette and fumbled around in his pocket for the packet for another. "I hope you'll come in on the side of the workers, Private Upton, even if your dad was posh."

"I need to find a job first. Can't get involved in anything political until I get a job. Start earning some money."

"What do you plan to do? Work in a bank or something? They say it's one of the great posh middle class things to do" Parker sneered.

"No. I'm going to get myself a job in teaching. Follow on doing what my father does."

"Doesn't pay much, from what I'm told."

High in the sky a squadron of British fighters was making its way over the Channel to France, but Upton wasn't paying much attention. Life, he knew, would never be quite the same after what they had just done. It was shameful, yet he had relished every moment of it. If word ever got out, he knew it would destroy his mother. And he knew it was not over. He remained in a state of excitement, nervous and shameful at what he had done yet longing somehow for a repetition. He hoped that other opportunities would arise while the hot summer continued, and started to fantasise as to other things he and Parker might be able to do together.

Upton and Parker made sure the signals post

required their attention frequently over the next few weeks, the gormless Captain Davies gullibly accepting their claims of maintenance problems. Blissfully for Upton, they repeated what they had done three more times before Parker suggested sexual congress. It was a criminal offence, Upton knew, meriting a long prison sentence, yet he yielded with alacrity, for Lance Corporal Parker had groomed his man well and had other plans in mind. Fortunately, or unfortunately depending on the point of view, the unit moved on and Parker was not heard of again; this was autumn 1944.

Upton couldn't sleep. He knew it was now a matter of self-control. Beyond the warm, inevitable embrace that he would receive from Brother Tertius towered the grim figures of the Abbot and Brother Secundus with their rabid, manic disposition to mete out the most fearsome punishment for the slightest deviation from monastic life. Even more worrying was the fact that he could be set up by Rosie if he didn't take up her advances, as obviously must have happened with Everett, if he was of the same persuasion as Tertius. It had him sweating; he would be trapped whichever way he turned. He had sworn, on being demobilised, to hide away in the depths of the country to shake off and obliterate his homosexual urges. He had taken a teaching job in the remotest part of the Fens, to embrace a semi-monastic way of life in order to purify his thoughts. It had never dawned on him that a boys' preparatory school, based in a former monastery in a remote part of the fens, might be the very hive of debauchery and depravity that he was now so eager to escape from.

★ ★ ★ ★ ★

"That girl's wearing silk stockings!" declared Brother Quartus, tucking into his scrambled egg on toast at breakfast two days later. "I wonder how she got them! You know what they all said about the Yanks in the war!"

Rosie, who was within earshot, put down the tin teapot and strolled over to the table where the monks were sitting. "You got a problem with my stockings, Brother Quartus?" she asked. placing her hands roughly on his shoulders and digging in her finger nails. "Think I'm not posh enough to wear silk?" She ground into his neck with her fingers.

"No, no Rosie. I was just admiring them" replied Quartus, choking and trying to push her hands off him. "Very nice, very nice indeed."

Rosie lifted a leg onto the spare chair at the table. "Got 'em as a present from a bloke I met in a pub in Branchester" she said. She pulled up her skirt to reveal the stockings, which stopped half way up her well-formed thighs. Upton was pretty sure, from where he was sitting across the table from Quartus, that she wasn't wearing any knickers. It prompted an unexpected frisson of desire.

"Mind you, I 'ad to 'earn 'em!" she said. She looked defiantly at the assembled company and grinned. She knew it would annoy them, especially old Tertius. "Got 'em for fuckin', if you want to know! And boy, have Yanks got big choppers!"

"Miss Robinson, that's enough!" Tertius interjected sharply.

The girl turned her eyes to him and strode round the table to where he was sitting. "And what do you know about fuckin' then, you old poofter? Or any of you for that matter, you fuckin' heap of faggots? Bet you lot wank every night!" she shouted across the table. "You've never seen a girl with 'er legs apart, thrust right back, knees beside her elbows!"

"That's quite enough disgusting language for one day, leave the room at once!" snapped Tertius.

"Not bloody likely! You're all at it." She fixed her eyes on Quartus. "I've 'eard you touch up the boys in the gym. Feelin' their willies, touchin' their bottoms. All the boys know! You wait till the Abbot finds out. He'll have Secundus tan your arse like you'll wish you'd never been born! And if no one else tells 'im, I bloody well will!"

She turned to Upton. "You're new here, aren't you? Bet you've got somethin' to hide. No one comes to a dump like this if they 'avn't got something to hide. You a woofter an' all?" She thrust her face close to Upton. She was wearing scarlet lipstick and soaked in cheap perfume, "Bloke before you was a woofter. I knew Secundus was looking to punish someone so I told 'im he'd tried to roger me. I watched Secundus give 'im a right good tanning. Cor, you should 'ave 'eard the bugger 'owl!"

She lowered her voice to a whisper, loud enough nevertheless to further annoy Tertius. "If it's girls you like, Brother Upton, I'm always ready" she continued into his ear, "anytime, any place. I 'ad one bloke on the altar in the chapel. Abbot didn't 'arf go crazy when he found out!"

She looked up and laughed at their stony faces. "Anything that goes on 'ere I soon know about. And if it doesn't I'll still make it up anyway!" She started to leave the room, then turned and lifted up her skirt, confirming Upton's suspicions. "That'll give you lot something to wank about tonight" she declared, kicking open the kitchen door.

The monks sat in silence; Campbell and Jenkins seemingly more depressed than ever as an unstoppable flow of cryptic little messages were now left routinely on the blackboard of whichever class they were destined to be taking.

"Don't say I didn't warn you" declared Tertius

solemnly to Upton as they left the room. "She's very, very dangerous!"

"But who is she, Tertius, and why does the school continue to employ her?"

Tertius looked at Upton in his usual mournful, hangdog way. "No one really knows. It's always been something of a mystery to me. But then so are Brother Secundus and Miss Tremble for that matter."

THIRTEEN

Oldham had a friend, a tousle-haired tough by the name of Davenport. Davenport had always been a rebel who loathed authority and took any opportunity to create chaos. He was said to be the result of an affair between a master of hounds and a colonel's wife at Catterick Camp, north Yorkshire, just before the war. He had had little experience of the comforts of home life, having been moved constantly as his parents were posted around the globe by the military. He had little empathy with his father, who suspected his mother's infidelity but couldn't prove it so took out his ire on his son. Davenport was quite fearless; he was impervious to punishment and had a backside that was crisscrossed with the marks of his various beatings. His speciality was blocking up the lavatories with paper and flushing all of them at the same time to cause a flood.

Davenport and Oldham decided that it was now time for a major operation to be launched against Miss Tremble, an operation which would both humiliate her and give the boys a chance to find out what she was hiding in her rooms. It would involve a number of others, boys they could trust, and had to be kept ultra secret to avoid detection by the prefects.

Oldham believed that someone more senior should be brought on board, for advice if nothing else; Ambrose was selected. The time of the attack was planned for just after sundown, before the doors were locked and bolted by Leno and Romano, during evening prep and ahead of supper. The day chosen was a Tuesday, the day the weekly post was received from Horkinge.

Oldham had asked Carps to help him make a particularly powerful catapult, as he wanted, he said, to try to bag one of the rabbits that infested the grounds. Carps had obliged him, using the same design he had given Ward the previous term. As Ward fiddled with the various types of elastic to give the best propulsion, Bennett was working quietly in the corner, experimenting with fuses intended for the Jetex engines which everyone was putting into their model aircraft. He had to install or meld these into the candles he had stolen from the chapel.

The Oldham/Davenport plan called for six other participants; three to ensure doors were open to help Oldham and three others to assist Dudley in the commando raid on the matron's room. An air of intense excitement imbued the teams as Oldham sneaked out of a window in the changing rooms and hid in the bushes, ready to fire. The chime of the school clock would be the signal.

In her room, Miss Tremble sifted through the day's mail. The post was only delivered to the Abbey once a week. She opened all the correspondence for the boys and read it. Letters for the monks were steamed open and then carefully sealed down to avoid suspicion, though communications from various magistrates' courts for Campbell were passed, opened, to the Abbot.

Two items of post held Miss Tremble's interest that afternoon. One was an official communiqué from a firm of London solicitors, on heavy cream laid paper and with an address in Lincolns Inn which looked very important. It advised the Abbot again that their client Mr Everett, lately in the school's employ, was looking for increased damages and compensation for serious assault and grievous bodily harm arising from an attack perpetrated upon him by one of the monks.

The other letter was from Mrs Hingham, asking why her little boy had not yet written to her as she had been told he would. Miss Tremble always destroyed letters that conveyed any form of motherly sympathy for her charges, occasionally substituting such letters, as best she could, with a replacement, which she signed off as realistically as possible with the sender's name. She knew that most of the boys guessed these letters were fakes, but it didn't worry her. Outgoing mail taxed her more, for she would send formal letters to parents whenever boys wrote anything uncomplimentary or incriminating about the school. Vetting correspondence was a good conduit to the Abbot's study, where she would recount to him all that she had gleaned from the boys' letters.

Silently she smiled to herself on a job well done. Henry's letters, like most of those of the new boys, had been extremely rude about the school, about her, about the food and about the monks in general. None of these letters of course ever left the building.

Miss Tremble threw the new delivery of parental letters into a waste paper basket and put the lawyers' letter into the brown satchel which she carried everywhere. She planned to speak to the Abbot just before evening prayers, when the boys were having supper. She thought it best for Secundus not to know of this development in case he too suddenly decided to run away like so many others in the past; it would leave them even more short staffed that they were already.

Unfortunately Miss Tremble's plans did not go quite as she intended, for as she reached the door of her room, there was a shattering crack as one of the panes of her window smashed and a large round stone fell onto the carpet, leaving the floor covered in jagged bits of glass. Miss Tremble knew at once that it had to be Ward, for he had perpetrated exactly the same stunt in the previous autumn term. Like lightning she dashed to the window, to glimpse only the outline of a boy scurrying round to the back of the chapel. This gave her the vital seconds she needed, for she knew exactly where he would have to re-enter the building. Discarding her satchel and flinging open her door, she tore down the stairs, rushing through the common room and into the boys' changing rooms, where an unlocked side door opened into the yard.

Hiding behind the boys' clothes and towels, she waited... and waited and waited, her face contorted with fury. Her anger was not helped by the fact that she had to squat in considerable discomfort until she was sure the changing room had been vacated. For what Miss Tremble, in her arrogance, did not know was that Oldham and Davenport, with help from Ambrose and the other members of the team, had decided upon a different strategy. An outright assault would be launched to gain access to her room when they knew for certain she would not be there. The prime purpose was to find out more about her and her activities, and hopefully, thus armed, to engineer her demise by publicising whatever scandal or secrets they could discover, bringing ridicule and disgrace upon her. The strategy was therefore to keep the matron waiting in the locker room for as long as possible while her room was looted.

To keep her there, several boys were instructed to come in and rummage in their lockers, pretending to look for things, chatting and making as much noise as possible. This would allow Oldham to get back into the school building by a long and circuitous route, hiding in the Abbot's garage if necessary, to avoid any traps she or Secundus might have set. The other squad, the commando unit, had hid in the passageway. They had rushed into her room as soon as she came out, seized as much as they could and scooped up all the inward mail, including the letters in the waste paper basket and the contents of her satchel. They had then scampered off to the dorms, where everything could be stored either under the floorboards or above the ceiling. A watchman, with a hammer and a metal bucket, would sound the alarm if Miss Tremble was seen returning to her room.

The plan worked brilliantly. The obvious culprits, especially Ward, made sure they were seen engaged in other activities. This left Miss Tremble even more annoyed and frustrated, for she hadn't the slightest idea who her new secret enemies might be.

"Unbelievable!" declared Ambrose, as the paperwork was shared round. Among the plunder was Henry's letter from his mother, as were many others that had been intercepted. The prize however was the letter from the lawyers threatening action over Everett's beating in the previous term. Mowbray, Williams-Jones and Bentley, among others, were brought in for consultation.

"We've got three options, as I see it" began Bentley. "We could stick it in Primus' prayer book, knowing that he's bound to see it. He'll go crazy, knowing not only that it's real but that one of us must have put it there. Kite will get a roasting. Or, and this would be much more fun, we slip it into Secundus' house, which should scare the daylights out of him. Third option - we just destroy it and see what happens!"

He turned to Ward and the assembled company for confirmation and inspiration. "If the law can get Secundus, and Campbell is taken away for robbery, Primus will have to close the school" mused Ambrose with a smile. "He couldn't carry on with just Jenkins, Tertius, Quartus and the new man."

"You've got a point" said Williams-Jones. "Let's all think what would be the most damaging thing we can do from all three. Gosh, I can see a big Black Maria, you know one of those big Daimler ones, crunching into inner yard with bobbies fanning out through our class rooms to catch them all!"

Everyone burst out laughing at this. Votes were cast, and after considerable debate, it was decided to put the letter in the prayer book, before evening prayers, so that Primus had to see it.

To their chagrin, absolutely nothing happened. It was observed nevertheless that the lights remained on in the Abbot's study very late that night. Miss Tremble, her vigil abandoned, scowled in silence throughout supper and did not return to her room before lights out. Carps was summoned to repair the window, blocking it temporarily with plywood, while Leno and Romano were ordered to clean up the broken glass.

The impact of what had been achieved had yet to sink in on the perpetrators. In fact the Abbot now knew that the whole school also knew what Sebastian Everett wanted; vengeance, financial ruin and ultimately closure of the establishment. It was the worst recrimination from a monk's punishment he had ever experienced. It even surpassed his greater fear of discovery by his earlier foes before the recent war.

FOURTEEN

Miss Tapscott winced as she crossed the inner Abbey yard. Despite having now spent nearly four years at St Eusebius, she still found the systematic beatings imparted on the boys a spine-chilling experience. She shuddered as screams from the second-floor window of the Abbot's quarters echoed round the yard. It seemed now to be an almost daily ritual as the school settled into its seventh week of term.

For Martin it was an even more terrifying experience, for it was his first experience of being beaten. He knew he had been arraigned on completely spurious and fabricated charges dreamed up by Brother Secundus, against which there was no appeal. "Attitude" and "Lack of spirit" were the charges laid against him following an unsuccessful rugger match against distant neighbours, Grenham House. He was the fourth boy to be caned that morning.

"Shorts off" commanded the Abbot "Take a position on the stool!"

Martin shook with fright as he took down his shorts. The stool, a small wicker affair, was placed by the window, not so much for the boys to be seen and heard by any onlookers who happened to be passing in the yard below, but in a position that would allow the Abbot, a right hander, to administer the cane or birch with the maximum impact upon the victim's backside.

Martin had never been beaten before. He found it absolute agony, as if a red hot iron had been placed upon his backside. He just screamed - and screamed and screamed.

In the yard below, as they walked to morning class, Brother Secundus turned to Upton with a huge smile beaming across his face. "You hear that, Brother Upton?" he asked in his clipped accent. "That, my friend, is the sound of the imposition of discipline at Saint Eusebius School!"

He could see that Upton was somewhat taken aback. "For in this school, may I remind you, my friend," he continued "all success is achieved through pain. *Flagellatum vincit omnia*! Those that do not meet our standards will be put to the birch or the cane, as often and as harshly as may be necessary to ensure that we will always win in our endeavours, be it in the challenge of the exams or in the more physical field of the games in which we challenge our competitors!"

Upton remained silent, speechless, as more shrieks reverberated round the yard from the direction of the Abbot's window; evidently a number of boys were being put to the cane. The pitiful cries were clearly some sort of elixir for the senior monk as he waxed lyrical upon the benefits of corporal punishment.

Two boys passed, juniors, their eyes averted, as they too heard the noise emanating from the Abbot's rooms.

"The Abbot has been far too slack this term, Brother Upton" Secundus continued. "How many boys have you reported from your class, for example, who have escaped the punishments they should have received? Boys are like racehorses; they can win the race, but it needs a good jockey to administer the whip when necessary! Do you not agree, my friend?"

It was just what the Abbot had said on his first day, thought Upton. He was not impressed at the monk's choice of words. Boys, he realised from his short stay at the Abbey, were sensitive, and blind brutality was not the way to get the best out of them.

"Well, none actually, Brother Secundus, sir" he replied, ignoring the senior monk's crass philosophy. "Some of my pupils are quite spirited, but in matters of academia they have all done extremely well."

"Academia? Forget the classroom crap. Sport is all that matters, Upton, not stupid books. Sport - win, win, win. Games are the conduit to victory. You are failing, man. You are failing. It is impossible for boys to be good. They have to be flogged, even if they think they are doing well. It's like a racehorse, as I said."

"My pupils regularly score nine or ten in my weekly exams. No one gets less than eight."

"My point precisely. He who only gets eight must be chastised! How else can we be sure of getting entry into the public schools? Eight is for me a failure, only eighty per cent achieved, twenty per cent lost. Do you know, Brother Upton, that Brother Jenkins has boys in his class who simply cannot do maths? They can't even do basic arithmetic! They have no aptitude for numbers. Groist man, if we are to let this go on we will have no bankers or accountants left in this country."

"They are good at other things? Languages, art, history?"

"Maybe. I don't know. I don't care either. You can't go out into the world just doing the subjects you like! God help us. Where would we all be?"

"Doing well in our chosen professions, for a start, sir."

"You are full of shit, Brother Upton. Full of shit, if you believe that sort of thing."

"My father used to teach history. Some of his students have become the best lawyers in the country. Many were quite useless at maths and science, he used to tell me."

"Crap!" The big monk increased his pace, forcing Upton to almost run to keep up with him. "If you believe that sort of rubbish you will never be a teacher, at least not of the calibre that we require at this school."

"Perhaps I'd better pack my bags." They had almost come to the parting of their ways.

"That's your choice, Brother Upton." Secundus stopped and sneered. "But let me tell you this. If we think you are not fit to be a teacher, we shall sack you without any pay whatsoever. Colston, Haines, Lysander - we sacked the lot of them. They didn't get a penny. We didn't even pay their bus fare to the station!"

He turned on his heel and swung away, towards the memorial hall and his awaiting class. The school clock tolled the quarter hour.

* * * * *

In her room above South Dormitory, Miss Tremble searched frantically to identify what had been taken by the boys. To her surprise the Abbot had been more concerned about how the letter from the London lawyers had come to be put into his prayer book than by the contents, and the implied threat that lay within it. It was the second they had received. He had dictated a letter to her, in front of Brother Secundus, which denied all knowledge of the alleged assault, backed his deputy to the hilt and challenged the alleged plaintiff to take his case further. He had then spent the next hour trying to work out who the culprits behind the assault upon his matron were and why they had done it. The only solution he could arrive at was mass punishment of all the boys who could possibly have been involved.

That, however, would include Ward, and would be a transgression of the agreement he had been forced to agree to, reluctantly, with his father, that on no account, was the boy to be beaten.

The telephone rang in his study and he picked it up, shooing the cat off his desk. "Yes?"

There was a long silence.

"Yes? This is the Abbot speaking." A further pause. "One of my monks? But that's not possible!" More silence. "I am sorry to hear this. Perhaps you would be kind enough to write to me with your complaint so that I may look into the matter further." He slowly replaced the receiver. Reaching into the small recess on the left hand side of his desk he extracted one of Lord Ward's bottles of Irish whisky. He poured himself a very large glass, neat with no water or soda, and sat back in silence to ruminate on what he had just been told.

★ ★ ★ ★ ★

Calm of a sort returned to Saint Eusebius the following day. It was evening, with the light fading fast. The boys settled into their homework time and hobbies and the monks relaxed before attending evening prayers. It was the hour between five and six o'clock, before school supper, when the rigours of afternoon sport had been forgotten and there was time, for once, to relax.

Or so it might have seemed. In the classroom on the first floor, hobbies for the seniors were well advanced. Bennett, nicknamed 'The Professor' for his fastidiousness in everything he did and his ability to get all his work correct, played with the soldering iron which he, as a senior, had exceptionally been allowed to use. For Jenkins, supposedly in charge but casually reading the *County Racing News*, Bennett's project was to weld small pieces of metal to create a track for someone else's model railway. Bennett was, in fact, experimenting with electrical wiring, the school's wiring; a massive short circuit, with subsequent sparks, was part of his long-term pyromaniacal projections for the school's demise.

On the floor below him Henry read and re-read his mother's letter, which he had hidden in his French grammar book. He began to write out, very carefully, for his writing was not that good, almost everything that he could remember that he thought he had told her about his life in the preceding seven weeks of the term. He knew he had to concentrate, for Ambrose had told him that he hoped to have the letter sent off secretly the next day. Ambrose told him to write about the cruelty of the monks, Kite, the food, the cold and how his bear had been confiscated and nearly destroyed. He was also not to tell anyone what he was doing.

The master in charge of his class, Brother Tertius, looked at his charges with benign affection, pleased that so many little boys appeared so devoted to their work. Quietly he made sketches of how he might portray Brother Upton in his work of art for the memorial hall window.

Brother Secundus, in his quarters in the gatehouse cottage, harboured other, less charitable ideas. The school second eleven had not done well that afternoon, and some encouragement was in order. Carefully he wrote down the names of the boys he intended to beat the next day; Langthorne, the captain, would get four, the others two. He tore off the list and put it into a small drawer in his desk. Punishment would be administered before lunch, in the changing room. He smiled to himself; it should certainly improve their performance against Headlington House two days later.

Miss Tremble, still seething at her humiliation, scratched around in her room, endeavouring frantically to gain an idea of what else, apart from her satchel, had been stolen by the boys. She had grilled Ward, Bentley and Williams-Jones, but all had cast-iron alibis; there had to be another gang at work, and she was determined to get the prefects to find out who they were.

Upton found himself fortunate to be forgiven supervision duties, and sat in his room in Herga reading a copy of a work of Dickens that had been lent to him by Brother Tertius. Suddenly he was startled by what he thought sounded like a cry of pain, someone in trouble perhaps, and he went out into the passage to see what it was. Miss Tapscott, he knew, would be organising the boys' supper, and Campbell and Jenkins, as far as he knew, were over in the school.

He heard the cry again. It came from the bathroom; someone, though he couldn't think who, must be in trouble. The door was locked. Stepping back across the hall he hurled himself at it, quickly bursting it open. The bathroom was full of steam, there was water on the floor and a hot bath had clearly been used. There, in the swirling steam, was Brother Quartus, stark naked and clearly aroused, was bent over one of the senior boys, who quickly turned his head away. Upton saw in a flash that it was almost certainly Thompson-Brown. They were like a pair of copulating dogs he had once seen in France, engaged in activity of the grossest indecency, and committing an offence that would earn Brother Quartus a lengthy stretch in prison for buggery if he were ever to be found out.

Silently Upton returned to his room; his worst fears about his teaching colleague had been confirmed. He wondered what, if anything, would happen next. Had Everett been doing the same, he asked himself?

He recalled the words of the Abbot, of his loathing in particular of sexual misconduct between men, monks, and the boys, and his statement that there was no sexual impropriety in the school. It made him wonder what else the headmaster was unaware of; Rosie? Secundus? Campbell? Jenkins?

★ ★ ★ ★ ★

The match against the school's traditional bitter rivals, Headlington Hall, had started well, with Saint Eusebius scoring quickly in the first fifteen minutes. Langthorne, who had gone down with a severe cold, had been replaced as captain by Bentley. Primus and Secundus, watching from the touchline, appeared satisfied with the performance, at least until the beginning of the second half, when Headlington scored with a brilliant header by one of their team. This was followed by a clever move on the part of their opponents when Taylor, a comparatively new member of the team was skilfully made offside by Headlington and the resultant penalty resulted in a draw at full time.

Exhausted, the school team squeezed onto the benches of the ex-Army one-ton truck for the long journey back to Horkinge.

"At least we didn't lose!" said Harper, one of the fullbacks, "which is a lot better than we have ever done before with them."

"We didn't win though" sighed Elmden. "And in Secundus' eyes that is all that matters."

"He'll beat us then?" asked another weary voice.

"Any excuse will make that brute get out his cane. Just wait till we get home!"

They did indeed not have long to wait to hear the

reaction of the Chief Disciplinarian. He was standing outside the door of his little cottage as the truck, driven by Romano, passed through the arch into the outer quadrangle.

"Oh, God, he's got his cane out already" shouted someone from the back of the truck. "This looks bad news".

It was indeed. The monk didn't waste his words. "That was a bloody disgrace" he yelled at the exhausted team in his clipped accent "I would have thought that after your last performance and my reaction to it you would have done better. Clearly I have failed in my work and I now have even more stimulation to hand out."

"But sir, we didn't lose!" Davenport dared to venture. "We held them throughout most of the day, even though they were stronger and more experienced than us."

This seemed to drive the monk into a frenzy. "Didn't lose! Didn't lose!" he shouted at them all. "What the 'ell do you think the bloody game is for? To draw? A draw is OK is it? No wonder you bloody British are no good at war. Fair play? Just a game? Give the others a chance? Be nice to prisoners?" He spat on the ground in disgust. "All games are war, do I not have to remind you again. Get into the changing rooms immediately and remain in your clothes."

Silently the doomed team walked to receive their

punishment. The monk continued to harangue them. Nothing of their performance had pleased him, not even the first two goals. "Headlington were weak and stupid to let you score. It was no success on your part that you scored!"

"Lying bastard" whispered someone under their breath.

The retribution was remorseless. The whole team were given four vicious strokes of the cane, except for Elmden, who got six for his failure to inspire as captain.

"One day I'll kill that bastard" declared Davenport as they nursed their bruised and battered bodies "Even if I have to come back to this school with a shotgun to do it."

"You wouldn't be alone, I can assure you" added someone else.

Ward smiled secretly to himself. Only he had access to a gun in this place. Maybe one day he might just have the chance to use it.

* * * * *

"Primus seems really worried, as if something awful has happened" declared Ambrose to Carnforth and Rice as they all prepared for bed that night. "It could be Jenkins this time" suggested Rice, not without a hint of hope in his voice. "You remember what happened with

Tomlinson last term? Maybe he's in trouble somewhere else, did something over the Christmas holidays."

"What about Primus himself? We all saw the letter we put in his prayer book about Everett. Legal action sounded very serious. Perhaps he's going to have to get money to pay for a lawyer."

"Rosie says Secundus beat Everett. She watched it all from a hiding place. He put up a terrific fight, but he and Kite overwhelmed him, tied him up and they really whipped him."

"Who told you this?"

"Leno. Rosie told him what she saw, and in great detail too."

* * * * *

In his classroom the next morning, Brother Jenkins had other problems. Another poem had been written on the blackboard; the fifth in the last week. Someone he knew must have it in for him and be trying to draw the Abbot's attention to his foibles. He felt sure that almost all his pupils hated him for the way he beat them around the head and pinched their bottoms, but this was not going to change; it was the only way he knew how to keep order or indeed to teach: *Taffy was a Welshman, Taffy was a thief, Jenkins is another one, so we all believe*, it said. Hurriedly he wiped out the offending ditty, praying that the Abbot would not have made one of his regular inspections of the classrooms.

The Abbot had not seen it, but Miss Tremble had. She had never cared for Jenkins; it could be useful ammunition in any future confrontation.

FIFTEEN

The ecclesiastical rigours of Lent had been imposed upon the boys with ruthless efficiency; all puddings were forbidden for forty days, as were meat and soft drinks. Bread and water became the staple diet, with watery soup for lunch and the usual dripping on toast for supper. By way of contrast, no such hardship seemed to have been imposed upon the monks, and deliveries of meat continued to be made to the school kitchens under the generous rationing that was granted to schools throughout the country. Foraging for food thus became something of a necessity for the boys, since Rosie, an obvious source for stealing food, was only prepared to co operate for favours in kind to those she fancied. Thankfully, however, there was another option open to the starving inmates.

A warm fire burned in the grate at Gatehouse Cottage. It was Sunday, late afternoon and half an hour before evening prayers. Nellie Marshall, Mrs Carps, was clearing away the six empty plates while Carps sat reading the Sunday papers, his feet inches from the grate.

"We've got to find another way of getting rid of that

woman" Mowbray declared as he wiped his mouth with his handkerchief. He and the others relished the Carps' 'tea', on this occasion a pheasant casserole, and made regular visits to the little house when the monks weren't looking.

"Well, no one ever ate my cake by the look of things!" sighed Williams-Jones.

"Lot of dead rats round back of boiler house, Jones" shouted Carps from behind his paper. "Reckon they threw that there cake of yours out with the rubbish!"

"Glad to know I have been of some help then, Carps."

"Abbot's cat's not looking too good neither."

"Oh, I do like that pussy, Harry. He's the only friendly thing in the place" declared Mrs Carps, coming over to where they were sitting and still wiping plates.

Ambrose looked up hopefully. "Could you do me a favour, Mrs Carps? Only something simple. Posting a letter from one of the boys?"

"Course I can, Ambrose. And I've got a stamp if you need one."

"No need, thanks. We stole a whole pile from Kite. When we did over her room."

"Yes, you should have seen what Ward and his team did!"

"You lot are turning into right little criminals. It'll be the end of you."

"We're in a prison camp as far as we're concerned. Nothing wrong with trying to destroy the place.

Melville's uncle was a prisoner in Colditz. He told me what they say in the books is all true. About destroying the castle. Bennett's got plans."

"Talkin' bout criminals" interjected Carps from his place by the fire, "I gather the Army's having a big purge round these parts, well all over the country, to catch them buggers what deserted and the like. Bloke told me in the pub last week they've been working over deserted farmhouses in the Fens all over Lincolnshire, Norfolk and even Cambridge."

"Gosh, d'you think some of the monks are deserters?" Williams-Jones and Ambrose looked up enthusiastically.

"Not this lot they ain't! Old Tertius was invalided out with shell shock in 1940 and Jenkins was discharged a year or so later after serving a short sentence for theft. Don't know nothing about Campbell."

"Brother Secundus? He must be a Nazi!"

"That South African bloke was in the colonial service, missionary or something. Saw his reference papers myself." Carps lowered his voice. "Secretly, between just you lot, I think he's secret service or something. Him and that Rosie."

"Rosie? The four boys cried in unison "She's the school prostitute! Everyone knows that except Primus. Leno and the other wop give it to her regularly. Right Ward? Ward's seen them doing it, haven't you?"

"In the shed, next to Primus' garage" affirmed Ward, still eating his hot jam roll and custard. "What's more, I saw Leno doing it once on the back seat of Primus' Rover. Oldham and Napier say Secundus has had her too."

"Disgusting talk! Whatever would your mothers say?" said Mrs Carps over her shoulder, returning to the kitchen.

"Did we tell you about Everett, Carps? He's threatening legal action for assault! We liberated the letter from Kite's office."

"Not surprised. Won't get him nowhere though." Carps folded the paper. "You see Abbot's got everyone under his thumb here. Got some sort of magic spell over all the people round about. Everett can shout blue murder about having a sore arse but no one's going to believe a word."

"Honestly Harry, you shouldn't use such language in front of the boys" shouted Mrs Carps from the kitchen.

"Don't worry Mrs Carps, we hear a lot worse from Rosie when she's doing it."

"Well, I'm truly shocked."

"Know that little boy I'm asked to look after, Mrs Carps? Little Hingham?" said Ambrose

"Oh, poor little mite. He always looks ever so unhappy." she replied.

"Kite stole his teddy bear, threw it on the rubbish tip."

"Served him right" said Mowbray. "I remember him clutching the thing on the school train. Pathetic!"

"He could be a useful weapon in the war on Kite. By the way I got him his bear back. We've hidden it till the end of term."

"So?"

"We all know Kite intercepts letters. Hingham hadn't had one from his mother so far this term until we liberated the last one from Kite. I bet she hasn't had one from him either." Ambrose reached into his coat pocket and drew out a limp envelope. "So I asked him to write down everything he thought he had told his mother since term started - the beatings, Kite, the fate of his bear, Jenkins, Campbell, the awful food and endless, useless chapel." He handed the envelope to Mrs Carps; it already had a stamp. "So I was wondering, Mrs Carps, if you could possibly give this to the postman when he comes next week, once he's been up to the Abbey?"

"Of course, my dear. No problem at all. I'll put it with the other letters for him to take tomorrow."

Half an hour later the boys left the warmth of the little gatehouse cottage; darkness had begun to fall. In the distance the school bell chimed the quarter hour.

"How do you know the postman isn't a stool pigeon?" asked Ward. "You heard what Carps said about Primus having everyone in his pocket."

"Risk we'll have to take" muttered Ambrose as they took the short cut back across the fields. "You noticed I had typed the envelope. Took me hours."

"Kite's typewriter?" asked Mowbray.

"Yep. It took me four days! Noticed how I was late for lunch three times last week? I knew she'd be in dining hall dishing out the muck" Ambrose declared.

"Talking about muck, wasn't that a super tea! One of the best Mrs Carps has ever done" enthused Mowbray.

Williams-Jones was tagging along behind the others. "Pity we didn't have a chance to see the guns this time" he said.

"Guns?" Mowbray asked, laughing.

"Isn't that right, Ward?" declared Williams-Jones.

"You bet. He's got a Mauser, a Luger with ammunition and several other types. He's even got a Sten gun!" Ward replied, full of enthusiasm. He didn't mention his own .410 however. That one was strictly a secret between him and Carps.

"Cripes. We could kill 'em all with a thing like that!"

"I'd shoot Kite if I had one" said Williams-Jones. "Does Carps have any other ammunition?"

"We'll have to ask, won't we?"

"Could we steal some? Use one of his guns?"

"That would be disloyal. To Mr and Mrs Carps I mean. No. We'll have to find some other way to get rid of the lot of them."

Silently they trudged back for evening chapel. Ward

now had hiccups from eating too much too quickly, a self-inflicted penalty for endeavouring to overcome his constant pangs of hunger and starvation.

SIXTEEN

Upton eyed the letter with suspicion. He had never received mail at the school, and he had gone to great lengths to make sure that no one, besides his mother, knew where he was. This letter was most certainly not from her. It could be from their solicitors or their bank manager, however.

He examined it carefully and then slit it open. His heart froze; it was from Parker. He had not heard from him since he had received a letter in 1945. He had left the army, he said, and was now actively engaged in trade union and local politics. The letter, friendly in tone, bore no hint of malice, nor did it refer in any way to their past association. Parker was apparently intending to stand as a Member of Parliament, if he could find somewhere to adopt him as their candidate.

Vaguely he asked if Upton could help him on this, when the school holidays came round. He gave a telephone number where he could be contacted. The address at the letterhead, Upton noted, was from a trade union office somewhere in Holborn.

Leaving the letter on the table, Upton went

nervously to his diary and checked holiday dates, dates when he could possibly go to London to discuss the campaign with Parker, assuming he had found a possible seat by then. He read the letter again. No, there was absolutely nothing in it to allude to their past, but the memories came flooding back. Their time in the Army, their afternoons in the sun, Parker easing off his shorts, the mutual admiration of each others' bodies. It was everything Upton hoped he could now be free of. It worried him that the man had tracked him down, for, in taking such care to hide himself, Upton realised that Parker too must have spent hours in diligent search to seek him out. Why? Was his motivation sexual? It seemed unlikely. Political objectives? Possibly. But how, or rather where, would he come in?

It was sinister that the letter appeared so innocent, so undemanding, and yet the man had blown his cover. There was only one thing this could imply; Parker wanted something, almost certainly something illegal, and he was going to blackmail Upton if he didn't get his way.

He was wondering what on earth this could be when there was a quiet knock at the door. It was Brother Tertius. He looked rather worried, in his sad, spaniel way.

"Did you get a letter today, Charles?" he asked. "I saw Miss Tapscott bring something to the house. Usually they are demands from debt collectors or the courts for Brother Campbell or Brother Jenkins."

"Yes I did. From an old acquaintance in the army."

"How nice. No one ever writes to me."

"He's planning to go into politics. Wants me to help him with his campaign if he can find a seat."

"There are some fine safe Tory seats in the Home Counties and of course round here too. I had a distant cousin who was the member for somewhere near here. North Norfolk East, if my memory serves me right."

"My friend is Labour. He hates the Establishment. He wants to fight the Conservatives tooth and nail. He's very bitter. His father and grandfather were both miners. His grandfather died in a pit accident somewhere in County Durham."

"Oh I am sorry to hear that. But you're not Labour are you, surely Charles?"

"Haven't given it much thought. What about the Liberals? They seem a nice lot."

"They'll never get to power! Not with the way we are structured in this country. You have to be either Labour or Conservative."

"You asked about the letter?"

"Oh yes. It's only a small point, but all our correspondence is supposed to be shown to the Abbot. Didn't Margolis and thingy tell you about that?"

"No."

"Oh well, I don't suppose it matters."

"To tell you the truth I rather got the impression that

someone might have steamed open my letter. The envelope felt extraordinarily damp – even for these parts!"

"Good heavens, what an awful thought. It would have to be Miss Tremble. She receives and vets all the letters, letters to the boys, bills for the school, all the stuff for Brother Campbell. I can't imagine that she'd have time to do something like that."

"I find her very sinister. The boys seem to hate her universally. I was wondering how good she was at her job, so many of them seem to look so ill all the time."

"She's rather brutal, I agree, but the climate here is dreadful. Blame for the way she conducts herself must lie with the Abbot. He hired her."

"Has she been at the school for long?"

"Came to us around 1940 I think. The previous matron had married and wanted to live where her husband worked."

"I heard about the suicide last term. Chadwick, wasn't it? Terrible story."

"Miss Tremble always puts the bedwetters in the North Dormitory. It's the coldest. Chadwick was also denied food because he had taken some cheese up to his dormitory. He was so hungry, poor little fellow. There were three of them who couldn't control their bladders. One boy, Painswick, told his parents in the summer holidays that Brother Quartus regularly touched his genitals in the gym class; they took him away at once. Another little fellow, Broxbourne, was also removed, which then left Chadwick on his own."

"He killed himself?"

Tertius looked down at the carpet and clenched his hands. "Yes. It was awful. He was found by Clarendon, the head boy. He had hanged himself in the locker room. We had to have an emergency service in chapel and everyone sang as loudly as they could. The Abbot told the boys it was an accident. Everyone prayed very hard for his soul."

"Miss Tremble? She must be held responsible, surely?"

"Not a hint of remorse."

Tertius was obviously not easy with this. He continued to clench his hands, twisting his fingers together. Upton sensed a pent-up emotion which he felt compelled to conceal.

"In fact it was rather the reverse" continued Tertius after a pause. "Miss Tremble gave the impression that if a boy cannot survive Saint Eusebius Abbey he's not going to survive in the real world. Biology, survival of the fittest and so on."

"I find that disgusting, don't you? I bet she didn't say that to the parents!"

"Yes I do" said Tertius, haltingly. "All of us are to blame, some more than others."

"Secundus?"

"A shrewd guess, Charles. Yes. Very much so. Secundus and Tremble are not very Christian, in fact not Christian at all."

Upton decided to change the subject. "Is it possible to telephone from here? I really ought to let my mother know what I am doing." He obviously didn't want to state the real purpose; a white lie to the old monk seemed harmless enough.

"All calls from Herga are supposed to be routed through Miss Tremble, who has the switchboard in her room. Secundus and I have separate lines however. You could certainly call from my room if you like."

"I'd like to take you up on that."

"Tonight?" Tertius asked, eyes looking hopefully at Upton.

"Not tonight. Daytime would be best."

"Oh, all right then."

"She's quite odd. Calls at night are best avoided."

"You haven't forgotten what I asked you?"

"About modelling for the Saint Eusebius picture?"

Tertius beamed. "Exactly. I've done some outline sketches of how it might look."

"Too cold, George, too cold to do anything like that at this time of the year."

"I have an electric fire in my room here. No need to go across to Drawing School."

"I would prefer to wait for warmer times. I'd very much appreciate using your phone, however."

Tertius fumbled in his pocket. "Here's a spare key" he said. He handed over a small key which had a brown string loop attached. "It was Sebastian's. We used to have such lovely evenings together."

Yes, thought Upton, I bet you did.

★ ★ ★ ★ ★

"I've seen the ghost again! And Sutcliffe's seen it too!" said Formby.

"Yes. It came out from somewhere near the kitchen and drifted over towards the gate that leads to the fields" confirmed Sutcliffe, to Formby's delight. Now perhaps they would believe him.

"It was a sort of grey thing. I mentioned it to Brother Tertius and he thought it might be the soul of one of the monks who were murdered here when Henry the Eighth's troops destroyed the original monastery" continued Sutcliffe

"Gosh, how creepy!" said Lewis, joining in.

"Did anyone discuss this with Mr Natterjack?" he asked.

"Why waste the time? Is it always the same time, Formby?"

"Think so. Well more or less. After Kite has done her round of inspection."

"Wouldn't it be super to actually meet it! See what it's made of" continued Lewis.

"Not me. Ghosts are supposed to be very cold. My grandfather said they used to get very cold air, a sort of presence, when they lived in a very old house near Tunbridge Wells. He never liked being near them at all" Sutcliffe declared.

"We must find out what it is. Do you think any of the seniors know about this? Ward, Williams-Jones?"

"Might be one of them! They're always sneaking out after lights." laughed Lewis.

"What? You mean it isn't a ghost at all but someone at the school?" Formby asked rather sadly

"Possibly. You never can tell" continued Lewis, warming to his theory.

"Oh no" sighed Formby, now visibly depressed,

"I know it must be a real ghost. All old churches like this have them."

No one believed him. Lewis probably had a point. Silently, everyone went back to bed.

★ ★ ★ ★ ★

Two days later, Upton found himself landed with Brother Quartus as his companion in the procession into chapel. They were singing one of the hymns Upton had now got to know quite well.

"Not a word, old man, not a word will you?" Quartus whispered into his ear, leaning across. He had terrible halitosis and reeked of bad breath.

"The other day? In Herga?" replied Upton.

"We chaps have got to stick together. We all have our secrets, old man. Bet you do too, otherwise you wouldn't have come to this bloody dump."

"Speak for yourself, Brother Quartus. My past, what little there is of it what with the war, has no secrets. My father's been killed and my mother's in a loony bin. I'm here for spiritual relief."

"Like hell you are!" snapped Quartus as they began the final verse of the hymn. "You're the same as me, as all the rest of us, just as your predecessor Everett was, just as Jenkins is and just as Brother Tertius is. Though from the goings on in his room with Everett last term, he clearly prefers the older male."

Quartus returned to the hymnal and sang with extra gusto as the hymn came to an end. Upton, worried by this caustic observation by a sodomite, an overt paedophile and one of his fellow monks, deigned not to look at him.

As they filed into their allotted places on either side of the nave, he began to break out in a nervous sweat. He felt vulnerable, desperately vulnerable, but at least he had rung the union headquarters, spoken to Parker and fixed a tentative date to see him. No one, he vowed, must know why he was going to London; least of all any of the teaching staff.

★ ★ ★ ★ ★

Veronica Hingham recognised the childish writing at once and tore open the little envelope bearing the Horkinge postmark. Silently she walked through the hall into the little sitting room, reading her beloved's missal as best she could. Tears welled up in her eyes and she flopped down into a chair. She read and re-read the news of how he was getting on at school. The masters, brutes for the most part; the matron, a vicious creature, quite unlike the image that she had formed from the letters that she had received from her, both before school started and now, from time to time, in poorly-typed bulletins. Very little food and endless cold. She also read how Royston had been taken away but had been rescued by a nice senior boy called Ambrose, through whose help this letter was being smuggled out.

The War Office was being extraordinarily evasive as to what Colonel Hingham might be doing and when he might be home on leave; he himself had told her many times not to ask too many questions. Peace in Europe was by no means certain and the political situation was volatile.

In desperation she turned to her brother Gilbert. They had to go down and see for themselves what was going on at this so-called illustrious preparatory school the sooner the better, for Veronica feared that if he was left to his own devices Henry might try to escape, get lost, be drowned or even murdered by the gypsies and army deserters who were said to infest the Fen country.

"Leave it to me. I'll take a day off next week" he assured her at once. "We'll go down unannounced next week, either by train, or in my old car, if I can get some petrol coupons from my contacts in the City. And if I can get it started and out of the garage."

"As soon as you can, Gilbert. I'm having terrible nightmares."

SEVENTEEN

Brother Secundus lay naked, face down, tied to the bed, writhing as Rosie meted out his punishment. Rosie had been brought up on a farm, and she knew a thing or two about the whip. She had watched her guardian load horses into boxes for the local hunt, encouraging the beasts to board with savage blows upon their rumps. The horses used to buck and kick; Rosie thought it thrilling. Now, as she started the evening's entertainment, naked except for her American high-heeled shoes, her new silk stockings and her scarlet suspenders, she calculated carefully the best way to bring discipline and pain to the pathetic brute who was so keen to allow himself to be humiliated by her. She had already given the big monk seventeen strokes on his large white behind and blood was beginning to flow. *Crack, whack, thwack* went the whip. She gave him a hard forehand, a quick backhand and another forehand.

"Groist Rosie!" groaned Secundus in his heavy South African accent "'ow much more do you intend to give me?"

Rosie walked across the room and lit a cigarette.

They were in the small bedroom that lay directly above his study. She had drawn the curtains and was fairly sure that no one could see them, or maybe even hear them, as a small gale was blowing again outside. She watched as the monk twisted his head to see her naked body.

"Release me! I've had enough!" moaned Secundus.

"Fuck that. We haven't even started, darlin'. Your punishment is for me to decide!"

She blew smoke into his face, raised the whip again and began to thrash him, all over his back and rump. Mercilessly she continued for five more minutes, landing her strokes where she considered it would hurt him most. Blood now flowed freely from the earlier wounds. Secundus howled for mercy, genuinely this time. He tried to rise, to stop her, but the ropes tying his wrists to the bed, held fast. That was another skill that Rosie had learned on the farm, tying up nervous and bad-tempered horses. Silently she drew on her cigarette and then started to burn him, lightly at first, on the buttocks. Secundus screamed. He really howled.

"Quiet! You'll wake the bloody Abbot! Think what you did to Everett!"

"Fuck the Abbot! Fuck Everett! Untie me, let me go!"

"When I'm ready." She now touched the underside of his leg, where she knew the skin was particularly sensitive, and burned him again twice. Secundus flinched, broke wind and began to tear at the bed, trying to break free, lashing out with his legs.

Oldham and Davenport, oblivious to the gale, couldn't believe their eyes. They watched in stunned amazement through the small skylight that lay directly over Secundus' bed. They couldn't quite see what Rosie was doing, as their line of sight was blocked by the woodwork of the ceiling, but they could hear the monk's shrieks of pain.

"We'd better get back. Before someone comes out to investigate" said Oldham.

"If it's anyone it'll be Kite."

"The last person we want to run into. Listen!"

A door was being opened somewhere out of sight, round on the far side of the buildings of the inner courtyard. The Abbey clock struck the half hour. Then there was total silence, apart from muffled noises in the bedroom below.

"What shall we do? Do you want to risk crossing directly back to the dorm?" said Oldham. He had always been adventurous, and this new discovery, of the secret lives of Rosie and the monk, had raised his adrenalin even higher.

"Who came out and where have they gone?" whispered Davenport, also on a high. "Think Stalag Luft. Is it someone on guard we don't know about? At least they don't have searchlights!"

"But we do have a moon, of sorts" answered Oldham. "Let's risk it."

"OK."

The boys crawled back along the guttering of the gym until they reached the drainpipe. They descended very carefully, Oldham first, Davenport on guard until they safely reached the ground. Then they started back for the window they had left open in the kitchen.

"Down!" Oldham signalled frantically to Davenport, who was just behind him. "Look!"

A figure was coming towards them, dressed in what looked like a shroud.

"It's a ghost! Formby said he had seen one this term" Davenport whispered.

They watched, hearts beating, as the apparition drew near, moving steadily but silently over the gravel. It was only about fifteen yards from where they were hidden when it stopped. It looked round nervously. There was the sharp click of a door being opened. The boys heard the noise too - someone coming out of the Abbot's front door.

The ghost turned. It started to run back to the school. Seconds later there came a piercing scream.

"Let's get out of here." Oldham was on his feet, running as fast as he could for the shadow cast by the kitchen building against the moonlight. They stopped in the shadows. Someone was talking very loudly, very close by. It came from exactly the place they were heading for. Two voices; a man and a boy.

Davenport eased himself forward, flat on the ground, his back against the brickwork. He felt his heart pounding with excitement. He gasped with astonishment as he peered round the corner of the building. Ahead of him was Primus, in a sort of robe. He had his back to him. On the ground lay the shroud. Before him was a boy, though he couldn't quite see who it was as the Abbot's sizeable girth blocked his view. There was clearly a serious row going on. Everyone knew that to leave the school at night incurred the most severe beating, ten strokes at least and probably with the cane.

Davenport crawled backwards to Oldham. "It's Primus. He's caught the ghost, but I can't see who it is."

"Ward?"

"It's not his voice."

"Let me have a look" Oldham slithered past him and slowly peered round the corner. He came back at once.

"It's Thompson-Brown! Wow, Primus has stripped him naked!" He went back for a further look, then signalled frantically for them both to freeze. The Abbot, gripping Thompson-Brown by the arm, started to drag him towards his quarters. The head boy was pleading, begging for mercy. As they passed out of sight, Davenport and Oldham raced for the kitchen window.

"Can we save him? Primus will show no mercy."

"The fire alarm! We'll set it off as soon as we get close to dorm. He'll have to let him go."

Oldham produced a little pocket knife. Quickly he unscrewed the glass that covered the alarm and pressed the red bell hard. Both boys had their cover stories well prepared in case Kite appeared.

"It doesn't work!"

"Try again."

Oldham pushed the red knob with both hands. There was silence. The alarm was useless.

★ ★ ★ ★ ★

Judkin, deputy head boy, his rubicund face beaming at his unexpected promotion and good fortune, carried the cross for Morning Prayers. Thompson-Brown, the school was told, had been taken very ill most unexpectedly and had had to be rushed to hospital during the night. No symptoms were mentioned, but it was thought that he had suffered acute appendicitis. Oldham and Davenport watched in silence as the great deceit was played out. What fascinated them, given that Secundus was engaged in activities of a very different nature with the school tart, was what Thompson-Brown was doing, had been doing in fact all term at that hour, and who he was going to meet.

No one was ever to see Thompson-Brown again. Lurid stories were put about, however, by Ward, after whispered details from Oldham and Davenport, that some form of ritual flogging had taken place in Primus' study, a re-enactment of the very martyrdom of the saint himself, with Thompson-Brown tied, spread eagled to a fearsome frame of torture that was hidden behind the book shelves in the Abbot's room. Thompson-Brown had been flogged to death, and his body had been disposed of, probably somewhere in the school grounds, by the Abbot and Kite.

It sent a frisson of fear through the boys, touched with a tinge of eroticism; visits to watch Secundus and Rosie were now to become *de rigeur* for those privy to the secret but, to avoid sharing Thompson-Brown's fate, a new route had to be found to reach the little cottage. Ward took charge of the plans after being briefed by Davenport; a new, longer but potentially more dangerous route was suggested. It should keep them clear of Kite.

★ ★ ★ ★ ★

"Why do you have bruises on your thighs and backside, Wrightson?" demanded Miss Tremble as the latter stood nervously before her for morning showers.

"Brother Jenkins did it. He does it to all of us!"

"Stop lying. One of the boys has done this. Who? Come on. Don't hold back. I shall find out anyway. Nothing escapes me in this school."

"I am not lying, Matron! Look at all the others. He's a horrible teacher and loves giving us pain if we don't do our lessons correctly."

Miss Tremble growled and pushed him away. To her annoyance, she saw that at least ten other boys had similar bruises. She would have to have a word with the Abbot.

★ ★ ★ ★ ★

In his dorm later that morning, during break, Bennett prepared the equipment he knew he needed to secure his objectives. Petrol was the only solution, he had decided, after a number of earlier experiments in hobbies class had failed. There was only one place he could find it, and that was in the Abbot's car. He could siphon it out, but what was really taxing him was how to store it in small quantities around the buildings without being detected before the chosen day; the day of the ultimate conflagration.

EIGHTEEN

Gilbert Mortimer dropped down into third gear to take the road marked to Spalding and the Fen country as they swung off the A1 north of Peterborough. For him it was a joy to take a day off from the City and to give his precious pre-war treasure, his Bentley, a good run in the country. Veronica, silent and brooding beside him, took in nothing of the delights of the drive; the wide open spaces, the little puffs of cumulus in an azure blue sky and the lovely old red-brick villages through which they passed.

"They'll let me see him, won't they?" she said, twisting her hands nervously and looking imploringly at her brother for a positive response.

"In my day parents were not permitted to come and see their children without the express permission of the headmaster. I have no idea what this new man is like, but I reckon our chances are fifty fifty."

Gilbert was not a man given to sentimentality. He had had a tough war, been wounded twice and had himself been to a strict prep school. Veronica looked at him imploringly.

"Fifty fifty? Surely they wouldn't stop us?"

"Boys' schools are very tough on visits, or at least they were before the war. It just wasn't done. Parents were officially allowed to visit once a term, twice in the long summer term, and to attend carol service before the Michaelmas term came to an end. Visits like this were only accepted in the case of a severe illness."

"What about if someone died? Say Henry's father had been killed?"

Gilbert looked at her disdainfully. "The head man, in this case the Abbot, would call the boy in, tell him what had happened, maybe allow him two days off to attend the funeral, but otherwise it was back to work as if nothing had come to pass."

"That's awful! Barbaric! I can't believe it."

"It's the way it is with boys' preparatory schools. Sentimentality, remember, is deemed to be a vice, not a virtue. Not good for making something of a man."

"This happened when you were a boy?"

"Oh, yes, all the time. I was sent to a place in East Kent. It was always horrendously cold in winter with endless North Sea winds. We had two deaths from pneumonia while I was there, it was quite common."

Veronica fell silent. She still clutched the letter that Henry had smuggled out with Ambrose's help. Poor little boy, he sounded so miserable. This boy Ambrose seemed to be the only person he could trust. She wondered what he would look like. The food sounded so awful, and everyone being beaten all the time.

The Bentley purred along the empty road, touching sixty on the straights.

"Did you ever get beaten, Gilbert, during your time at school?" she asked.

"Good Lord yes. All the time. Hurt too. Our headmaster was a man called Bickersteath, Prebendary Bickersteath, a typical sado-evangelist who saw Satan in everyone's backside. He cut your bottom to ribbons. Didn't help me with either algebra or parsing of French verbs!"

They were coming to a junction. "Which way, dear sister?"

Veronica pulled out the map and tried to work out where they were. "According to this we shouldn't be too far from it now. Apparently the monastery stands out among all the flatlands and the Fens. It's on some sort of hill or knoll."

"They always were. Monks knew a thing or two when it came to building on a flood plain."

"Little Hickstead, Muckrinton and Horkinge next the Sea, that's what we want isn't it?"

They pulled off to the side of the road and Gilbert got out to admire the scenery. He lit a cigarette while Veronica studied the map. It was a fine, sunny day, warm for a change, with daffodils in full bloom. Gilbert remembered the area from his wartime training as a gunner. The endless canals across the fens; superb country for defence.

He took the map from her. "We don't need to go all the way to Horkinge, it's way over here on the coast. If we take this road we should come out just about at the right place." He put his arm on her shoulder. "Don't worry Veronica. It'll be all right, don't you question it."

They drove on in silence, both lost in thought, for about a quarter of an hour.

"Ah, this looks like the entrance" said Gilbert suddenly. The Bentley slowed as they saw the sign to the school. A woman working in the small garden of the gatehouse waved as they passed. Veronica waved back.

The car started to climb the long twisting drive to the Abbey and the school.

"Nice-looking old soul, that woman at the gatehouse" said Gilbert, slowing to pass through the outer portal. "There doesn't seem to be anyone around. Guess they're all in class." He looked out of the window, admiring the playing fields. "Super set of grounds here. No wonder they've got such a good reputation for rugger."

His sister stared blankly at the grim-looking pile they had arrived at, impervious to her brother's enthusiasm. Somewhere here, in the depths of these grey granite buildings, would be her dear little boy. Where, oh where, could he be?

Gilbert eased the Bentley through a second arch that led into the inner quadrangle. He pulled up before what he took to be the headmaster's quarters.

* * * * *

The Hillard & Botting Shorter Latin Primer was a tough book, engineered by the printers to withstand considerable punishment from those destined to learn from its pages. It was dark blue, with a thick cardboard cover, and well glued together. The corners of the book were particularly strong. Robust would be a better way of describing it. For Jenkins, ordered by the Abbot to take junior Latin, it was also a weapon of enforcement, a weapon of punishment, and he had developed a skilful backhand flip with this book, sending it hurtling across the classroom to strike any boy he deemed to be misbehaving or not paying attention.

It was Wednesday morning, a bright and sunny one, and they were almost halfway through the term. A subtle change in the atmosphere as the end of term drew near had seen silent optimism replace the earlier weeks of gloom. It was at last also getting slightly warmer. Henry found Latin very difficult to understand. The verbs, the vocabulary, the syntax, all left him greatly confused. None of this was helped by Jenkins' Welsh accent and his terse use of words. He spoke only once upon a subject, gave immediate instructions as to what was to be done in class, and retreated to his desk, where he would usually spend his time reading the *Racing Post*. Woe betide any boys who took this insouciance for inattention, for Jenkins kept an eagle eye on his charges.

At the far side of the room Humphreys was sobbing. He rubbed a large red mark, just below the ear, where the primer had caught him when he had stopped momentarily to look out of the window. Such a fate had not yet befallen Laurie, who kept an eagle eye open for anything motorised that moved. Laurie was a cheerful little junior who saw himself as a truck, or rather as an integral truck and driver unit. He would change down before ascending the stairs and always put on the handbrake before answering a question if spoken to when moving. On the football pitch he lived in a world of his own, changing gear up and down relentlessly, occasionally steering to avoid a pothole. In class he kept his engine in neutral until the bell rang. Miss Tremble, deeming him to be quite barmy, left him to his own devices. Tertius felt pity for him, while everyone else ignored him. Jenkins had another missile at the ready in case of misbehaviour.

"Look, someone's arrived! Wonder who it is?" whispered Laurie, nudging Henry, who was struggling with his parsing. "Never seen that car before."

"Silence!" barked Jenkins, putting down the *Racing*

Post. "Get on with your work, all of you." His thick, hairy fingers reached for the blue book on his desk. But no one now paid him any attention; all eyes were on the yard and the new arrivals. No one ever drove up to the Abbey in term time, except for the black police car, but even that had failed so far to take any of the monks away.

A tall, elegant woman with a large brimmed hat surmounted by an enormous feather climbed out of the car, followed by a beefy, florid-faced man in a dark brown tweed suit. Miss Tapscott, emerging quickly, was giving directions to the Abbot's door.

"It's someone's parents" whispered Davidson "I wonder who they are."

Henry, who had been watching with only mild interest, suddenly realised the new arrivals were his mother and his Uncle Gilbert.

"It's my mummy!" he shrieked with undisguised glee, making a rush for the door. Jenkins, wasting precious time by despatching the Latin Primer at his friend's head, leapt from his desk amid the chaos, but he was too late. Henry tore out of the room and raced down the stairs. If he could get out through the side door leading from the yard to the gym, he could intercept the pair and plead for them to take him home.

His luck, however, was out. The door was locked and bolted from above, far out of his reach. He turned back as the couple were waiting to be let into the Abbot's rooms, and rushed through the dining room, out through the washrooms and round the back of the school. He had just managed to get the last door open when a hand wrenched him by the hair.

"What the hell do you think you are doing, Hingham? No one's allowed to leave the building during class!" The heavy hand of Miss Tremble held him in an iron grip. She knew Henry might try to bite her as he had done so once before, so she kept his hair pulled back hard as she frogmarched him back through the school. "It's my mummy! I want to see my mummy! Henry wailed, but he was being dragged further and further away from where he knew his mother was. "My mummy's come to take me home because you are all so beastly to me!"

"Rubbish, you ridiculous boy! Everyone's happy here. You've told your parents so in all your letters every week."

"Not me. Not me. I hate you all. I wish you were dead! You evil woman!"

Miss Tremble tightened her grip on Henry's hair and twisted her fist. He began to howl and scream, but he was powerless to do anything as she dragged him to her dispensary, a dark and forbidding room underneath the stairs.

"If your mother wishes to see you, which I very much doubt if she will, you will be brought out to meet her" hissed Miss Tremble.

Brother Secundus, passing in the passageway, grinned with amusement to see Miss Tremble opening the door to her dispensary and dragging Henry inside.

Within the dispensary was another room, little more than a cupboard. She unbolted the door and flung Henry head first into the darkness, stepping back before he could attack her, and slamming back the bolts.

Henry continued to scream and bang on the door, but Miss Tremble put on the radio as loud as possible to drown out his cries.

There was a knock. She opened the door to reveal Miss Tapscott.

"I thought I heard a boy crying out in pain? Is everything all right?"

"You heard nothing of the sort. It was something on the radio" Miss Tremble snapped, slamming the door in her face with a bang.

NINETEEN

The Abbot stared at his new arrivals in amazement. No one had ever dared to come to the school unannounced in this manner. It was disgraceful behaviour, he considered, and the woman was clearly emotionally unstable. He tried to hide his anger.

"Had you told me you were coming Mrs Hingham, I would have arranged for your son to be here" he said.

"You mean he's not here at the school? I demand to see my son!"

The door to the Abbot's study opened and Brother Secundus entered unannounced. He dropped heavily into the third chair before the Abbot's desk, stretched himself and yawned.

"This is Mrs Hingham and her brother Mr Gilbert Mortimer, the boy's uncle. Apparently there has been a complaint."

"A complaint? What about? Us?" The deputy headmaster glowered at the new arrivals. "What a load of rubbish. This is the finest preparatory school in the country!"

Gilbert leapt to his feet. "This letter, smuggled out of your school, contains a first-hand account of one of the most appalling stories I have ever heard. It's worse than Dickens. All your prayers and beatings! A disgrace. This place should be closed down, on health grounds if nothing else." He waved the letter in front of the two monks.

"Let me see it!" Secundus put out a hand.

"Not bloody likely! This is going to our lawyers."

"And, pray, what do you mean by that?" asked the Abbot, feigning calmness despite his anger. "you must be aware that we are still recovering from a most terrible war. Our budgets for everything are very restricted. We hardly get enough rations to feed the boys, let alone ourselves."

"If I may say so, none of you look to be exactly starving!"

"Flippancy will get you nowhere, Mr Mortimer."

"How dare you make such accusations about our noble school!" interjected Secundus. "Why did you ever allow your nephew to be sent here if you harboured such doubts about our professionalism?"

"You're a qualified teacher, Brother Secundus?"

"Of course."

"I shall check the facts on our return to London. Now where's the boy?"

"This school has been grooming the cream of the British upper classes for over a hundred years" declared the Abbot. "We have five holders of the Victoria Cross, thirty-one MCs and countless hundreds of medals for lesser gallantry among our old boys. Go down into our Memorial Hall and look for yourself!"

"We want to see the boy. Go and get him" insisted Gilbert.

"I have written to my son every week of term, yet he says in his letter that he has never received any of my communications" said Veronica, addressing herself to the Abbot and ignoring the leer on the other monk's face. "Furthermore, until this arrived I had never received any news of him other than typed notes from this matron of yours telling me how happy and content he was when quite clearly he was not!"

At that moment the door opened and Miss Tremble strode in.

"Ah, here is our matron, Miss Tremble. You can ask her about your boy" said the Abbot. Miss Tremble walked over to him and whispered something in his ear. She turned to Veronica and Gilbert.

"You wanted to see your son, Mrs Hingham? I am afraid that will not be possible."

"Why?"

"The doctors have decided that he may have German measles. We played Havering Lodge last week and two of their boys have gone down with the infection."

"Well he must be in a ward or something? Where do you put the sick boys?"

"We don't. Dr Wallace looks after them. He has a spare house in Horkinge."

"Good. We'll go and see him there!"

It was clear that this was the woman who had treated Henry so badly. His comments about her had been damning.

"That won't be possible" continued Miss Tremble, her thin pasty face tensed with anger at such impudent interrogation.

"Why not? He's either here, being concealed from us by you, or he is where you say he is with this Dr Wallace fellow in Horkinge. Am I right?"

"No you are not. Dr Wallace is concerned about him. He said he would take him into Branchester to see a consultant."

"That's miles away. Don't you have someone nearer?"

There was a moment's silence. The Abbot was not pleased with the way things were going, especially with Mortimer's threat to pass his nephew's letter and a record of this visit to the educational authorities. That was the last thing they needed right now what with Everett, Campbell and now Thompson-Brown's forced confession of his relationship with Brother Quartus. He was beginning to wonder what else was going on behind his back.

"And what qualifications do you have, Miss Tremble, to be matron at this school?" demanded

Gilbert Mortimer in the cut-glass tones of authority. At this question Miss Tremble appeared to lose her self control.

"Five years' training at the London Hospital, four years as a nurse. Then with the RAMC in the war" she snapped back at him.

"Good" Gilbert declared, noting what she had said in a little book,

"I shall check with them when we return to London."

"Go ahead!" she hissed through clenched teeth. The Abbot winced. Bad publicity was the last thing they needed.

At that moment the telephone rang. The Abbot picked up the receiver and listened for a moment. Then he spoke quietly in Spanish before quietly replacing the receiver. Veronica burst into tears. "I've had enough of this pathetic, deceitful, libellous rubbish!" she yelled.

Secundus rose from the chair and beckoned Miss Tremble to follow him. "One day I'll thrash that bloody child of hers" he declared in a stage whisper to Miss Tremble. Then he banged the door shut and stumped off noisily down the stairs.

★ ★ ★ ★ ★

"We've got to do something! Kite's locked him up in her dispensary."

Ambrose, Ward and another good friend, Hetherington, were in earnest discussion at the bottom of the stone stairs to upper school. It was break. Jenkins sloped past, skulking. "No whispering in break!" he growled.

"You've got three minutes" Ambrose continued. "We can't get him out because Kite has got the key. Miss Tapscott had a copy but she's lost it."

"Carps lent me a chisel. I'll get it" said Ward. He ran off towards the washrooms.

"Where's Kite now? asked Hetherington.

"In an emergency meeting in Primus' study. It sounds as if a frightful row is going on. With his parents."

"Good. It'll give us time."

Ward came running back with his treasured chisel and a screwdriver. "Think this might be better. We need to loosen the screws."

"She'll go ape!"

"Good. Let's hope she has a heart attack and dies. Ambrose, quick, silence the school bell. It'll give us a few minutes."

Ambrose ran up the stairs till he was above the offensive clock and pushed the arms back ten minutes, which made a horrible grinding noise. Then he ran back down to the others.

"Someone watch Primus' door" he said. "They'll have to come out that way."

The handle of the dispensary came off very quickly, but the lock took longer to spring back. Hetherington ran back.

"Quick! They're coming out. Kite's at the back."

The boys ran into the dispensary and pulled back the bolts on the cupboard door. Henry started screaming.

"We're coming to rescue you, Hingham" shouted Hetherington. "Your mummy's still here!"

The bolts sprang back and Henry shot out like a cornered rabbit.

"Quick. Through the window!" Ward helped him out. Henry's mother and uncle were already in the car and the Bentley's doors were closing as Henry appeared in the yard. Miss Tremble raced across the gravel in a desperate attempt to intercept him, but the little boy kept on running, dodging, weaving to get past her. The Bentley accelerated out of the inner courtyard and passed through the arch. He could see his mother inside, a handkerchief covering her face. Uncle Gilbert, grim, sat staring straight ahead. Neither of them looked in the mirror.

"Mummy! Mummy! Stop please, stop!" screamed Henry, but the car was picking up speed. It turned and began the long descent to the gate house and the public highway.

It was Secundus who finally caught the boy. He took a short cut across the fields and intercepted him just before the stone bridge over the stream. Warned by Miss Tremble, he held him in a steely grip and started back to the school. Then he marched him straight to see the Abbot.

★ ★ ★ ★ ★

"I'm going to check this place out as soon as we get home" muttered Gilbert to his sobbing sister. "Five years in the army taught me how to spot a liar, and that lot were lying through their back teeth."

"Perhaps we could go into Horkinge and see this Dr Wallace?"

"Why not. We've come all this way. It will be interesting to see if he knows anything about the boy. My gut feeling is that they were making up their stories as they went along. Didn't care for that South African monk. Struck me as a charmless brute."

"The matron had written such comforting things about Henry. Now we know it was all lies."

There was a further, sharp bend before the gatehouse of the grounds. Gilbert slowed. Another car, a black Wolseley, was climbing up towards them. It was a police car, and the driver made a signal for them to stop. Gilbert wound down his window.

"Very sorry to trouble you sir," said the driver "but we're looking for a Mr Rhodri Jenkins, who we believe is teaching at this school. Do you know where we might find him?"

Gilbert and Veronica shook their heads. "I'm afraid we have just had a most distasteful meeting with the headmaster, the Abbot. We met a monk with a South African accent, but no one else apart from the matron, a Miss Tremble."

"Ah, what a pity."

"Drive up to the Abbot's quarters, officer, and he'll be able to help you" said Gilbert. "It's through the archway and across the inner courtyard. By the way, perhaps you could help us, are you local?"

"We're from Horkinge next the Sea, sir. We cover this area."

"We're trying to find a Dr Wallace who apparently tends to the needs of the boys at this school. I was wondering if you could tell us how to find him?"

The two police officers conferred and shook their heads "No doctor of that name in Horkinge, sir. There's Watson, Robins and Wellgood-Williams in one lot and Thompson, Radcliffe and a junior bloke in the other group. Never heard of a Dr Wallace. Sure he was in Horkinge?"

"That's what they told us, up there in the Abbot's study."

"Perhaps they meant Muckrinton, but that's a strange place for the school doctor to come from. Sorry."

They let the police car pass and watched it climb towards the school. "As I suspected" sighed Gilbert, easing off the handbrake, "there's not a word of truth in this. Let's hope Henry succeeds in smuggling out another letter. His first certainly had them rattled, set the cat among the pigeons. First thing I'm doing when we get to London is to check up with the London. Tom Kemp, the senior orthopaedic man, is a good friend. I don't think that bitch ever went near the place."

★ ★ ★ ★ ★

"So you've no one called Rhodri Jenkins on your staff, then Abbot?" the police officer asked.

"We did have a man of that name working for us here last term. Called himself Blodwen or something, not Rhodri. What, may I ask, is the purpose of your call?"

"It's a confidential matter, sir. We would like him to help us in our enquiries into a number of public order offences. We are acting on behalf of the Oxfordshire constabulary."

"Could you tell me the nature of these charges? Nothing involving boys I hope, since we are so vulnerable at this school."

"I'm afraid we're not at liberty to say, sir. Thank you for your time." The officers turned towards the door. "By the way, we found a couple in a car at the bottom of your drive who were looking for a Dr Wallace. We were wondering why you gave them that name? There's no one practising of that name in Horkinge, as I'm sure you know."

"They must have misheard us. Dr Watson is the man who comes here occasionally."

"Thank you."

The Abbot watched as the police car slowly turned in the yard and made its way to the drive.

"Get me Brother Jenkins!" he barked into the direct line to Miss Tremble. "And make sure that Hingham child is punished most severely for being such a nuisance."

★ ★ ★ ★ ★

"I think we've been lucky" said the Abbot three days later, helping himself to another slice of the game pie which the Montrose-Wilson's little boy had brought to the school. "If that Hingham boy had been seen by his parents, God knows what sort of a mess we would be in."

He was greatly perturbed by the pending litigation from Everett and had a growing feeling of unease that the future of the school could be extremely bleak. He watched Secundus as he devoured yet another huge plate of food. There were only the three of them present;

Tertius claiming a bad cold and Quartus feigning another engagement, knowing full well that his presence with the other monks would not be welcome, and the junior masters had not been invited anyway.

"No one can intimidate me!" laughed the big, beefy monk, helping himself liberally to the claret donated by Ward's father. "I don't care for people who turn up unannounced and start asking personal questions. I smashed a bloke's brains out once for daring to ask me about my private life."

"An African, no doubt" sighed the Abbot.

"No. One of you English as a matter of fact. He was hospitalised for five months."

"You weren't charged?"

"No one dared to testify against me" he smirked, as if enjoying some private joke.

Miss Tremble, already into pudding, took another large slice of brown plum cake. "I do like Lent" she beamed. "It gives us a chance to use the rations where they rightly should be going. That was excellent game pie if I may say so, Abbot."

"Has anyone seen Jenkins?" enquired the Abbot.

"Disappeared from his class as soon as that police car arrived. Old Tertius said he thought he saw him running off across the Fens."

"It's not the first time it's happened" sighed the Abbot. "This time they were acting for the Oxford force.

I wonder what they wanted?"

"You'll have to get rid of him, Abbot. And Brother Quartus too, especially after Thompson Brown confessed."

"We can't afford to go on losing staff. Brother Quartus will be dismissed at the end of term. We shall not pay his wages. I'll have to replace him though."

Secundus was pleased that the other monks had declined the invitation and that there were only the three of them. There was something private he wanted to know that tickled his fancy, that oozed from his sadistic mind; the punishment accorded to the former head boy.

"How many strokes did you give that Thompson-Brown, Abbot?" he asked quietly, his face betraying the lupine look of a wolf which had somehow just missed the opportunity of killing a particularly fat sheep. "We should have had a school flogging, you know. We haven't had one of those for two terms now!"

The Abbot looked at his questioner with the sudden aloofness which the monks knew signalled his displeasure at both a question and the tone in which it had been asked. "It would have been most inappropriate under the circumstances" he declared. "People, the boys, would have asked what he was being punished for. Expulsion was my only option."

"We shall have a flogging soon, Abbot. Don't you

doubt it! I'll find the excuse" declared the Chief Disciplinarian, charging his glass to the brim. The Abbot fell silent, watching his two greedy members of staff helping themselves liberally to the spread that lay before them. His disdain for both of them was growing daily, especially for his deputy, whose sadistic, brutal obsession with corporal punishment had now landed them in such a precarious position and rendered them vulnerable to a lawsuit which could potentially bring about the closure of the school. He had never had much confidence in Brother Secundus, who, hiding under the mantle of the Jesuit doctrine, overtly used his position to satisfy his lust for cruelty. He wondered what else the man was engaged in within the confines of the school.

His attention turned to Miss Tremble, who had dropped some food on the floor. He knew that she too was loathed by the boys and most of the staff, but she was different; the price for earlier salvation in a very different world.

"Delicious plum cake, you must try some" said Miss Tremble, emerging from beneath the table with the rescued morsel. She passed the plate across the table to Secundus, who took the proffered cake and hacked off a sizeable portion with his knife. "Ah, a feast in Lent! How I love it!" Miss Tremble muttered, crumbs dribbling down her bony chin.

★ ★ ★ ★ ★

"Look, Look!" shouted Williams-Jones as he stood at the dormitory window in the darkness a little later that evening. The other boys rushed to join him. They were astonished and delighted to see below them, crawling on hands and knees around the dimly-lit inner courtyard, the form of Miss Tremble. She was groaning horribly and seemed unable to get to her feet. As they watched, she collapsed in a paroxysm of vomiting.

Outside the door to his cottage Secundus too lay curled up in agony, a thin moon shining down upon his waxen features. Others too had heard strange noises; little faces appeared at the windows. Harding was roused from his bed.

"I've done it! I've done it! shrieked Williams-Jones, bouncing up and down on his bed with glee. "Now let's see if all their wretched prayers will come and save their skins!"

Oldham wanted to go out there and then and cut the matron's throat with the knife he had stolen from Leno in the kitchen, but wiser hands held him back. Bennett watched the unfolding drama in silence from a window further along the dormitory. His plans were becoming clearer by the day. The removal of the odious Kite would greatly assist in the final preparations.

TWENTY

Woburn Square, London, had once been one of the most attractive Georgian squares in Bloomsbury. Delightful four-storey houses surrounded a small green garden. A Victorian church dominated, built half way down the east side of the square. But by the end of the war, thanks to its proximity to the major railway stations much of it lay in decay. What had not been destroyed by enemy action was about to fall to the bulldozers of London University.

Upton made his way along the south side of the square until he found the narrow black door of number 55. Scruffy pieces of paper identified the individual flats. Flat 3 was not shown; Upton pressed one of two bells which carried no identification. After a long period of silence an old woman, her hair covered with a scarf, opened the door. She was smoking a cigarette. She stared at Upton for some moments, as if deciding whether to be friendly or not.

"You come to see the poof?"

"Sorry. I'm looking for Mr Parker's flat."

"'E's the poof. All the men what come here are

poofs." She continued to eye him suspiciously. "Or bloody commies. You don't look much like a poof, nor a commie come to think of it."

"I fought with Mr Parker in the war. I was passing. Heard he hadn't been well."

"Poofs, queers, nancy boys, they're always bloody ill. They're…" She changed her mind, as if not wishing to continue with her diatribe. "It's the other button. Doubt if he's in though."

Without further ado she slammed the door. Upton heard her struggling slowly up the stairs. He waited a few moments before ringing Parker's bell.

Parker appeared instantly and ushered Upton in with almost manic urgency. "You got that ghastly woman! I must get this bell marked properly." He said. He led the way downstairs over threadbare carpet to a small, one bedroom basement flat. Signs of damp were evident throughout.

"Make yourself comfortable. Tea or coffee? Both are muck. Can't afford much, you know." A packet of powdered milk lay open in a tiny, squalid little kitchen.

Parker had aged since Upton had last seen him; his face was sharper, the eyes more ratlike. He had developed some sort of skin disease and had a nervous twitch beneath the left eye. His clothes were none too clean, and his trousers were clearly the lower half of his demob suit.

"How's life? You a monk! I can't believe it" he said. He scratched around for some tea as the kettle boiled on the hob. "So isolated, so removed from real life. It took me long enough to find you."

"And how did you find me?" Upton wanted to know, as he had gone to considerable lengths to make sure Parker did not know where he was. Now, as he feared, blackmail was in the air. Upton wondered what he wanted. It couldn't just be sex.

"Pretended to be from the army. Located your mother. I remember you told me she'd moved. It took me months." He grinned, not altogether without malice.

"So here I am. What do you want?"

Parker eyed him lasciviously. "You've not forgotten, surely? Those happy days in the army?" He sat down beside Upton on the battered sofa and put a hand on his knee. "Plenty of it at the school then? They always say boys' schools are the worst, or best, whichever way you look at it."

"No time for anything like that, Parker." Upton wondered why they never called each other by their Christian names. "For one thing it's much too bloody cold. Wind off the North Sea. We all have to dress in monk's clothes, habits as they call them. Food's terrible."

"And pay? What do they pay you?"

"Not a lot. Food and lodging's included of course."

"You could do with some more? I could help."

"I took the King's shilling, not Uncle Joe's!" Parker removed his hand and reached round for some papers. "It's not what you think. We're being chased by the security people."

"MI5? Why? You must be up to something."

"It's the big strike we're working on. Coal, trains and the docks. All together. The workers united. Attlee's government is full of poodles. The Conservatives are plotting everywhere."

"1926 didn't do you lot much good."

"My lot? You're in this too, Upton." Parker rummaged in the pile of papers. "Here you are, my friend. Fully paid-up member of the Wales and Western Communist Party. Here's your card. Five shillings a year. I've paid on your behalf." Parker's eyes veritably twinkled with malevolence. "I'll keep paying for you, or would you like the membership to be sent to your school? All those white, tight-arsed little boys running naked before you everyday. I bet someone's buggering them, if it's not you."

"I didn't come all this way to hear this nonsense." Upton stood up and walked over to the window.

"They'll spot you, Upton. This place is staked out day and night."

"So?"

"They'll track you. Follow you on the train. Find out where you work. All our members in the Rhondda are marked men, ditto Durham."

"And then? I've done nothing wrong."

"Your word against mine. And that's before any sex charges. You could go down for five years."

Upton saw the danger. If Parker had already started the membership and had a card to prove it, what else was he hiding up his sleeve? He couldn't just walk out. He had to know more.

"So what is it you want?"

"Your skills from our signals days. You were a clever boy in the field."

"Out of practice now."

"It's the location that matters to me. Not new technology. I have to be able to communicate with the brotherhood without interception of third parties. Your Abbey might be the missing link between Durham, London and South Wales."

"You've lost me."

"I'll explain everything over a bite to eat. There's a noisy little caff not too far from Russell Square station. Even if they follow us they won't be able to monitor our conversation. When's your train back?"

"I plan to take the five o'clock from London. It'll take four hours with all the changes but at least I'm spared evening prayers."

"Come on. Let's go." Parker put on an old army overcoat. He grinned "Officer's uniform. Gives status. Got it from the Salvation Army!"

They ran up the stairs and out into the drizzle. Upton looked back. The old crone was staring from the first floor window. Maybe even she was MI5. He kept his thoughts to himself as they headed off to Russell Square.

★ ★ ★ ★ ★

Upton rubbed his eyes as the train sped north into the gathering darkness. The cheap brandy Parker had insisted upon had had a deleterious impact upon his judgement. He knew he was caught between a rock and a hard place. Morton's fork. The choice was stark. Exposure on the one hand, with immediate loss of job, maybe a court case if Parker turned really nasty or cooperation in what appeared to be a mild matter of internal communication. So long as that was all it was. Parker would be sending medicines, for Upton had recounted how Miss Tremble opened all their mail. His medicine would be for a stomach ailment, prescribed by a doctor in London. They would come in a large package. Hopefully they would defeat whatever limited medical knowledge the matron actually had.

Upton tried to clear his mind and go back over the conversation in the dingy café. What was Parker really doing? Was it legal, and if not, what would be the implications from his involvement in whatever it turned out to be?

The train stopped with a jolt. They had reached Newark. He scrambled out and ran as fast as he could across the platform to make the connection. He found an empty compartment in the non corridor train, collapsed into the corner seat and closed his eyes.

The brandy had only served to stimulate and agitate his mind. There was no one he knew in whom he could confide, not even Brother Tertius, nor Miss Tapscott to whom he found himself drawn more and more as an ally in a dangerous world. It was not that Tertius was such a great friend, but rather that everyone else was so awful; Campbell forever stealing little things, Quartus and Jenkins obsessed with their lust for pre-pubescent boys, two of them prone to drink, Secundus overtly evil and the Abbot a sort of self created saint presiding over pseudo-ecclesiastical chaos. Of the women, only Miss Tapscott bore any mantle of respectability.

Upton prepared to change trains again, but the last connection had been cancelled. To his annoyance he had to pay a hefty taxi fare. He reached the school well after eleven at night and climbed wearily up to his room in Herga.

A few moments later there was a discreet knock at the door. It was Tertius, dressed in his silk dressing gown with the front slightly open as always. He welcomed Upton back with his usual rather sad and lost demeanour.

"I've left my bath, dear boy, in case you felt the need" he said. "I imagine London was filthy, as always, and the trains equally so. I do so hope you had a good day." He paused, as if not quite sure whether to continue. "The news of poor Miss Tremble is not good, I regret to say. She remains in intensive care in the county hospital. But on a more cheerful note, Brother Secundus is back with us."

"A more cheerful note, Henry? Do you mean that?"

"Let us not wish ill of colleagues, Charles, no matter how evil at times they may appear to be!" responded Tertius. He paused for a moment and then added, slightly raising his eyebrows, "Oh by the way Charles, Brother Quartus has specifically asked not to be disturbed."

TWENTY-ONE

The Abbot waited a full week before calling Brother Secundus and Miss Tremble to his study. No one knew precisely what had caused their sickness, and the report from the county hospital confined itself to declaring that it had probably been the result of eating contaminated meat; there was a lot of horse meat entering the food chain under the guise of beef. No one suggested poison. The unexpected illness of two of the senior staff and the disappearance of Jenkins was adding to his problems. Jenkins was still absent, probably trying to evade the law, and Campbell had asked for leave again to appear before magistrates in Grantham the following week. The school was now seriously short of teaching staff; Secundus, Tertius, Quartus and Upton would have to undertake even more work. To his disgust the Abbot himself would be forced to take the senior boys in History and Latin. He drummed his fingers on the desk.

"How did the Hingham parents come to know so much about this school?" he demanded bitterly of his two staff members. "And why did they feel compelled to come and see me personally about the state of their boy?" The Abbot looked accusingly at them. Secundus and Miss Tremble sat stony-faced in the two leather chairs before his desk. Secundus, with his narrow blue eyes, squinted defiance.

"Any scandal will only be to our detriment" continued the Abbot. "You heard what Mortimer was threatening. Once news of our predicament becomes widespread, we will see a host of parents removing their boys from our care, a sad way for Saint Eusebius to end after seventy years of excellence. As for the bad food, forget it, it could have happened to anyone."

"We were deliberately poisoned!" growled Miss Tremble. "And I've a pretty shrewd idea who did it."

"Don't tell me it's the Italians and the girl?" the Abbot scoffed. Secundus kept his silence. He had a pretty good idea about what had happened. He had learned it from Rosie, but couldn't of course say how. Miss Tremble, her dark, brooding countenance if anything hardened by her experience, and still in considerable pain from stomach cramps, sat scowling. She too had some inkling of what had been planned for her after overhearing two of the senior boys joking about it in the changing room. It was the ignominy of being seen crawling across the yard in agony before the boys that had really irked her; quietly she was plotting her revenge. First, however, they had to break the wretched little Hingham boy. He had to be tamed, his spirit broken, irrevocably, irretrievably, and before the coming holidays. He must conform with his peers to be a true Saint Eusebian.

Miss Tremble did not betray her emotions or her thoughts to the Abbot, but she had come up with a brilliant idea, one to which only Secundus would be party. It would depend upon the timing of the Abbot's next visit to Branchester, which would provide them with the opportunity they needed.

"You know, Brother Primus, that I vet all the correspondence that enters and leaves this school" she declared acidly. "It is quite impossible for the boy to have written such rubbish to his parents."

"But he did. You saw the letter in the boy's handwriting" the Abbot snapped. "He wrote to his mother, to be precise; the father is still working for the government." The Abbot drummed a pencil on his desk. "Let me remind you, Miss Tremble, that it was the father who wanted the boy to come to this school, not the mother. She was, and remains, implacably against us."

"The uncle, or whoever he was, appeared extraordinarily well briefed" growled Secundus. "If we've got a spy in this place, Abbot, God help him when I find out who it is!"

"Beating up a suspect won't get you or any of us anywhere, Brother Secundus."

"I'm going to find out who tried to poison me!" squawked Miss Tremble. "It has to be one of our monks. But which? The new Upton fellow doesn't have the knowledge yet, Tertius is an old fat cat, it won't be Campbell, obviously, and I doubt if it could be either Jenkins or Quartus."

"We may be losing both Jenkins and Campbell anyway" replied the Abbot. "I've had another complaint. What makes you suspect Upton and Tertius?"

Secundus shrugged his shoulders. "Don't like 'em, don't trust 'em."

"That's no reason. For God's sake use some imagination. Phones?"

"One line. I control it" Miss Tremble declared icily. She stared accusingly at the Abbot. "It's not an option."

"Miss Tapscott?"

"Theoretically she could be our spy. Miss Tapscott has been here for over five years and we have had worse things happen than this. She's not going to jeopardise a good living for the sake of a small boy."

"The prisoners, then?" The Abbot glanced up enquiringly beneath his bushy eyebrows.

"Prisoners?" Secundus and Miss Tremble looked somewhat puzzled.

"Don't tell me you've forgotten our two Italian helpers, Leno and Romeo, or whatever the other one is called."

"Romano" replied Miss Tremble coldly. "Two of the laziest swines I have ever come across. No wonder they couldn't win a war."

Secundus shifted uneasily in his chair. They were better at it than he was, Rosie had taunted him, telling him she had been to bed with both the Italians. They had also had a threesome in a hotel in Skegness, she had boasted. He stared at the carpet and clenched his fists.

"This school is dominated by three boys, three post-pubescent youths, and I can't wait for their departure" declared Secundus. "But before they go, thinking they have got the better of us, I intend to cane them. To leave their backsides so scarred, so hard, that they'll carry their marks for years, maybe even for life." He turned his head and looked hopefully at the array of canes anchored to the wall behind him.

"And who are these boys you intend to beat, Brother Secundus?"

"Not just three, more likely five or six. We all know who the troublemakers are, don't we Abbot? Ward, Davenport, Williams-Jones, Ambrose, Penfold, Bentley and Mowbray, to name just a few. I could go on."

"Only five or six?" the Abbot rubbed his chin and laughed lightly to himself. Secundus would get his chance, so long as Ward was not among them. He did not disclose his thoughts.

"They are planning to destroy this school, by fair

means or foul" said Secundus. "We must be on our guard."

"Fair means, for destroying our school? I find that an odd choice of words, Brother Secundus. Foul I accept."

"Poisoning us until we have insufficient staff left is one of the plans" said Miss Tremble. "And I don't underestimate their skills at fire and pestilence."

"Pestilence? Fire?"

"Someone has access to our stationery supplies. That Rosie creature said she saw someone lurking in the supply room."

The Abbot's patience began to slip. "Let's get back to the main point" he hissed. "None of you seem to have the slightest idea how the Hingham boy's complaints got out of the school. I'll give you a week to find out. You want me to call in outside detectives to resolve this matter?"

"No. No certainly not!"

"Well then, make sure you get your facts straight, make sure you can pinpoint who helped the boy. How did he get a stamp, for example, in a school that has no cash allowances?"

"We'll do the best we can, Brother Primus, but don't count on it."

"And Miss Tremble, if the mother writes to him again I want to see the letter before you destroy it. Am I absolutely clear?"

"Of course sir. I'll do my best."

"You'd better succeed."

Outside in the yard, Secundus and Miss Tremble exchanged angry looks. It was raining hard, which served only to dampen their spirits.

"He's just arrogant enough to go and do something bloody silly like that, calling in a detective" said Secundus, turning up his cape. "Something that would fucking screw up all of us, maybe even himself included."

"The Abbot has a secret?"

"We all have secrets in this place, Miss Tremble. No doubt you are no exception. I bet Upton's hiding something too."

"I certainly have no secrets" declared Miss Tremble archly, standing on her dignity. She lowered her voice. "But I do have a plan for Hingham, and you are part of it, Brother Secundus." She looked at him with dark, salacious eyes. "The Abbot goes to Branchester on Wednesday. I'll let you know once I have decided when, and more importantly how, we are going to do it."

They parted, each stumping off into the wet, wrapped up in their thoughts.

★ ★ ★ ★ ★

The Abbot cursed as he drove onto the road to

Branchester. The car was again showing that he had almost no petrol left, yet he had filled up, with his precious coupons, the very last time he had used the car. He would have to have it looked at. Surely a Rover would never have a leaking petrol tank.

TWENTY-TWO

The celebrations of Miss Tremble's demise had called for a further raid upon the Abbot's whisky during his absence in Branchester. The boys sat sipping from a tooth mug which was passed round solemnly between them.

"Let's just hope she eats some more and dies" said Williams-Jones, passing the plastic mug to Ward. "In agony! As she deserves."

"You heard what she did to Hingham?"

"Poor little wretch. Locked up like some rabbit."

"No, I mean since then."

"No. What?"

"Apparently his mother and uncle came to see him to tell him his father had been killed. Somewhere in Europe. He may have been chasing Nazis or spying on the Russians. No one knows."

"Who told you this?"

"Ambrose. Hingham told him himself."

"Anyway, what did they do to him?"

"Secundus called him into Primus' study. Last week when he went to Branchester. Apparently he had Kite with him in case Hingham fainted or tried to attack them. They told him in graphic detail that his father had been shot by the Russians and his body had been thrown into a ditch. Hingham was really upset. Seems Kite recalled the whole thing with relish."

"She's not got over being bitten!"

"Is Ambrose going to be doing anything about this? He's Henry's guardian still."

"Haven't asked him. Think I should?"

"Dunno. Not much point. If his daddy's dead, he's dead."

Ward passed round the whisky. "You think it's true? They haven't made it up?"

"We saw his parents. It must have been important."

"Maybe they got the letter."

"Letter?"

"Ambrose got him to write a secret letter. He took it to Mrs Carps and she posted it. He told me."

"Gosh. That's brilliant."

"Heard about Upton's new wheeze?"

"Fifth form geography?"

"Everyone's into radio signals. It's super. He's set up an aerial in the old Abbey tower, the smaller one on the left. We can hear lots of foreign languages. He twiddles some sort of knob and we can hear what we think might be the army. Upton tells us we can't get America yet but he's working on it."

"Makes geography interesting at last. All Jenkins

ever did was to go round hitting you with those horrible atlases."

★ ★ ★ ★ ★

It had taken Upton several days to work out how he was going to get the fifty-foot transmitter wire up on to one of the old towers of the ruined Abbey. There was no way he could climb the structure, which was probably unsafe anyway, and no easy access to it either. Then he hit upon a brilliant idea. Some of the boys had been extolling the merits of archery to Brother Tertius the previous year and wanted to know if they could reproduce in carpentry the sort of bow and arrow that might have been used. Carps was brought in on the plan. He rather dampened spirits by pointing out that anyone with a physique less than that of either Secundus or the Abbot would be quite incapable of drawing the bow. To keep everyone happy however, he agreed to help the boys make two bows, with arrows, which were smaller than the originals but usable by the boys. Everyone had a great time re-enacting Agincourt and Crècy, with Tertius running round organising target practice.

At the end of the summer term the bows and arrows were put away in a cupboard in the carpentry shop and everyone forgot about them. That is until Tertius, apprised of Upton's idea, mentioned them to him. Tertius suggested in jest, on hearing of Upton's plan to liven up Geography, that it might be possible to shoot a line over one of the towers with string, to which an aerial might be attached.

All the class were brought in to watch the fun. In the distance Secundus scowled sullenly; such frivolity from a whole class on his precious sports fields was not to his liking, not in the fighting spirit of Saint Eusebius. It took fourteen attempts to shoot the line of string over the tower and quite a few minutes to pull the aerial, attached to the string, over the ruins behind it, since it snagged frequently on the stonework. When it had finally been fixed, Upton introduced his class to a new world of radio; signals were heard, the BBC Home Service picked up loud and clear as well as American forces radio. The boys were delighted.

Under cover of darkness, and sweating with nerves, Upton opened the first package Parker had entrusted him with and, attaching it, transmitted whatever secret message it contained. He had played his part in the great workers' revolution, he hoped, and trusted that Parker would now leave him alone.

It was wishful thinking. More packages arrived. He was forced to tell Miss Tremble that he had visited his doctor in London and was having to take some medicine on a regular basis. She seemed surprisingly indifferent. Upton knew that once Parker had tracked him down, it would be only a matter of time before the blackmail was renewed. He would be exposed as a communist agent in some traitorous plot. He resolved accordingly to seek an early exit from the school, even if it meant taking a loss of earnings and to seek advice into assisted passages to Canada or Australia on his next visit to London.

* * * * *

Upton, isolated from the real world in his remote post at Saint Eusebius, rarely read a newspaper unless it was an old copy of Miss Tapscott's *Daily Mail* or the *Horkinge Gazette*. Accordingly he was quite unaware of the growing militancy among the unionised manual workers and, more to the point, the penetration of the working class unions and the Labour Party by hardline pro-Soviet Marxists. Parker, already under observation by the security services, was now actively communicating with Soviet spies at the London Embassy, through whom he was instructed to ascertain details of British defence plans in the face of the worsening Cold War in Eastern Europe.

In London, at their offices in Gower Street, Commander Selincourt knocked on the door of his superior's office. It was a little after midday.

"Yes, what is it Chips?"

"Something rather strange, sir. Two things, to be precise. As you know we have been maintaining a very close watch on Soviet trawler activity in the North Sea."

"Operation Dogwood. Of course. What's developed?"

Captain Sands took the pipe out of his mouth and tapped it lightly on the ashtray. "We are receiving advice that two new, very long range and very sophisticated vessels have come into the area. We were asking ourselves why this should be so when the SIS people called to brief us on new radio transmission activity, from a location as yet undetected, on the North Sea coast, not too far from the Wash."

"Norfolk or Lincolnshire then?"

"Exactly. We are going to follow this one very carefully. Part of the problem is that the transmissions are made in a code for which we do not have the cipher. It could be a new NKVD network rather than the usual Soviet navy transmissions."

"Keep me closely advised, Chips. Times, frequency, squelched, position of receiving vessels."

"Of course sir."

Not more than a quarter of a mile from the Gower Street offices, Parker beavered away that night working on the next set of squelched tapes which he would be sending off to Upton. Covert Soviet support for the great Peoples' Revolution to come was absolutely critical for their plans to break the Attlee government.

TWENTY-THREE

The envelope Miss Tremble had been waiting for came ten days later. The handwriting was Hingham's mother's and the postmark was London. Carefully she lifted the kettle and began to steam open the smart cream vellum envelope. As the paper parted, she slipped a thin pocket knife under the fold and pulled back the triangular paper which had sealed the contents. She removed the letter carefully and laid it out on her desk. It was not long and would be relatively easy to replicate, though she did not have Mrs Hingham's expensive notepaper. She doubted that Henry would notice that the envelope did not match the contents.

She put on her glasses and began to read.

Darling Henry, Uncle Gilbert and I were <u>so</u> sorry not to have seen you darling when we came all the way down to Saint Eusebius last week. The matron told us that you were ill and had been taken to see the doctor in Branchester. I do hope you are better now, my little pet. Uncle Gilbert felt that the matron was lying and trying to cover up and he had a <u>really</u> tough time questioning some horrible big monk who *barged in on our meeting with the Abbot. Uncle Gilbert didn't like him at all and he didn't think much of the matron either.*

The words 'so' and 'really' had been heavily underlined. Stupid, sentimental cow, thought Miss Tremble as she turned the page and read on. Her pulse began to quicken.

Uncle Gilbert told me on the way home that he thought the whole school had gone downhill since Daddy was a boy there. The few boys we did see looked terribly cold and wretched; no one smiled. It wasn't right, he felt. He went on and on about the meeting with the Headmaster. He said something was worrying him. He's going to make some enquiries. He has old friends from the war in high places in Whitehall.

Miss Tremble's hand started to shake. She re-read the page again before picking up the second one.

He's going to ask them to start an investigation into the nasty big monk. He doesn't think a South African monk should be working in a remote school like St Eusebius unless he has something to hide. I don't know why. Everyone needs jobs now the war is over.

Happy, happy news! Daddy hopes to be back in England by Easter. Won't it be exciting to have him back with us again! Mr Binks has got a fur ball in his throat and has been very sick. All over the new cream carpet in your bedroom. Like me he misses you very much. With lots of hugs and big kisses from Mummy.

A tear had obviously fallen on the paper as she had

finished writing. Soppy bitch, thought Miss Tremble. She snatched up the letter, carefully locked her room and set off to find Secundus. It was just after two o'clock and games didn't start before three. On the way she picked up the blue shawl that always hung inside the dispensary and set out across the yard. It was raining, with a strong cold wind blowing in from the direction of the North Sea. Keeping close to the wall of the building she worked her way round the inner courtyard until she reached Secundus' quarters under the archway. She knocked loudly on the door.

"Who is it?" The voice was unmistakably Rosie's. It came from the first floor room. Miss Tremble looked up at the small window. She knocked loudly again. "Coming" said the voice. There was the sound of someone clattering down the wooden stairs. The door was flung open.

Rosie stood there looking dishevelled, her hair out of place, the buttons on her blouse paired with the wrong buttonholes and her skirt on the wrong way round. Her face was deeply flushed, but the blue eyes were as alert as ever.

"Yes?" she snapped.

"I must see Brother Secundus at once. It is a matter of great urgency."

"He's not here."

"Where is he then?"

"Dunno."

"Why are you here?"

"What's that got to do with you? None of your business what I'm doin' here."

"Yes it is! In case you had forgotten Miss Robinson, I could have you sacked."

"What for?" Rosie challenged, her blue eyes now hard and cold.

"Insubordination, for one. I'll find other reasons, you mark my words."

This heated exchange was cut short by the unexpected appearance of Brother Secundus. He was dressed smartly, as if for afternoon sports.

"What's going on? he asked, giving Miss Tremble a scornful look. "Trust you to turn up now when we've lost him."

"Lost who?"

"Whoever was breaking into this place. Rosie spotted him and gave chase. I came but I lost him too. Could be that bloody Campbell again."

Miss Tremble looked at each of them with disbelieving eyes.

"It's this" she declared, holding out Henry's letter from his mother. "You'd better take a look at it."

Secundus turned to Rosie. "Run along, Rosie. Many thanks for coming to my help."

"Not till I get a fuckin' apology out of her, I won't!" she snapped, grabbing Miss Tremble's blue cardigan and shaking her. "This bloody cow says she goin' to get me sacked for insu, insu..."

"Insubordination, you disgusting trollop."

"I'll sort this out later" said Secundus. "Let's not have a scene, especially where the boys can see us." He beckoned Miss Tremble into his study. Rosie turned and whispered, very loudly in his ear "I'm going to fuck with Leno and Romano while you're out with your silly games!" She pushed him away and ran back to the main building, skipping from side to side and singing to herself.

"That girl's a load of trouble, you mark my words Secundus" said Miss Tremble. "Don't let her try any of her revolting tricks on you."

"Of course not. I'm not stupid. That's why I beat that Everett fellow last term. If she engages in sex with those two greasy wops, that's her choice. You have a letter?"

"Bad news for all of us. Just read the damn thing. I knew that man was trouble. The sooner we get rid of Hingham, the better it will be for all of us."

"What, do him in? Don't be crazy."

"Of course not, stupid. Make them take him away."

"The Abbot won't go a bundle on that. Are you in a position to stump up for the fees we'll lose?"

"An investigation" continued Miss Tremble, waving the letter. "An investigation, Brother Secundus! None of us want that."

"I couldn't care less, Miss Tremble. I've nothing to hide." He stared at her with loathing. Her unexpected intrusion had wrecked his little tryst with Rosie. "So what are you afraid of, Miss Matron?" he sneered. "The truth about your medical qualifications? That boy's suicide last year? Your inability to stop Hingham writing some home truths about you to his mother?"

"Everett will get you for grievous bodily harm, you mark my words!"

"That's my problem, not yours."

"This man has contacts with Whitehall and the police. His cousin is a judge."

"So? With a bit of luck we'll get rid of that thieving bastard Campbell and, while they're at it the police could take away those perverts Jenkins and Quartus."

They glowered at each other, both aware that Hingham's uncle's intervention could indeed mean serious trouble for them both, though neither of them was prepared to admit it.

Secundus stepped back to the window to read the letter. It was indeed both threatening and malicious; against the two of them personally and against the way the whole school was run. Stupid bitch, daring to question their professional abilities, he thought to himself, but no reason to panic or to share the matron's evident unease; no doubt she, like him, had some dark deeds in her past she would like forgotten, but then so had almost everyone else who had been touched by the war.

"It's nothing but sentimental drivel" he said. "An attempt to boost the morale of her pathetic child entrusted to us for serious education."

"You're not concerned about some Whitehall judge being brought into this incident, mindful of Everett?"

"Of course not! This is all a bluff. Their word against ours."

"Right, if that's the way you feel, Brother Secundus, so be it. But don't say I didn't warn you."

Miss Tremble took back the letter and put it carefully in her pocket. Steaming with indignation at his treatment of her, especially in front of that disgusting slut Rosie, she stomped off back to her room in the school.

Secundus turned on his heel and slammed the door in her face. He was in a fury, but not about the letter or the threats contained therein. It was his masculinity that was being challenged. He knew Rosie meant what she had said.

He lashed out at his books, kicking them across the floor. Neither getting rid of Hingham nor the arrival of the letter was paramount among his thoughts.

TWENTY-FOUR

It was the third package Upton had received from Parker in as many days. He was worried that someone would begin to ask questions. This was not what Parker had said he wanted of him – it was supposed to be just the occasional message to be transmitted for the workers – but now he was being inundated. Moreover, he couldn't understand what the messages were, for they were always sent in code.

"Your doctors must be very concerned about your health, Brother Upton" Miss Tremble declared sarcastically, handing over five packages which had been collected for the weekly drop by the postman at the Abbey. "I trust your ailment is not so serious that the Abbot should be informed? We are after all as concerned about the health and well-being of our teaching staff as much as that of the boys."

"There's been a mistake, Miss Tremble. They keep sending me the same thing. I must write and tell them immediately."

No one, Upton felt sure, had yet seen him working at the foot of the tower to transmit the tapes, but he knew that sooner or later his luck would run out. There were far too many people prowling around for him to get away with it, even in the hours of darkness. He'd have to come to a compromise with Parker. Unfortunately the threat of blackmail, plus the uninvited membership of the Wales & Western Communist Party, with the incriminating card still in Parker's hands, left him little room to manoeuvre.

Another trip to London was essential; he would do it in the Easter holidays.

* * * * *

Miss Tapscott was thrilled. Her sister had never telephoned before, and though she had got the date slightly wrong, it was nice of her to think of her birthday. It was late in the afternoon and well timed, for she had plenty of time on her hands, plenty of time to chat.

"One of my hobbies, Melanie, as you may recall, is the archaeological history of this nation" her sister began. "I have been spending a lot of my time, when time allows, researching the designs of our churches – in England, initially, though I shall visit Wales and Scotland in due course – and I am thinking of coming up your way. I had a most fruitful time in the West Country. Devon and Cornwall are so rich in ecclesiastical history. I'm in regular contact with the Bishop of Truro."

Miss Tremble, listening in as always to calls to and from Herga which came through her, yawned with boredom.

"The wool trade saw of course the construction of some magnificent buildings in Suffolk and Norfolk and many in your part of the world. I am travelling with a dear friend, Mollie Walton, and we thought we'd probably make ourselves a base at Muckrinton. There's the George, which we have heard is very good."

"I wish I could help more, Lottie, but we are terribly isolated here at Saint Eusebius Abbey" replied Miss Tapscott. "I rarely leave the place, you know. The countryside is very bleak, nothing really but fens, lakes and broadland with the occasional small village."

"We'd love to meet you somehow, Melanie. Perhaps we could drive by, collect you and go off and have tea somewhere, say Horkinge next the Sea? As I recall, before the war there used to be some good places on the waterfront, the bit where all the mills and warehouses are and the ships tie up."

"That would be lovely, Do you have a date in mind?"

"Well, this side of Easter if possible as I've a commitment then which I must tell you about." An air of excitement had crept into her voice. "It's a man! And I am going to meet his parents!"

"Wonderful, Lottie, that's excellent news. Tell me more!"

"Let it wait till we meet. There's so much I've got to tell you."

Miss Tremble replaced the headset and yawned again. At least they didn't have a problem with Miss Tapscott, but why was Upton really getting all these packages? They had to be inspected. The Abbot would expect it.

* * * * *

The Abbot, however, had other problems on his mind. Despite the school being threatened financially by the over-zealous behaviour of the Chief Disciplinarian, he thought he might be able to contest Everett's allegations in that he had personally sanctioned the disciplining of the teaching staff, the junior monks, by whom no lapse in moral rectitude could be countenanced. The purity and probity of the staff were critical in maintaining the great and illustrious reputation of Saint Eusebius. The very thought that a member of his staff had engaged in sexual activity was an absolute abhorrence, and to have introduced Miss Robinson to carnal knowledge was truly satanic.

Brother Secundus had assured him that he had gone to great lengths to ensure that Miss Robinson was living a life of purity, as befitted any young person at Saint Eusebius. There was however another cause for concern, and this related to the Spaniard whom the staff had found prowling in the grounds. Who was he? Did he know something? Miss Tremble knew the facts, and she had had to be taken in to protect her from the cruel world they had all experienced in the previous decade; the war years and the 1930s. Silently he drummed his fingers on his desk.

"Are you all right, Brother Primus?" Secundus enquired solicitously, sitting before him in his study for their regular early evening review. He himself had not given another thought either to the Hingham letter or to the threat of litigation from Everett's solicitors in London. Maybe it was this that was taxing the Abbot.

Jenkins had returned, slinking back in the night; no one had asked any questions.

"We've got a serious cash problem" began the Abbot, in a surprisingly quiet voice, after several moments of deliberation. "It's not something that will necessarily lead to the closure of the Abbey, but it is life threatening all the same." He drew some papers out of the top drawer of his desk. "I have been to see the bank, and they are quite happy to let us continue. I have agreed to remortgage the premises, thus effectively passing ownership of the physical assets of the school to the bank. Our biggest threat now remains the Everett litigation." He looked at Secundus. "I have been to see our solicitors and they advise caution. There is, in their opinion, no protection from the charge of assault from the wording of the mediaeval charter of the Brotherhood. They point out that is a historical tithe with little or no meaning in the present world."

"But that's ridiculous!" interjected Secundus. "Everyone joining the Abbey knows the rules!"

"Do they, Brother Secundus, do they? Does Brother Upton know about this, for example?" The Abbot poised, knowing full well that it was he who had imparted knowledge of this punishment himself to the new master. "You bet he does! I warned him to leave Rosie alone, or else."

"There's nothing about any of the ancient obligations in the letters of contract that we exchange with our teaching staff?"

"I told him. Said I'd have him whipped if he tried anything immoral while a member of the Brotherhood."

"And his reaction?"

"He was strangely quiet. Didn't say anything. I got the impression that he was rather shocked. He must have heard about Everett from another source."

"You realise, Brother Secundus, that this is the second, no forgive me, third time that you have administered the mediaeval punishment upon a monk since you have been at the Abbey. That's three beatings in seven years."

"That's not many. I see no problem."

"Well, maybe you don't, but I most certainly do! If

we are forced to pay Everett compensation – and he is claiming permanent disability to injuries upon his spine – we are looking at maybe ten thousand pounds. A huge sum, more than five years' fee income. We cannot meet it. You could apologise, in person?"

"I certainly will not!" The Abbot's voice grew louder, harsher. He was now visibly angry at the attitude of his deputy. "It will do us little good. The man has permanent damage. He wants not only compensation but retribution!"

"You can sack me if you want, Brother Primus, but I will not apologise to that disgusting piece of human filth."

"I intend to put your pay into a compensation fund" declared the Abbot icily. "You are free to leave us if you want."

"Aren't you forgetting one thing though, Brother Primus?"

As the two monks squared up for confrontation, the door opened and Miss Tremble barged in.

"You've got to see this letter, Brother Primus" she declared, striding across the rugs to where the two of them were sitting. "It came two days ago. It's from Hingham's mother. Brother Secundus has already seen it."

"It's nothing to worry about sir," said Secundus. "Just speculative drivel."

"Don't bother me just now with trivia Miss Tremble" said the Abbot. "We have more important things to talk about. We have a financial crisis on our hands."

"The Everett lawsuit? I knew it would all go wrong."

The Abbot was unusually sombre, quite unprovoked by her rude arrival.

"No" he sighed at length, having clearly and carefully thought out his words. "No. This disaster transcends everything that may have gone before. We're running out of money."

Silence fell upon the three of them. Miss Tremble was trying to analyse what he might mean. She gave the Abbot's cat a discreet kick from under the desk, out of sight.

"I've just had a thought" she said, "Two of the boys, Lawrence and Hartley, have both gone down with measles. I've put them in quarantine in one of the isolation rooms. I think they could have contracted the disease from the match against Talbot House last week."

"What's this got to do with our cash problem, Miss Tremble?"

"Quite a lot."

"You mean close the school immediately, save on food and wages and send everyone home?"

"Good idea, Miss Tremble" interjected Secundus. "We can hold Quartus, Jenkins, Campbell and Upton's wages over until next term. They'll object of course. but stuff 'em!"

"No, no. I have a much better idea, quite the opposite to what you are thinking. You're coming from the wrong direction. What I suggest is that we cancel the Easter holidays of four and a bit weeks and go straight into Summer Term from Lent. We charge the parents an extra month's fees for having to keep them all here. Put up the fees anyway."

The Abbot looked at her quizzically, then sat back in his chair and put his arms behind his head. "You mean declare the school to be the victim of an unforeseen infection requiring its immediate quarantine?"

"Precisely. The staff, teaching and administration will not see any difference."

"And the boys? Some of them might have been looking forward to going home."

Secundus snorted. "Going home! The boys, the seniors at any rate who have been indoctrinated with our ideals, wouldn't dream of it. They love it here! Thinking of home is quite contrary to the philosophy of this establishment, Brother Primus! Surely you would agree with that?"

"Oh, yes. On that point I do. Some of the leavers will have to go of course, Ward for example, and Ambrose and so on. I shall announce that the school has been infected and despatch letters to all the parents tonight. The postman comes tomorrow."

They all agreed that it would be a cunning, albeit short-term solution. The boys would be informed of their decision before prayers that night. The relationship between the Abbot and his deputy remained fractious, however, and the contents of the Hingham letter did indeed strike home and remind them of their vulnerability.

★ ★ ★ ★ ★

News that there would be no holiday not unnaturally brought an immediate and hostile reaction from the boys. For Henry, still stunned by what Miss Tremble and Secundus had told him about the death of his father, life seemed more miserable than ever. For the others only a slight improvement in the weather, the appearance of spring flowers, daffodils and crocuses, heralded the prospect of better things to come; a respite from the hardship of the school.

It was among the members of the Lower Fifth that the pronouncement had the greatest effect. Ward and the seniors, the ghastly prefects, would be departing; it had been implied that they would not be facing enforced quarantine if their parents were prepared to take the risk of removing them. For the others, the prospect of another four months' incarceration was more than they could bear. Be brave, be bold, be risk takers, the Abbot had exhorted in his speech and this they certainly would.

"We're going to make a break for it, well before Easter" Davenport declared. "Primus and the monks get into a frightful religious frenzy as Lent comes to an end. If we get an extra day off class, and if we time it right and get away at dawn chances are they won't spot our absence until evening prayers." He looked round at the others. "You coming, Montgomery-Smith? Ambrose?"

"Davenport's going to play it straight, aren't you?" said Linforth. "He's going to leave in his school uniform and say he's on his way to visit his parents."

"I could say the same" grinned Montgomery-Smith, "though Galloway is a long way to go. My father's very stingy. I'm sure he won't want to spend the money sending me back."

"And you, Ambrose? What will you do?"

"What my father did in the Balkans against the Germans. Travel at night, lie low by day, get myself onto a goods train. You know that silly idiot Laurie, the one who thinks he's driving a lorry all the time? He says he thinks there's a train that shunts and collects wagons from Horkinge. He's not sure where it goes however, south to Norwich or north to Great Yarmouth. It leaves at ten at night. Wydmark's said he's coming with me."

"I've said I'll put dummies in their beds when Kite comes round" added Linforth. "She never looks too carefully at the fifth form boys anyway."

"What's happening to Bentley and Willington Rushton?" asked Linforth.

"Willy's chickened out. Bentley thinks the days are wrong" replied Davenport

"Wrong? In what way?" asked Ambrose, looking up.

"He says too many people will be around. I disagreed. The more the better. No one's going to challenge a little boy travelling on his own over the holiday" continued Davenport.

"They will round here. Everyone within five miles knows our uniforms. They'll ring Kite at once. Just you watch." joked Linforth "especially if we're known to be in quarantine. What a shame no one stole clothes from somewhere else, Smallwood House or Magdalene's."

"Everywhere round here is cut off by canals, lakes and swamps. We've got to use the roads, or run along the railway line at night. We'll need compasses." declared Ambrose.

"And maps and food?" suggested Montgomery-Smith.

The battered copy of *Farewell Campo Duce* was once again passed round for study.

"Don't think the obvious." observed Montgomery-Smith

"Meaning?"

"Hide in the mail van or, better but more risky, hide in Primus' old Rover – you know under sacks or something!" he continued.

"Bennett's told us he's almost drained the tank. Forget the car. It's used by Rosie and the Italians anyway!"

Everyone looked at Davenport in amazement. How did he come to know all this? He did, however, have a point. There was not much time to lose.

TWENTY-FIVE

Carps took the shoebox out of the drawer with great care and placed it on the table. Then he reached into the drawer again and drew out another box, smaller than the first but clearly much heavier. This he carried to a small table near the fire and put down with great care.

"Mind you don't go giving these boys the wrong impression, dear!" said Mrs Carps from her customary chair by the hearth. "We don't want the boys thinking we've a flippin' arsenal down here at the cottage." She looked up from her knitting.

"Course not, love. We can trust these fellers. Besides, it's their last term." He pulled a third box out from the second drawer of the chest.

"What's that, Carps?"

"Ammunition, young Ambrose, that's what that is."

The boys watched with fascination as Carps opened the boxes and began to bring out his guns. They were pistols, all of them, of different sizes and calibres. All were wrapped in newspaper and all were evidently well looked-after and oiled. Ambrose had brought Hingham down, to the dismay of the Marshalls.

"He's being deliberately starved by Kite, Carps, and I know he'd love a piece of cake, scones, toast, anything you've got going. They've just told him his father's been shot and that he will never see him again. He's very depressed."

Henry sat in silence, some way from the others, idly flicking through the pages of a car magazine.

"Do they all work, Carps?" asked Montgomery-Smith, wide eyed. He turned to Ambrose and Linforth "Just think of it. If we had this we could storm the school and shoot the lot. Well, Kite, Secundus and Primus anyway."

"You'll be doing no such thing, lads. I keep this lot under strict lock and key, don't I dearest?"

"I'll say that again. Carps is meticulous. Everything's locked up and we keep the key hidden from sight. It's them gypsies we have to think about. They've been breaking into a lot of houses round here. They attacked Round Tree Farm last week and stole poor old Giles Weatherspoon's twelve bore."

"Yes he had to report it to the police, for insurance if nothing else. Now the law's all over the place. They've been round here but I only showed them my shotguns, which I'm allowed to use in the Abbey grounds."

"Does Primus know you've got these guns?"

"No. And you're not about to let on to him neither!"

"Of course I won't" said Ambrose. "Tell us how you got them."

Carps puffed his chest out and took out the largest pistol. "This is an officer's Luger. Kills at fifty feet. An SS man was coming at me when we were fighting the Bosch in the Battle of the Bulge. You've heard of it?"

"The last German breakthrough! Yanks couldn't take the pressure."

"Too right, Carmichael. We were thrown in to counter-attack." Carps removed the paper from the pistol and cradled it in his hands. "It was him or me, the brute. Gave him a burst with my Sten gun. Squirted them. Took out three of the bastards!"

"Oh you lying so and so!" laughed Mrs Carps. "Last time you said you found it on a dead German and hid it from the sergeant so you didn't have to hand it in."

"That was this one" snapped Carps, not best pleased at his wife's interruption. He picked up a smaller, much neater little pistol. "Yes, this one I did take off a dead bloke. Much later, after we were in Germany proper. I think he was Hitler Youth or something. We threw grenades into the trench and then bayoneted the survivors."

"Cor, how super! Wish we could do that to Kite and Secundus!" trilled Ambrose.

"Horrible thing, war" said Mrs Carps, putting down her knitting to put some more coal on the fire. "They shouldn't romanticise it with all these books and films. We had a terrible time. Carps was nearly killed at least three times and we all got bombed, well those of us what was left in the cities did. My Aunt Vera got crushed to death when her house in Birmingham collapsed on her after an air raid. Not a nice war, no not nice at all. Right Carps?"

"She's certainly right on that one. Far too many friends got killed. You young people have no real concept . The noise and the smell. The smell of death all around you."

"Ambrose and I and three others are planning to escape, Carps" said Montgomery-Smith, changing the subject. "We might need your help."

"Help? My help? Surely end of term's just after Easter. Can't you bloomin' wait?"

"Hartley and Lawrence have got measles. Kite's got Primus to cancel the Easter holidays by putting us all into quarantine. They can charge our parents more money for keeping us here. We hate the place so much we're determined to break out" Montgomery-Smith continued.

"Endless swishings, the food's getting worse; Brothers Quartus and Jenkins doing nasty things to some of us in the gym" added Linforth.

"Ambrose plans to hide on a train to London. I'm heading for our home in Galloway" declared Montgomery-Smith with an air of confidence. He outlined their plans in detail. Mrs Carps watched incredulously. "Galloway? But that's in Scotland!" she protested.

"We thought you might be able to get us tickets" continued Montgomery-Smith.

"Tickets? It's not wartime, you know. You won't get shot. You boys have read too many war stories. We can't possibly do that. Be patient. They'll send you home as soon as the measles scare is over."

"Bennett's planning to burn the school down. He's been siphoning petrol out of Primus' car for weeks. It's all planned. Jetex fuses into a jar of petrol in the roof or where they store the paper."

"That's terrible. That's what they call arson. You could go to prison for that. Someone could get killed!"

"We hope it'll be Kite. Bennett's father was in the SOE. He was told how to do these things without leaving any trace" Ambrose added.

"Any other tricks in mind?" Carps looked up hopefully, a glint of humour in his eyes. "Tell you one thing boys, you won't get your hands on my guns, if that's what you have in mind."

"Never given it a moment's thought, Carps" lied Linforth convincingly. "Our plans are to get the school closed. Permanently, for ever, so we can all be sent to somewhere better."

"And what about us? cried Mrs Carps. "If you did that we'd all be out of a job. Have you given any thought to that?"

Five faces looked at her in unison, stunned into silence. No, they had never thought of that. The Carps were allies, not enemies. They would have to be protected. But how? What an awful dilemma.

They watched as Carps put the pistols back into the drawer of his desk and slipped the key under the carpet. Then, collecting little Henry, they made their way quietly back to the main school through the secret pathway through the woods that skirted the drive from the gatehouse.

TWENTY-SIX

Melanie Tapscott adjusted her hat and scrutinised herself once again in the mirror. This was a surprise, she thought to herself, for her elder sister Lottie rarely if ever communicated except at Christmas. She watched from her window in Herga as her sister's ancient Morris came up the rough track past the main school. She had told her sister precisely how to find her, for she had not been to the Abbey before. Locking her room carefully, mindful of Campbell's light fingers, she went out into the drive and waved. "Here I am!" she called.

The venerable car made a turn and pulled up beside the gate. Lottie, beaming, leaned across from the wheel and pushed open the passenger door.

"Jump in, Mel. It's great to see you!" she grinned. They embraced. Lottie looked so well and happy. "I want to hear all the news!" said Miss Tapscott. "Especially about your new man."

The car reversed with a crashing of gears, turned and started down the drive, Lottie swerving to avoid the worst of the potholes. "Funny thing I saw just now as I was coming up" she said. "There was a boy, medium-sized fellow with glasses, siphoning off petrol from an old Rover. I hope your charges are not planning to burn the school down or do something awful?"

"They're all very upset. The headmaster has cancelled the Easter holidays because we've got a case of measles."

"Surely they don't all have to be in quarantine?"

"They're letting the leavers go. Everyone else has to stay behind."

"What about the masters? Don't they have private lives?"

"Here? Good heavens no. Frankly I sometimes think they're all refugees from reality."

"They sound awful."

"They are, most of them. Brother Campbell must be a dreadful thief, if you will pardon my saying it, but we've had the police up at the Abbey several times this term. One monk disappeared very unexpectedly last year. I had to clear his room. There's another that I've heard does some very unpalatable things to the boys."

"How disgusting! What about your Abbot, headmaster or whatever he's called?"

"Primus? A dear man at heart, blessed with the highest standards of probity. Wounded in the Spanish Civil War, I believe. It's such a shame they're all so brutal to the boys."

"Well we don't want to become a nation of wimps do we! Our men did so well in the war."

"So tell me about your new man, I can't wait."

"We're getting married in May."

The great clock of the Abbey chimed midday. From behind a curtain in the pantry a few yards away, Miss Tremble watched with morbid curiosity. Visitors for the staff were few and far between.

"There's a very good place not far from Muckrinton, I've heard" said Lottie. "Might be better than the Waterfront in Horkinge. It's a pub run by someone I used to know vaguely during my time in the navy. I left Mollie Walton behind in London by the way, much more fun to be just the two of us."

Lottie was a short, thick-set woman with a much deeper voice than her sister. They really did not look alike at all. Few believed they were sisters. Where Miss Tapscott was quiet, retiring and shy, her sister was quite the opposite, gregarious, loud and rather sporty.

Lottie changed down through the gears, scraping them badly between third and second as they reached the gatehouse.

"George and I used to come up here before the war to look at birds" she said. "The annual migration from the Arctic was always a source of awesome magnificence, particularly in the area around Horkinge."

Once on the open road Lottie drove fast, almost dangerously, brushing the hedgerows with cheerful abandon as she swerved to avoid oncoming cars. "Tell me, how on earth do you survive up in a place like this? It must be so bleak in winter."

"I survive. My rooms are quite warm. I'm directly above the boiler room."

"Any kindred spirits? Anyone to play a hand of Bridge with?"

"Not really. The monks are steeped in religious learning. They're a mixed bunch. We have a nice new one this term. I have to confess that I don't get along with either the Abbot or his number two."

"They do a lot of corporal punishment, so I've heard. The school has quite a reputation, Melanie. They are all at it of course, but your place seems to be particularly severe."

"It's the ethic. Success through discipline and the acceptance of pain."

"All sounds very depressing. I thought we'd done away with fascism at last. Who was that sinister woman I saw peering out at me from behind a curtain?"

"Young or old?"

"Old I think, though I couldn't really see."

"Miss Tremble. The matron. Not a nice sort of person."

"And if I'd seen a young woman?"

"Then it would have been Rosie. She works in the kitchen. Dreadfully common."

"Do you have any refugees? Poles, people like that?"

"We've got the two Italians, ex prisoners of war,

Leno and Romano. They do all the dirty work. Don't seem to be in any hurry to go home."

"They were fascists?"

"I very much doubt it. They spend most of their time chasing Rosie, fiddling the ration cards and generally bumming around."

Lottie laughed. She was hiding her real reason for coming down to see her sister in the Fens.

"Let me bring you up to date. I've found a new man, I must tell you at once. Philip. He was also in the Navy. Had a lucky escape after Singapore."

They drove on, chattering like sparrows. After several miles Lottie slowed down and drew a small map out of the glove compartment. They had been driving about half an hour.

"It's somewhere round here" she said. "It's called the Speckled Heron, I think.

"What about that place? It says 'Restaurant' and something like that in small print underneath."

"That's it!" Lottie stopped and reversed, again with much grating and scraping of the gears. She backed up to a white wall where a sign said 'GENTS'. They climbed out of the car. Lottie shut the door with a sharp kick and led the way, striding over fresh gravel to the entrance of the establishment.

Inside it was cosy, warm and welcoming. A table for two had been reserved for them in a corner close to an open fire. They ordered promptly; mutton stew seemed to be the only warm dish on the menu and they asked for half a bottle of wine to accompany it. To Miss Tapscott's surprise her sister ordered a large gin and tonic. Pressed to keep her company, she accepted one too.

"So tell me Lottie, this work of yours keeps you in London most of the time?"

"It's all frightfully frantic at the moment with the new government demanding so much of us. I work the most terrible hours, I really do, but then I suppose I don't really have much option. I mean after the war service I've got to think of my pension, and heaven knows what sort of a world we'll be living in in ten years' time, let alone twenty when I should retire."

"Mama might leave us a little money."

"I wouldn't count on it. Not if she has to go into a home."

Miss Tapscott wrung her hands. "Yes. Yes I suppose so" she said.

"And you, Mel? How long are you going to go on hiding up here with all these awful monks? The whole school sounds quite frightful. I'm amazed it hasn't been closed or gone bankrupt."

"They have a huge turnover of staff. No one seems to be able to get on with either the Abbot, his second in command or the matron."

Miss Tapscott took a sip of her gin and tonic. What a treat, she thought, as the alcohol burned slowly down her throat. "We've got a sweet new young monk this term" she said. "His name is Upton. Such a refreshing change. Good looking too. He's managed to really inspire the boys. One of the subjects he teaches is geography and he has got them all entranced with foreign languages and so on."

"Foreign languages? Surely that belongs to the language masters?"

"Mr Jenkins and Mr Campbell? They're hopeless brutes, they hit the boys. Mr Jenkins, he's called Brother Jenkins officially, does even worse things to them, they say."

"How ghastly! You were saying about Geography?"

"Oh yes. Mr Upton has set up some sort of aerial in the school grounds that allows the boys to listen in to radio signals. It's mostly ships and so on, but it gives the boys some idea of the real world, where we export to and import from and so on. It makes the maps more realistic. What a shame such a talented man couldn't do something in Latin or Maths!"

"Where did this Mr Upton come from?"

"No idea. Some agency I should think. The Abbot has an awful lot of applications from rootless, unemployed young men roaming the country in search of gainful employment. The post-war diaspora of the officer class, you might say. Tell me about your new man?"

"Philip's serving in the Navy. With a bit of luck he might get a shore posting before too long."

Lottie elaborated on their hopes and plans. Miss Tapscott still wondered why her sister had chosen to do her research before spring had really arrived. She had a camera and a notebook and seemed to have her schedule well planned in advance.

They drove back to the school after lunch mostly in silence, each lost in their own thoughts. "Do you mind if I take a photograph of the ruins of your Abbey?" asked Lottie. "It would be so useful for my research."

"Of course not. The light's not bad today."

"Won't take a moment."

The car slowed as they approached the junction and the entrance to the school. "You're right, Lottie" said Miss Tapscott as the car turned into the long drive and passed under the arch by Carps' house. "I should rethink my life. Get away from this place. Find something more rewarding to do with my time."

"There are plenty of schools down in Kent and Sussex who would welcome someone like you with open arms. And the weather is a darn sight nicer than it is up here! I could help if you like."

"You have a point. Stop here Lottie, no need to go into the yard. This is an excellent place to take a picture of the ruins."

"Sure?"

"Yes, I'll come with you." They got out of the car

and walked across the grass towards the forbidding-looking remains of the original Abbey. Upton's wiring was clearly visible.

"Pity about your new man's wiring, but I guess he hasn't damaged the stonework. So glad someone has been able to inspire the boys" said Lottie. She took lots of photographs, declaring that the twin towers were a wonderful relic of the Gothic period. Then they pottered back slowly to the car.

"Let me know about the wedding date!" said Miss Tapscott, giving her sister a kiss and waving as Lottie turned the car. Slowly she walked back to Herga and to her little room, suddenly overwhelmed with a terrible sense of emptiness. What was the point of it all? Lottie had been right; there must be a better life somewhere else, but where? Where could she go? It seemed a hopeless prospect.

The school was strangely quiet, quite deserted. Then she remembered that evensong had been brought forward by an hour that day.

The organ started to play a hymn, and singing wafted across the bare green grass where a few daffodils struggled to survive the vagaries of the boys and the weather.

TWENTY-SEVEN

Miss Tremble sat in her usual place as the senior boys paraded past her for morning showers. Their seniority entitled them to warm water. Carefully she studied their genitalia for any signs of abnormality. She was surprised that a number of boys seemed to have a redness of the penis. It puzzled her.

"Ward, Harding, Ambrose! How do you come to have this inflammation? She pointed at the offending organs.

"Brother Quartus makes us do gym in the nude" Ward declared. "He makes us jump over the vaulting horse and that's why we've all got this redness. It's what the Spartans and the Romans used to do for their games, at least that's what he says."

Miss Tremble looked each of them up and down. Knowing their penchant for dishonesty, she knew this was unlikely to be true, but on the other hand, given Brother Quartus' penchant for unusual athletic interpretation, she realised it might be. She turned to the line of hot and cold taps behind her, shut off the warm water and waved them through.

"Great thinking Ward. Thanks" said Harding.

"What if she checks up on us?"

"Chances are she won't. She hates Quartus as much as we all do." declared Wydmark with a grin.

That afternoon Brother Quartus was amazed when the boys suggested vaulting in the nude. It didn't take much persuasion for the muscular paedophile to give his approval.

"If that's what you want, we'll try it out" he beamed. It never occurred to him, as he carefully handled the boys over the vaulting horse, that the Abbot might be watching this bizarre interpretation of the ancient sport of the Grecian Olympiads. The Abbot, who by chance was present in the gym, swore lightly under his breath. He would have to get rid of this monk, especially in the light of what Thompson-Brown had revealed.

★ ★ ★ ★ ★

Henry was very pleased with himself, for he had perfected a way of creeping out of the school when no one was looking in order to go and see how Royston was surviving in his new hiding place in the headmaster's garage. He planned his visits carefully, as Ambrose had advised him to do, choosing times when he knew both the monks and Miss Tremble would be busy; either just before meal times or after tea, when they were all given half an hour to pursue hobbies, making model aircraft or trying to paint in an informal class run by Brother Tertius.

Henry had begun to come to terms with the fact that he would never see his father again, and that, unless something very unexpected were to take place, he would be forced to stay in the school for months and months without being able to see his mother either. His hatred of Miss Tremble, as the harbinger of bad news, grew daily, not least from the pleasure she had obviously taken in telling him how his father might have met his end. This abhorrence grew even further when the matron decided to force upon him evil-tasting medicines which made him want to go to the lavatory. They gave him a permanently sore bottom, which she examined every day in her customary callous way. Royston was all he had to remind him of home and of happier times.

The route he took varied, depending upon the time of the day. The Italians had seen him, and the cheerful girl who brought in the meals had hidden him once in an outside shed when Miss Tremble had appeared unexpectedly. He had also come across a much older boy doing something to the Abbot's car, but he had found a good place to hide and had not been detected. The boy seemed to be taking something from the petrol tank. Perhaps he hoped the Abbot would run out of petrol and be murdered in the depths of the country; he wondered who he was and what he was planning to do with the fuel he was stealing.

Henry had not been able to check on Royston for over a week. This time someone had removed the ladder Ambrose had used to place him high up and out of sight under the eaves of the garage. Henry managed to find an alternative way to see that his bear was safe, but it took much longer and meant climbing along a beam high above the car.

He had almost reached Royston when he heard a challenge from the ground. "What on earth you think you are doing up there, Hingham?"

It was the one voice he dreaded, that of Miss Tremble.

"Just playing hide and seek" he stuttered.

"You should be in class, doing your hobbies."

"This is my hobby. I want to be a mountaineer when I grow up."

"Get down here at once!"

"I can't. I'm stuck."

"Leno!" she bellowed at the passing Italian, "get me a ladder at once. I have this ridiculous boy pretending to hide to escape his work when he should be studying."

"Of course, Signorina Tremble" replied Leno, returning after a few minutes with a large wooden ladder, which he placed against the beam.

"Wait!" she ordered the Italian. She climbed swiftly up and seized Henry by the leg. Henry started to howl and wouldn't let go.

"Leave me alone!" he shouted at her, but she only intensified her hold. "Why are you here, Henry? What are you hiding now? It can't be that ridiculous bear, I threw it out." The matron's grip intensified, as did the pressure she applied to his leg. Henry felt himself starting to slip. The piece of wood he was holding onto was giving way in his hands

"Catch him, Leno! Make bloody sure this ghastly boy doesn't damage the Abbot's car" she roared. The Italian, short and thickset, held out muscular hands to catch Henry as he fell from the beam. He could see he was cut.

"He is hurt, Signorina Tremble. I go get some plaster."

"You'll do nothing of the sort, Leno. Hold the boy while I climb up and see what the hell he was doing here."

"But he hurt, signorina. He hurt bad!"

"Too bad. It's time he suffered. Hold the ladder."

Miss Tremble climbed up; she seemed surprisingly athletic. At the top, to her fury, she saw the purpose of Henry's visit. In falling from the beam he had unwittingly removed the wood that was hiding Royston.

"You deceitful, disgusting little creep!" she roared. "You got that thing back out of the rubbish tip!" She reached out and threw the bear down onto the ground. "Give me that knife, Leno!" she commanded.

"No!" shrieked Henry. "No! He's not done you any harm!"

"Why 'e no be allowed to keep a 'is bear, Signorina Tremble?"

"Because, Leno, not only is this thing forbidden here but the boy is in an area of the school that is out of bounds. Hold him!"

Taking the Italian's knife, she slashed at Royston. One by one she cut off his arms and legs and threw them to the four corners of the garage in fury. All the while she was staring with undisguised hatred at Henry, held fast by Leno.

"This will teach you not to try to outwit me, you vile child! From now on you are to be placed under direct supervision at all times during the day. Next term I shall ensure that you will be beaten. I only regret that the rules of this establishment forbid such punishment for new boys. Leno! March the boy back to the house."

Henry glowered at her in cold rage, ignoring the blood trickling down his leg. But just then, something quite unforeseen happened. He realised he had grown up. He was no longer a child, no longer the timid little boy who had come down on the train from London. For what had happened had been a transformation of his psyche; he was no longer a child but a boy, a boy who was afraid of nothing, not of her, not of the school, not of the downside of risk. Unwittingly, unconsciously, he had suddenly grown up. He had realised that only deceit, dexterity and ingenuity would see him through his time at Saint Eusebius.

He scowled at her with undisguised hatred. She had now killed his beloved Royston, irretrievably and irrevocably, and for this she would have to be punished. All through supper that night, Henry brooded on what to do next; how to wreak vengeance on this ghastly woman.

"Cheer up, Henry. Whatever's got into you?" It was the friendly voice of Ambrose. He put his hand on his shoulder and led Henry into a nearby empty classroom.

"She found me visiting Royston and cut him up him" he declared bitterly. "I had been so careful to try and keep him until the end of term."

"I'm sure you'll be given another one for Christmas. When's your birthday?"

Henry turned away and looked wistfully out of the classroom window. "You know something, Ambrose? I don't want another bear. I've grown out of fluffy toys. It's what you all said on the train." He paused, as if wondering how to continue. "But you know, like all of us here, I really do want my revenge on Kite."

"Too true, don't we all!" laughed Ambrose. "I'm sure your parents will give you something more grown up. Tell you what, write another letter telling your mother what Kite has done, and I'll make sure it gets posted by Mrs Carps."

"You're very kind Ambrose. Don't do anything that might get you into trouble."

"I won't. By the way, Mrs Carps thinks you ought to come down and have another nice secret meal with us, next Sunday just as we did last time."

"That would be lovely. I can't wait!"

TWENTY-EIGHT

Brother Tertius looked greatly distressed, for the Abbot had made a troubling announcement after prayers the previous day. This was to be Upton's first experience of a formal school flogging, and he had heard from Brother Tertius about the ritual involved; the singing by the assembled school of *Rule Britannia*, *Land of Hope And Glory* or some other so-called patriotic song to drown out the screams of the victims as they were dragged to the birching block, where the boys, kneeling, placed their heads between the legs of the Assistant Chief Disciplinarian. Quartus had played this role with relish, but the Abbot had now appointed Miss Tremble to the role.

The concept of formal flogging had been brought to the school by a monk, a former master at Eton, where such rituals were regularly enacted. Upton, with the other monks, stood at the back of the memorial hall. The rest of the school were lined up in ranks, facing the stage upon which stood the flogging block. Secundus, the Chief Disciplinarian, his huge frame draped in black, swished wildly in practice with a new birch he had made out of six long whippy twigs cut from the willows down by the beck. The doomed boys stood with drooping heads to one side of the stage of the hall; they would be called forth one by one for their punishment. Once it had been delivered, they would be sent into solitary confinement in a room adjacent to Miss Tremble's. They would be denied food for twenty-four hours and would survive on water only.

For formal floggings the victims were required to wear nothing but a coarse robe, made from old jute coal sacks and dyed black. Miss Tremble, the kneeling victim's head clamped between her legs, would pull up the garment, giving Secundus free reign to administer his punishment on bare buttocks. The Abbot, seated on a high chair at the back of the hall, would give the signal to Secundus to begin when he considered the singing to be robust enough to drown out the cries of the victims.

There were three candidates for the ultimate of school punishments; Berkeley, who had been caught placing bets on horses, Hook, who had attacked the communion wine and consequently passed out inebriated in Jenkins' class, and Miller, found pilfering food in the monks' kitchen the previous night.

Ward and Williams-Jones shivered. They too had been party to the raid on the communion wine which had gone down so well after Mrs Carp's mutton stew; it was unfortunate that Hook had consumed so much.

Taylor, too, had had a lucky escape. He had located where the Abbot stored his whisky. He had missed exposure by a whisker, but had spent a very uncomfortable half hour under a sofa while the Abbot prepared his notes for the afternoon's Latin class. All felt great sympathy for their friends destined for the block.

The Abbot gave the signal. "Hook!" called out the Chief Disciplinarian. The terrified boy, just turned eleven, shaking with fear, made his way forward and mounted the stage. He gingerly knelt on the block as Miss Tremble seized his robe and pulled it up over his head, revealing his thin white behind. Secundus, his narrow eyes burning with concentration and eyeing his victim's naked, quivering body much as a mediaeval executioner might have done, rushed at the kneeling youth and dealt him two vicious blows, a right and a left with a backhand. The blows drew blood immediately. Hook howled with pain, screaming for mercy. Secundus stood back, admiring his opening strokes as blood rose from the welts. He loved this; it was the best thing that ever happened to him at the school. Only he, he knew, had the real art of inflicting maximum pain over the longest period of time.

He advanced again, repeating the first two strokes. Hook wriggled and yelled, trying to escape from the fearsome chastisement, but Miss Tremble held him fast, a few drops of blood now spattered on her face.

Secundus added a single blow, lower than the other two, taking the skin off Hook's thigh. Hook felt as if his entire backside was on fire.

"Six or eight? What do you reckon?" whispered Williams-Jones

"Eight or ten for this! Never less in a formal flogging!" Ward whispered back.

"We must help them after this!"

"Precisely." Ward held up a tattered sheet of the songs they had to sing. "I've got a plan. I'll tell you at prep."

"Get down boy!" barked Secundus as he delivered the sixth stroke across Hook's backside. "I haven't finished with you yet!"

Two more strokes landed on the unfortunate wretch as he sobbed and screamed. *"Land of the free, land of hope and glory, something, something for me"* sang the school.

The Abbot raised his hand, Secundus nodded and Miss Tremble released her grip. Hook ran sobbing from the stage, through the door into the changing room and collapsed in a heap.

"Miller!" barked Secundus once again. The second boy to be flogged shuffled nervously up onto the stage and was seized by the matron. Upton felt physically sick, as he knew Tertius did. He could see that Secundus and Miss Tremble were visibly relishing the event. Jenkins and Campbell, having both quietly returned to the school, sang discordantly beside the Abbot's chair.

The Abbot watched, impassive, much as the prison governor would watch a hanging, a job to be done, a ritual to be observed. Upton wondered what was going through his mind and what effect this would be having on the psyche of the boys; certainly it was a deterrent but did they have to witness such overt cruelty and humiliation?

Miller received the same eight strokes as Hook, but the Abbot commuted Berkeley's punishment to six strokes.

"Awful, quite awful" observed Upton as he and Tertius walked down the corridor to lunch. "Why all the ceremony? What if the parents heard about all this?"

"Oh, they were probably beaten just as hard in their time" sighed Tertius. "It's in the tradition of Saint Eusebius. Martyrdom by flogging, all that sort of thing."

"They don't seriously expect someone to be flogged to death?"

"Oh dear me no. Saint Eusebius was flogged to death for his belief in Christ. Here the boys are flogged for genuine transgressions, the weakness of the flesh. All Christians are born sinners, as you know."

"Miller was scavenging for food, poor little fellow. Hardly a sin to be hungry, surely? Especially here, seeing what they're fed in Lent!"

"He should have had the fibre to resist such temptation. Others do."

"You support this form of punishment then?"

"It's a necessity, I am afraid to say, Brother Upton. Yes, punishment must be meted out for the sins of the flesh. It is the very essence of what we are here for. Boys must be prepared for manhood. The suffering of pain is but a mere part of this process. The boys were fortunate today; Secundus was lenient with the birch. He usually extracts a dozen for transgressions of such magnitude."

"You shock me, Brother Tertius. Secundus is a sadist. He clearly revels in every opportunity he has to flog the boys."

"Ah, that is a sad fact, I do concede. No pleasure should ever be derived from executing whatever punishment must be given. I don't think the public hangman enjoys his job."

"Well, he must do so to some extent, or he wouldn't do it, would he?"

"You've got a point."

They walked slowly along the corridor to the dining room for lunch, each lost in his own thoughts. Upton wondered how this sad old monk could reconcile himself to being part of such a brutal establishment.

The smell of boiled cabbage permeated everywhere at this time of day; the soup, the remains of the greasy mutton stew that had been given to the staff the night before, was being ladled out by Romano and Rosie. Upton tried to avoid her eye as she ladled out his bowl, but she managed to spill some of the evil-looking liquid on his cassock. "Oops! Silly me!" she said.

"Don't worry. It's nothing."

"You'll have to take it off and wash it now, won't you!"

Upton ignored her, moving on to pick up bread, She called after him "Tell me if you need any help, in taking it off I mean." She gave a knowing grin.

Secundus, coming to collect his food, scowled as Upton crept to his appointed table. *"Benedictus benedicat"* sang the Abbot. *"Benedictus per te, Tua"* chanted the school in unison. A small boy, his eyes red with tears, served up butter and brought round salt. New boys and lower boys served everybody first, starting with the monks, before being allowed the measly remnants of whatever was left over. This being Lent, there was not a lot of choice. One small boy, his head bent over as the result of a huge boil that was sprouting where his collar rubbed his neck, brought round cups of tea. Upton noted that Miss Tremble did not appear to take the slightest interest in his plight. Sneezing and coughing, as always, dominated over conversation.

Upstairs, the three boys who had been flogged sobbed quietly. After their chastisement Miss Tremble had painted iodine upon their wounds. It hurt almost as much as the flogging, as the stinging returned with their every move. They too smelt the cabbage as it wafted up to their incarceration.

"I'm hungry" moaned Hook, but no one took the slightest notice.

Back in the dining room the hatred for the Chief Disciplinarian was growing by the minute. "Look at Secundus grinning like a monkey" said Dawson. The boys turned to see him in animated conversation with Miss Tremble.

"He's always in a good mood when he has handed out a thrashing, haven't you noticed?" said Hook.

"One day, someone will kill that man" declared Ward with unexpected gravitas, once more wiping the sides of his bowl with a tiny piece of bread. "If I wasn't leaving I would do it myself."

"Do it when he is doing it to Rosie!"

"Who's going to watch next time?" Heads came together, whispers were exchanged. "There can't be more than two of you at a time. Oldham said the roof was none too good."

"Rules out Carmichael, Ringmer and Oxley then! They're too fat and heavy" warned Ward.

They laughed; voices were lowered again.

"Any news about the escape plans?" asked Dawson.

"They're waiting for a full moon. It's vital that Kite's disabled on the night they go, or at least distracted" Ward replied.

"Thought it had been decided that a daytime escape would be better – on a Sunday when we don't have either class or games?"

"We're looking at the book. The big question is the loyalty of people outside this place. If Primus has them all in his pocket no one will get anywhere" warned Harding.

"They're thinking of hiding in the post van or the one that comes to deliver food twice a week" said Ward.

"They don't work on Sundays. What a bore. Couldn't Carps be asked to help?" suggested Harding.

"He'd never want to take the risk. It's bad enough getting letters out of this place. Carps won't want to lose his job, or his home for that matter" Ward replied.

"Who's helping? Who's chief coordinator?" asked Dawson.

"No one's been chosen yet. Ward thinks it should be Carmichael, don't you?"

"He's head of the Lower Fifth scheme. Ambrose wants to be clear two days before Advent Sunday."

"Two days before we were originally due to break up?" queried Dawson.

"Yeah. The others think that's a good idea too."

"We've got something more serious to consider right now though. How are we going to get food to those poor wretches in the punishment room?" sighed Bentley, joining in the conversation.

"Not an easy operation. Kite's locked them in, she's got the key on her. Look, it's on her belt. We could never get hold of it" Ward declared candidly.

"No copies anywhere? In her dispensary for example?" asked Dawson hopefully.

"We think, but are not sure, that Primus might have copies of all the keys, but they would be buried somewhere in his study. We would never have the time to search the place and find them – assuming they were even there." Harding declared.

"So it's got to be a window job then" suggested Bentley with a broad grin.

"Window?"

"Lower a bucket down to the window. We'll get some food from Rosie."

"From the roof you mean?" gasped Dawson. "Wow! What a risk!"

"There's an emergency exit onto the roof from the passageway outside classroom B. Someone would have to be helped with a chair, you could never just climb up to it. That part's not so difficult" suggested Davenport. "I've been up there once myself. The route to the window is quite easy – so long as we get the right one and don't hang a basket in front of Kite's."

"That'd be disastrous!" laughed Harding.

"I've got a plan for disabling Kite" whispered Bentley, as heads came together again. "I got the idea from one of the escape books in the library. I think they did it in Germany but maybe it was Italy. Anyway what I'm planning, or thinking of at any rate, goes like this, and in this order." He started to elaborate. "First, we must remove the light bulb at the top of the stairs just outside Kite's room. You know how she rushes out and tears down those stairs. Well, stage two is this. After we know she has gone to her room – to steam open our parents' letters and so on, when she'll be thinking of other things – we place a thin wire, and I've already got that from Leno as he thinks it's for the model aircraft I am supposed to be making, across the top of the stairs, about four inches above the top step. She'll never see it in the dark, and then hopefully she'll trip and fall down the stairs."

"Cor! Golly, if she broke her neck! Terrific!" Everyone broke out laughing.

"Let's hope. Anyway the third part of the plan is this. Someone's got to get Kite to come roaring out of her room like she did the last time you shot the window out with your catapult, Ward."

"I might miss in the dark, but I'll give it a try. Got the Abbot's cat the other day – it didn't half move!" They all laughed. "Basically I want three volunteers for the rescue. I'll go up on the roof with the food, if someone can help me. Someone, ideally you Ward, gets outside and blasts Kite's window, and a third person, and this is very dangerous, tries to get Kite's keys off her as she lies wounded on the stairs."

"That's much too risky. No, someone does have to be hidden outside the incarceration room to warn them to open the window. Who's going to do that?"

"I will" volunteered Davenport. "Anything to help against the enemy."

"Suppose we set off the fire alarm? Won't that make her let them out?"

"I wouldn't count on that! She'd rather let them burn. We know it doesn't work anyway."

"Quite a lot of people prowl about at night. We know where Rosie goes but Kite herself has been seen in the grounds and then there's Upton."

"Upton?"

"Oh, yes. He's been seen slinking off towards the tower. With packages of something."

"Golly. The radio mast! Is he Secret Service you think? What a fab idea. All the police closing in on Secundus, Kite, Primus too perhaps!"

"You remember Rudolf Hess? Who flew here in secret in the war? It's all hush hush but maybe Primus and Secundus are senior Nazis who were ready for the invasion but who are now disguised to avoid capture. They might even end up being hanged!"

Everyone beamed at the thought. "I'll need a bucket and a rope though" added Bentley, "and of course some food."

"Romano will come to our assistance. I liberated a bottle of Campbell's whisky when he wasn't looking. They're on our side."

"God help us if they're not. At least prisoners weren't flogged at Stalag Luft."

"No; they were shot! For heaven's sake be positive."

★ ★ ★ ★ ★

Upton had come out in a cold sweat as more and more packages arrived. He knew he had no way of stopping Parker without calling him. He decided to borrow Tertius' bicycle and ride to the nearest call box, which was half a mile from the school. He'd tell him they were becoming suspicious and were talking of calling the police. So rising early, a little after five, he let himself our of Herga, rode to the box and made the call. A disgruntled Parker answered after several minutes; Upton had the impression he was not alone at the flat.

"They've discovered what we're doing" Upton whispered. "There's talk of the police being called in to investigate. Don't send any more packages until I tell you the coast is clear."

He could hear Parker snigger and could imagine the smirk on his face, even at that hour of the morning.

"Too late, matey. You're too late. I sent another seven packages off to you last night. Be a good boy and do as you're told. Wouldn't want any trouble now, would we?" In the background there was the sound of a kettle coming to the boil.

"I won't send them, Parker. Not until the coast is clear."

"You may not have the option, Private Upton. Remember what I said. You're a card carrier now. Don't forget your part in the coming revolution!" The line clicked off with a buzz.

★ ★ ★ ★ ★

In her room, Miss Tremble opened the third of the latest lot of packages which had been brought up that afternoon for Upton by the postman. They all seemed to contain some form of coiled tape. She looked at them under a magnifying glass, but was none the wiser. She put the third one down, with the others, in a drawer in her desk. She wasn't quite sure how to tell the Abbot about this, because she couldn't work out quite who Upton was and why he was working at the school. Now that the packages had started arriving, she wondered what his game plan was. Did he have accomplices, and if so what were they looking for?

She opened the fourth package, which contained something different from the others, although it was undoubtedly some part of the radio transmitter Upton was using for his geography classes. Just as she leaned forward to examine it more closely, the glass of her window shattered with a tremendous bang, showering her with shards.

Miss Tremble was becoming used to this. Ignoring several minor cuts from the glass, she leapt up with lightening speed, rushed to the door and shot off to the stairs, cursing the lazy Italians for failing to replace one of the light bulbs. But her right foot caught on something at the top of the stair. She lost her balance and fell heavily and painfully on her elbow.

It didn't take her more than a few seconds to realise that this must be yet another ploy to get her out of her room. An accomplice of Upton's, perhaps? She clambered back up the darkened stair, nursing her elbow, and scurried back to her room. To her surprise, and indeed dismay, there was no one there. She looked around, but it seemed nothing had been taken.

She left her room, locking the door very carefully, and slowly and cautiously descended the stair, taking great care to avoid any other booby traps or tricks. Once on the safety of the ground floor she made for the staff quarters, calling for Leno or Romano to come and help at once. This was the break Davenport had been waiting for. Creeping to the incarceration room, he whispered to the inmates, telling them to open the window. Then, in the darkness, hearing the sound of approaching steps and Kite's voice, he quietly removed the wire that had snagged the matron, rolled it into a neat coil and slipped away into the body of the school.

* * * * *

Charles Cottesmore, Captain of Games, slept in the privacy of a small, exclusive dormitory which was reserved for the prefects and the head boy. It was a third-floor bedroom above the main classrooms of the east block of the outer quadrangle, away from the rest of the school and opposite to the chapel. Access was by way of a separate door to the main school, locked by the senior boys at night from inside, and safety was provided by an iron fire escape tacked on to the outer wall of the quadrangle which gave out onto open grassland facing out onto the Fens. It was from the small ground floor door that Thompson-Brown had made his fateful exit dressed as a ghost on the night of his capture by the Abbot.

Cottesmore slept deeply, for he was exhausted after the school's match against Lowgrove, a match which Secundus had warned must not be lost on any account or there would be fearsome retributions for the team. To everyone's amazement they had won three-two after a nail-biting finish; it had been an away fixture with a long bus ride of almost two hours each way. Brother Quartus, determined like Brother Secundus to see excellence in all the school's sporting activities, had singled out Cottesmore for extra training, seeing his potential as an athlete as well as being a first class student; long sessions in the gym had become the norm.

There was however a darker side to the monk's attentions, for after Thompson-Brown's expulsion, Cottesmore had become the prime object of his carnal desires, notwithstanding the boy's persistent refusal to visit his room in Herga. Endless entreaties, offers of snacks and even of drink had all been rebuffed. The more Cottesmore resisted, the more the fire in Quartus burned, until his lust had become obsessive. It consumed him, absorbed his mind and obliterated all rational thought.

Brother Quartus had been very careful in his research. He determined now to visit the boy in his small, exclusive dormitory. He had made a reconnaissance of the bedroom while the boys were in class and, aware that the front door was locked at night, for Thompson-Brown had told him so, had calculated how he might reach the room by way of the fire escape, a thin iron ladder that ran up the side of the building to the window. For security the ladder did not quite reach the ground but stopped some feet short of it, a rope being fastened to the last rung to allow final escape. The great advantage of the fire escape from an intruder's point of view was that it could not be seen from any other part of the school, and this served Quartus well, for he had been able to hide a small stepladder which he had found in Herga against the wall from, which he could seize hold of the bottom rung of the ladder and, being extremely fit, thus haul himself up to the dormitory window.

It was a bleak night, dry and cloudy but windy, as Quartus, overcome with burning lust, let himself out of his front door at Herga. The school clock had sounded eleven and all was darkness save for two lights, one in the Abbot's rooms and the other in Miss Tremble's. As he left Herga another figure could be seen moving in the dark, but this he assumed was probably Campbell foraging for something to drink and he paid it no notice. He carried a small torch but knew the route well, round behind the back of the school and only intended to use it once he reached his objective.

Placing the ladder upright, he seized the fire escape and started to climb. The ladder shook a little as he advanced stealthily up the side of the building, but it held his weight. He paused and watched as he reached the bedroom window. To his dismay, and cursing his incompetence for not having thought of it when he did his reconnaissance, the window would not open. It was disgrace, he thought, for had there ever been a fire, the boys would not have been able to escape. Using his considerable strength, and slipping a small penknife round the edge of the window where it had been painted over, he slowly succeeded in opening it a crack. Slowly, slowly he prised open the window as the school clock struck the quarter and then the half hour.

Cottesmore's bed was nearest the window, he knew from his research, so it would be easy to slip into the room. His heart racing, adrenalin pumping, he quickly flicked on his torch.

To his horror, he saw that the boy in the bed by the window was Judkin, not Cottesmore. The head boy had swapped with the captain of games. Judkin, a light sleeper, woke unexpectedly, saw the torch and let out a scream.

Quartus slipped back hastily through the window and started to clamber down the fire escape. But the iron ladder was rusty and ill-maintained. It snapped suddenly and broke away from the wall. Very slowly, with the terrified monk reaching with desperate fingers, the rickety old ladder swung away from the building and accelerated towards the ground. Quartus's body struck the hard earth like a sack of potatoes. The impact broke his back at the same moment that his groin was pierced through by one of the rusty spars.

Judkin, convinced by Cottesmore that he had had a bad dream, went back to sleep. Someone else shut the window. In the rising wind, no one heard the agonised monk's dying cries.

TWENTY-NINE

It was raining again as Gilbert Mortimer parked his Bentley in Victoria Road, Kensington. It was too difficult to drive into the mews in the dark, but fortunately he knew of a little flight of steps which allowed pedestrians to pass from the street into the tiny mews.

He knocked quietly and was warmly received by his sister. She had been expecting him after his call earlier in the day.

"You've come round at a very opportune moment, Gilbert, for I have only this moment received another letter smuggled out by my Henry from that dreadful school. Drink?"

"A whisky wouldn't go amiss. With soda if you've got it?"

"Think so. Gave the vicar one earlier in the week, but there's still something left in the siphon." There was a hiss as she filled a large glass with Bell's.

"There you go, cheers."

"So what's the news? "

"I've spoken to Richard. He's with the embassy in Paris, hopes to start extended leave next week. He's agreed we should move Henry somewhere more civilised. He's contacting the Dragon in Oxford and some schools in East Kent. I told him what a poor impression we had received on our visit to Saint Eusebius and how they had obviously lied to us about Henry being ill and so on."

"More than that, Veronica, but go on. I'll tell you what I've found out in a minute."

"Henry's letter is very revealing. The whole place seems to be turning into some sort of torture camp with bullying, floggings and beatings. There's a very nice couple who live in the gatehouse at the bottom of the drive. They've been very kind to Henry, especially after our visit when that matron woman seems to have decided to single him out for punishment by way of starvation! Henry goes there, with the senior boys, for secret meals. He has a mentor, a chap called Ambrose, who's done a wonderful job in keeping his spirits up. The matron found his teddy and destroyed it, which caused great grief and consternation, but Ambrose has been a tower of strength."

"He shouldn't be having a teddy at his age, Veronica, but go on. By the way, delicious whisky!"

"So glad. Yes, let me continue. We've received a letter from the Abbot telling us that, as the school has had to be quarantined for measles, they are proposing to cancel the Easter holidays and go straight into the summer term. They have asked us to stump up extra money for the time the boys will now have to be with them."

"I wouldn't fall for that one! They're short of cash. Plain as a pikestaff."

"We haven't. Richard and I are going to drive down and rescue Henry as soon as he comes over from Paris. It should be just about the time they were due to break up anyway."

Gilbert put down his glass and pulled a piece of paper from his pocket. "Let me tell you my news. Remember I wanted to ask Tom Kemp at the London if they had ever had a Miss Tremble as a trainee nurse before the war. Well, he told me something very interesting. Yes, they did indeed have a young nurse by that name. She was small, petite and very conscientious."

"Doesn't sound much like the creature we saw?"

"She wasn't. I'll tell you the rest. The real Miss Tremble volunteered for the Far East. She left London from Tilbury on a troopship in 1941. It was torpedoed off Singapore by a Japanese sub. There were only twelve survivors, and Nurse Tremble was not among them."

"So who the hell is this woman at the school?" Gilbert shrugged his shoulders. "And who the hell are all the rest I ask myself? The Abbot seemed sound enough, but who knows. That dreadful South African brute certainly must have a dark past. We didn't really see the other masters but I bet they all have murky secrets to hide."

"So they lied to us, all of them! Read Henry's letter. They kept him away from us, deliberately. Because they knew he would blurt out what a bunch of scoundrels they all were."

"We should tell the police."

"Why bother. We're bringing him home. End of story."

★ ★ ★ ★ ★

Lottie checked the copies of the photographs she had given to her boss the moment she got back to London. It had been a hectic twenty-four hours, as the laboratory people saw little reason to share the sense of urgency of her request. Shunning the lift, which was unpredictable at the best of times, she sprinted up the three flights of stairs to her boss' office. Selincourt held out a hand.

"Congratulations, Mrs Walpole. You did a wonderful job. We knew there had to be something there for the Russians to have suddenly put so many of their trawlers in the area. Trouble was we couldn't find the source of the transmissions. What a lucky break we had with your sister."

The commander was a submariner, and like so many of them he was a huge man, six foot four with bushy eyebrows and the sort of voice that left no one in any doubt as to who was in charge.

"I'm so glad to have been of help, sir" said Lottie. "I know Melanie won't mind helping us if there is anything else we require."

"No, Mrs Walpole, that won't be necessary. Now we know the source of the transmissions, half our work is done. Much more important to us, at this juncture, is that we find out the source of the information that's being passed to the Soviets. The encoding is of particular interest because it is of a very sophisticated nature, prepared by someone who has had considerable experience in this field. We are working on our records."

"My sister didn't have much to say about the teaching staff except, as I say, that a new man had joined this term, the Lent term, who had rigged up the aerial for his geography class."

"Did your sister mention a name?"

"Oh yes sir. He's called Charles Upton. She said he was a very nice man."

"Most traitors and spies are! Does the name ring a bell with you, Captain Sands?"

The senior officer shook his head. "No. None at all. We'll have Navy check all the records of those who might have been so trained and who have recently left the service. We'd better speak to our colleagues in the Army and the RAF, the latter might be a good place to start."

He turned and walked over to the window, puffing on his pipe. "Surely our friends in SIS should be brought in too?"

The captain grimaced. He had never cared for the rival service. "Yes, Chips," he sighed. "You'd better get them in as well."

* * * * *

Two days elapsed before the body of Brother Quartus was found. Leno was prowling the grounds with the pistol he had taken off the Spaniard, looking for rabbits, when he stumbled across the blood-soaked corpse. No one had asked about Quartus and why he was suddenly absent. The general feeling among the boys was that he had done a Campbell and fled the premises before the law could arrive to arrest him for some earlier misdemeanour.

The Abbot, however, had other thoughts. He knew all about Brother Quartus' sexual depravity with Thompson-Brown and guessed that there must be others in the school, either enrolled or who had left, who had been targets for the monk's carnal desires. Quietly he arranged with Mr Natterjack for a private burial in Horkinge churchyard for Brother Quartus. The boys were informed that he had died of a heart attack while exercising in the school grounds. No one believed a word of it, but no one on the other hand had the slightest idea what had really happened.

Life went on as usual; Miss Tapscott was called in

once again, this time to clear Brother Quartus' room at Herga.

* * * * *

Bentley signalled for Williams-Jones to follow. It was a few days after the disappearance of Brother Quartus. They were out on the roof, safe, they hoped, in the knowledge that Kite was engrossed in checking for anything missing from her room. She would be so puzzled about it that there was a fair chance she would not come out later and patrol the grounds.

They were taking a new route, pioneered by Oldham and Davenport, which involved climbing two vine-covered drainpipes with a difficult descent onto the roof of Secundus' cottage. It called for a fair degree of fitness and strength; Ward had procured a screwdriver and a jemmy from Carp's workshop. The school buildings were barred and bolted. From a small window directly above the Abbot's study, they climbed out, dropped onto the flat roof of the Memorial Hall and crawled round the side of the building, keeping themselves hidden behind the gothic crenellations out of the line of sight from the Abbot's study windows.

A gentle wind was blowing, and the school was covered in darkness save for a light in Kite's room. Williams-Jones crept along behind Bentley, carrying the coil of rope they would need to let themselves down onto the roof of the monk's quarters. Rosie had been seen heading towards the building; hopes were high that some seriously exciting viewing might be on offer. Their hopes, however, were dashed. No one came up into the bedroom.

However, the sounds of a furious row were coming from the ground floor.

"Quick, we'd better scarper" whispered Bentley. "She could come out at any moment. If he comes out too our line of retreat will be cut off."

They had started to climb up the rope when they felt something move above them. "Oh, gosh, the chimney's shifted!" hissed Williams Jones. "It could come down at any moment. On a quiet night like this Secundus will go berserk."

Bentley reached the parapet and pulled himself over, then pulled on the rope to ease the strain on the aged chimney. Williams-Jones had almost made it when the chimney began to topple. Bentley pulled him clear, grabbed the rope and they ran, not bothering to attempt to hide. The chimney slowly and majestically toppled on its side and fell with a thunderous crash through the roof of the monks' sleeping quarters.

From the safe distance of the crenellations the two boys squeezed each others' hands. "On a normal night the brute would have been right there with Rosie" said Bentley. "What a thought, the naked monk and the school tart! Now he'll think it was an assassination attempt."

Lights began to shine and torches flashed. The Abbot opened his window and called out. Miss Tremble, quickly awake, once again rushed out across the quadrangle. Rosie, scantily dressed, was last seen heading for the woods.

★ ★ ★ ★ ★

"What a dreadful thing to have happened." Brother Tertius stepped back to admire his artistic handiwork. It was a few days after the drama of Secundus' chimney. He had finally got his way with Upton after weeks of cajoling and inducement. Upton, naked save for a cardboard halo, stood at ease, relieved at being allowed to abandon the painful pose Tertius had demanded of him. He was to be the new Saint Eusebius, and it was this picture that would one day hang in the memorial hall.

They were in Tertius' large, comfortable bedroom. The gas fire had created a tremendous fug; it was the warmest Upton could recall being since his arrival at the school.

"The poor man might have been killed, indeed I am sure he would have been had he not been studying downstairs well after all our bedtime. I do admire his duty and his dedication to work."

"His beating of the boys?"

"Let's not touch upon what I know you find to be a distressing and distasteful matter. As I have repeatedly told you, it is in the tradition of the school. I suppose that, if one were to dislike it so much, one would have to leave."

"Not easy in these troubled times. Secretly, between the two of us, I would if I could."

"But that would be terrible! You're thinking of leaving us so soon, before even one term is out? You can't be serious?"

"I have a problem, of which fortunately you are unaware. Let me put it briefly – I'm being blackmailed."

"Whatever for? You can't have done anything?"

"It was in the war. My stupidity. I got too close to somebody."

"You were in the Navy? It was quite common for men to fall in love when they were faced with constant and terrible danger. I see nothing wrong."

"It's illegal, George. That is the crux of the matter. For a man to, er... have relations with another man. Maybe some day everyone will all be free to go and live in a country where it is allowed – like Germany before the Nazis came to power. It was nothing depraved, like Quartus and that boy."

Tertius looked perplexed. "Quartus and what boy? I'm not quite sure if I know what you're alluding to.

"You didn't know? Didn't I tell you? No, I suppose I didn't. I was too shocked at the time. I came upon them in the bathroom. They were like dogs coupling in the street. It was quite revolting, to me anyway."

"Well yes. I agree that inducement to such immorality and at such a tender age is not acceptable at all. This was Thompson-Brown, I assume?"

"Yes, I'm sure it was him, someone blond anyway, Quartus had him bent double. You must be right in your assumption, because the Abbot expelled the boy shortly thereafter."

"I wonder what really happened to Brother Quartus? He always seemed so, how shall I say, self confident and pleased with himself" sighed Tertius

"Not a nice character. Not a nice person at all."

Tertius, leaving the picture, came across and put his hand on Upton's shoulder. He had never touched him before, certainly not when he was naked. Upton felt a frisson of mingled excitement and revulsion.

"That trip I did to London was to see the blackmailer as a result of his threats to me."

"And you didn't resolve it?"

"Sadly, no. I found him repulsive, disgusting, filthy. He tried to seduce me after a rather alcoholic lunch. I refused him. He smelt of tobacco and bad breath, something I had never noticed before. He repelled me."

"He couldn't accept this?"

"He's moved into very left-wing politics. He's

pretending to support the Labour Government, but I suspect he is closer to the communists. He may well have something going with the Soviets, but I'm not aware of it. He worships Stalin."

"Most unfortunate! So how is he blackmailing you, this man in London?" Tertius put both hands on Upton's shoulders and started to massage his neck. "You don't mind?"

Upton shook his head "No, not at all. You are giving me great comfort, To tell you the truth. Without you, I have no one to turn to. I'm terrified that Miss Tremble will open one of the packets the wretched man keeps sending me and see what they are."

"And what are they, if I may ask?"

"You promise you won't say anything?"

"Of course not." Tertius continued to massage, moving his hands up and down Upton's back. "It will remain a secret between us."

"He is sending me encrypted messages which I have to transmit from the aerial I set up on the towers of the ruin. I have no way of knowing what they actually contain, but they are, according to him, special communications between units of workers' unions in Scotland and Wales; coal miners to be precise. They say it's vital that the security people do not know what's being planned."

"Another general strike, no doubt. That's the last thing we need!"

Tertius sighed and Upton felt him kiss him very lightly on his neck.

"It is so good of you to let me paint you for the portrait" said Tertius. Upton detected that, underneath his habit, he had a large erection. Tertius ran his hands over Upton's body and then down to his thighs, taking care not to touch his genitals. Experience had taught him that the younger man would eventually, almost certainly, succumb. His priority was to overcome Upton's fear both of his blackmailer and of the Abbot's hatred of homosexuality. He needed to calm him, ensure him that he had nothing to be concerned about and to give him the confidence to be sure that he would remain on the staff of the school.

"We should have worked on the picture, you and I, much sooner than this, but hopefully, now that we shall not be bothered by the Easter holiday, we will be able to make great strides." He continued to run both hands down Upton's thighs to below his knees, bringing them back up and over his buttocks, kneading them softly and gently. Such practice had worked with Everett; it should work with him.

Suddenly, quite unexpectedly given the lateness of the hour, the calm of Herga was shattered as the front door bell sounded. At the same moment the school clock struck ten.

"Damn and blast!" muttered Tertius, removing his

hands. "It must be that wretched Campbell losing his keys again. Wait, Charles, for I shall return forthwith." Straightening his habit to ensure that nothing would betray him, he opened the bedroom door. The front door bell continued to ring loudly. He stumped off down the stairs shouting "Coming, Brother Campbell." Vexed by this unexpected intrusion, he flung open the door.

It was not Campbell who stood before him, however, but Miss Tremble. She seemed particularly agitated.

"Yes? What can I do for you, Miss Tremble?" he demanded of her acidly.

"Is Upton here?" she barked, holding a large package in one hand. "This thing was delivered to us this afternoon. I want to see that man immediately. All this nonsense has to stop!"

The monk stared at her amazed. "Am I to be my brother's keeper, Miss Tremble? I only assume that Brother Upton has returned to his room, for I cannot imagine where else he might be."

"Sending secret signals to persons unknown would be my guess, Brother Tertius! Are you people here in Herga so isolated that you don't know what's going on between your fellow monks? I am astounded at you, you of all people who have a senior position in this school. Now where is Upton?"

They both called his name, Tertius loudly, hoping to give Upton a chance to dress. He appeared a few moments later looking hot and flustered.

"Yes Miss Tremble what is it?"

"This!" she snapped, thrusting the package into his hands. "It was delivered to us this afternoon for your urgent attention. What on earth is going on, Brother Upton? No one receives anything like this at this school. And don't tell me that these are more of your so-called medicines!"

Upton hopped from one foot to the other. Well aware that he had come close to being seduced by Tertius, which was the last thing he wanted, he had found the interruption something of a relief as well as a threat. He realised that he would have to come clean with this fearsome gorgon.

"No, Miss Tremble, they are not. It is all a ghastly mistake. Someone I know in London is sending me a series of tapes which I am supposed to transmit. In fact I have been putting them in the rubbish bin, as I shall indeed do with these."

"Oh no you won't! You won't get away with this as lightly as that, Brother Upton. You must show them to the Abbot and give a full account of your movements." She paused and scratched her head. "On second thoughts I shall do that, now that you have told me what they are."

She snatched the package back from Upton, to Tertius' astonishment. "Tomorrow morning, first thing" she called back over her shoulder, as she strode off into the darkness of the grounds.

"Come, my friend, for we have much still to discuss" Tertius whispered, putting his arm on Upton's shoulder. But the fire had gone out, and now Upton's demons had returned. Upton spent the entire night wondering what "punishment" Secundus would extract if he were to be brought into the picture by the Abbot.

* * * * *

Plans for the escape were well advanced, and messages prepared to be sent by telegram back to the school once they had made their home run safely and successfully. The first escapers were to be Ambrose, Dhering, Wydmark and Montgomery-Smith. Ambrose and Dhering were going to wear their uniforms and get away the night before the other two. Montgomery-Smith and Wydmark hoped that the ensuing chaos when the first two were found to be absent would give them the chance to slip away in the confusion.

Bentley, who had never favoured this timing, planned to walk out a week later, saying he was going to visit the doctor; he had managed to steal £2 from Jenkins' coat when it was hanging in the gym. The

Welshman had gone crazy.

"Serves him right for hitting us all the time!" laughed Pychley, one of the unfortunates whom Jenkins, like Quartus before him, was so obsessed in punishing.

In the hobbies room, Bennett perfected the cut into the candle which he had removed from the chapel. He had already established that the fuse would catch fire once the wick had reached it. He had calculated that he needed one inch of candle, after lighting it, before the fuse was reached and that the fuse would take three seconds to reach the petrol in the jam jar. They had gone over it all five times and so far only one failure had occurred.

Bennett was now confronted with two problems; finding the right place to start the conflagration and choosing the right time, so as to cause maximum damage without endangering either boys or monks. Carps had advised, unwittingly, that if one wished to burn a house down without a trace, the place to start the fire was in the roof. Bennett found this all extremely taxing, as well as dangerous, for it involved very careful research and reconnaissance in the area of the school forbidden to the boys.

He finally settled upon a storage area which appeared to contain boxes full of old exam papers, school accounts and staff reports. The advantage of this was that not only did it cover a large area of the roof, but it was easily accessed by a back stairs from the kitchen; one fire, one candle, would lead to another. Three candles should create enough flame to spread to the other places where jars of petrol could be put in place. It would have to be done when they were in chapel, when the boys would all be safe, the Abbot would be unable to see what was going on and everyone else would be distracted. The only other option was to wait until there was to be another flogging, but everyone hoped this would not come about, not least because both he and the escapers might themselves be the victims.

The day before the escape, Ambrose sought out Henry.

"I might have to go away suddenly, to hospital, if things go on as at present" he said, without elaboration. "But in case I don't see you again, as it is my last term, I just want to say how sorry I feel that I let you down about your bear. It was all my fault. We should have kept him in the school somehow, but I really couldn't think of where to put him."

"Don't worry Ambrose. I'll get my revenge on Kite one day, when the right opportunity comes up."

"We tried to cripple her putting wire across the stairs outside her room the other day but she only hurt her elbow. You and the juniors will find a way of bringing about her fall. Good luck!"

They had reached the bottom of the stairs that led

up to the senior boys' dormitories. Ambrose patted Henry on the back and sprinted up to his room.

THIRTY

Carps had made a very good job of repairing the roof of Secundus' little gatehouse cottage. With the help of Leno and Romano he had enlarged the skylight, improved the drainage and rebuilt the chimney, using old bricks and some wood found behind the school garage. Oldham and Davenport had done a reconnaissance run, using their old route along the inside of the battlements. Ropes hidden from sight were now fixed in place for subsequent viewings. There was only one fly in the ointment; Rosie and Secundus appeared to have fallen out, as they had stopped their usual trysts.

Late that night, the escapes went ahead as planned. Ambrose, Dhering and Wydmark separated and went their respective ways, Ambrose and Dhering to the station, Wydmark lying up in a farm and riding Jenkins' stolen bicycle by night. No one missed them until morning prayers, when Montgomery-Smith also made his escape.

All hell broke loose. No one had ever run away from Saint Eusebius before. It was not only wholly against the spirit of the school, to lead, to serve and to obey no matter what the consequences, but the Abbot saw it as a personal affront to his authority and his ability to administer the school to the standards of his predecessors. No one had ever absconded during Taylor Bradford's time as headmaster. What, the Abbot asked himself, had so provoked the boys to act the way they had when half of them were leaving anyway?

Games were cancelled that afternoon, lest any other boys tried to escape. Montgomery-Smith's absence had added to the general confusion, but word was put about by the seniors that he had said he was not feeling well and might have collapsed in the grounds. Leno and Romano were despatched to conduct a thorough search. Panic set in among the senior staff; the Abbot, Secundus, Miss Tremble and the elderly Tertius were all running round searching classrooms, dormitories and any possible hiding places. The discovery of the dummies in the beds only worsened the state of paranoia, and Bennett, researching possible sites for the planned conflagration, had a narrow escape hiding in a cupboard in the Abbot's quarters.

The police were called in to find the boys, a move which Ward considered a very bad sign. That night, before prayers, the Abbot warned that if anyone else tried to escape they would be severely punished and would be beaten personally by the Chief Disciplinarian until they fainted from the pain. Pointing to the window in the chapel, he reminded them of the fate of Saint Eusebius, who had been flogged to death for a far more noble cause; the espousing of the Christian faith. All the seniors shivered, everyone praying that the missing four would get through, but few doubted that someone would be caught, given the wildness and bleakness of the Fen country.

Secundus was clearly in high spirits. He marched round the school grinning from ear to ear, and few doubted that he would make an assignment with Rosie if they were back on speaking terms. Lots were drawn to witness their tryst, and Ward and Carmichael won. They crept out onto the battlements and took up positions on the roof just after nine that night. They were not disappointed. Rosie, her well-rounded young breasts bouncing, sat astride the monk, twisting, grinding, heaving, riding up and down, all the while digging her fingernails into his shoulders.

"What an enormous dick he's got!" whispered Carmichael.

"Like our horses in Ireland" said Ward." I've seen them do it loads of times. Gosh, he's changing position."

Two pairs of eyes watched intently as the huge monk, naked, rolled Rosie onto her front and mounted her from behind. Huge white buttocks, already lined with whip marks, were thrusting and heaving, faster and faster. Rosie's moans became little grunts and squeals.

"Is he hurting her? D'you think he'll kill her?" said Carmichael. Ward shook his head.

"I've seen them at it like this lots of times. She loves it. When a woman is being really fugged she lets out great cries of ecstasy."

"Never heard my mother do that."

Ward looked at him sadly. "Not everyone makes a noise, mind you. Rosie is still very young" he whispered diplomatically.

They inched forward for a better view, but this was a disastrous mistake. Seconds later, just as the huge monk and the nubile serving girl were reaching orgasm, the new roof, with its thin glass and cheap construction, caved in. Ward scrabbled back but Carmichael, losing his grip, crashed down in a shower of splinters and broken glass upon their steaming, sweaty bodies.

"Run for it!" yelled Ward from the edge of the gaping hole. "I'll let you in by the gym."

Ward ran back along the battlements, abandoning any attempt at concealment. He dropped down through the opened window and ran through the school, picking up a heavy fire extinguisher as he did so. From the gym window he could see Carmichael limping across the grass; he was cut badly. Taking the fire extinguisher, Ward smashed the glass in the window of the door and opened it, unlocking the bolts. He had hid the fire extinguisher and turned to go back to the dormitory when suddenly the lights came on and the grim figure of Miss Tremble barred his way.

"Just what are you doing Ward? Here, and at this time of the night may I ask? Are you trying to run away too?"

"I saw Carmichael sleepwalking, Matron. I tried to stop him but he's crashed through the door and he's terribly cut."

Miss Tremble, seizing Ward by one arm, dragged him away from the door. She put on the outside lights and at once saw the broken glass and the bleeding figure of Carmichael.

"Get back to your dormitory this instant!" she snapped. "Leave this to me!" Letting go of him, she opened the door and pulled up the stunned and wounded Carmichael. She marched him peremptorily to her dispensary and slapped iodine on his face and arms, heedless of his cries of pain.

"If I find out you too have been trying to escape, I'll see you're severely beaten, Carmichael!" she hissed as she hauled him to the headmaster's quarters. Then she resumed her search for any other missing boys.

★ ★ ★ ★ ★

The following day dawned grey and cloudy. The

thoughts of the seniors were with the escapers; lowers and juniors just wondered what all the fuss was about as they shivered in line waiting for chapel.

"Look at Secundus!" whispered Bentley, as the big monk strode into chapel, his face covered in plasters. All the seniors knew what had happened; Ward had told them. The big worry was what was going to happen to Carmichael, now placed in isolation somewhere in the Abbot's quarters. One of them had heard Secundus telling the Abbot that he wanted him beaten and put in isolation.

"They're keeping Carmichael locked up so he doesn't tell everyone what actually happened, but thanks to Ward we all know." Mr Ainsley struck up one of his regular hymns, *Let us with a gladsome mind, praise the Lord for he is kind, for his mercies...* "There won't be much of that round here if they catch anyone" whispered Carnforth.

The boys shuffled forward to yet another uninspiring session of morning chapel. In a last desperate attempt to save his friend, Oldham had slipped a note into Secundus' prayer book. It said tersely "If you beat Carmichael we shall tell the Abbot what you do to Rosie". To his chagrin he watched as the paper slipped unread to the floor and lay at the big monk's feet.

★ ★ ★ ★ ★

Brother Campbell was in a vile mood. Someone had broken into his room at Herga and removed yet another bottle of whisky; an empty had been propped up against the door on the running board of the Abbot's Rover. To increase his rage, a mysterious hand had again written: *Hickory, dickory dock/The mouse ran up the clock/Campbell's a thief/We know and believe/he'll soon be back in the dock.* Sixth Form Latin was never his favourite class. He found the boys rude, uncommunicative and wholly resistant to his whacking them over the head with their books; wrecked copies of the Kennedy Shorter Latin Primer lay in various corners of the room.

"Who wrote this?" he snapped, as the perpetrators hurriedly wiped their hands on their shorts to remove the chalk. "No one leaves this room until I have an answer!"

His threats were interrupted by the sound of wheels on gravel. A large black police car had stopped before the Abbot's door in the inner courtyard. "Anyone you know, sir?" said someone jocularly in a stage whisper. Sadly, before anyone could laugh, the cowed figures of Ambrose and Dhering appeared. The police seemed concerned at the welfare of their charges, while the Abbot was smiling and Miss Tremble, who had come out beside him, appeared to be giving her assurance that the boys would be well looked after.

"They're doomed men for the Lubyanka" someone whispered, as Campbell furiously erased the offending verse from the blackboard. "Get back to your work!" he shouted, evidently relieved at what they had all just seen. "And translate what I have given you today."

He pulled out an old copy of the *Racing Times* and sat back in his chair, wiping his brow with a dirty silk handkerchief.

★ ★ ★ ★ ★

No mention of the escapers was made at lunch, nor were they seen. A quick reconnaissance by the Lower Fifth established that they were not being held in the usual punishment rooms at the top of the building. No one knew where they were. Ward looked puzzled; this had never happened before.

They were sitting gloomily at lunch in the dining hall waiting for rice pudding when suddenly the door opened and Leno ran in. He was carrying a piece of brown paper, which he handed to Brother Tertius, who opened it at once. It was a telegram.

"An urgent telegram for Carnforth" he declared, to the surprise of everyone "Come and get it, will you?"

Carnforth got up from his bench at the far end of the room and went to collect it. He opened it and read it out aloud: "Your horse just came in first in the St

Leger, Wydders." He shouted to the others at his table. "He's made it! He's made a home run! Yippee!"

The senior boys, except for the scowling prefects, all rose as one and applauded. "Silence!" boomed the Abbot in a commanding tone. "This is wholly irregular, Brother Tertius. You know perfectly well that telegrams are never to be given to the boys directly, no matter how urgent they may appear to be."

Tertius, buried in confusion, began apologising profusely, while Miss Tremble, sensing a code, guessed the true content of the message. Campbell, silent at the end of his table, made no comment; he knew the St Leger was not run at this time of the year. He wondered why on earth the boys should have been so excited, so ecstatic. It was but a brief respite, a short flash of sunlight on an otherwise world of darkness. Before Grace the Abbot rose and addressed the school.

"Classes, after chapel tomorrow morning, are cancelled" he began. "We have a serious infringement of discipline to consider. As you know, a number of our boys have, contrary to school rules and against the spirit of Saint Eusebius, deserted their comrades in arms, ignoring their duty to serve, honour and obey. They have left the battlefield of the brave to pursue the route of the coward. They have crept away from the gunfire of the battle of life, from the eternal war of justice and peace between the forces of good and evil, to seek refuge as cowards, hiding miserably in their pitiful need for self-preservation. Tomorrow an example will be made of those boys, as we pursue our route to righteousness."

"They're not going to shoot them, are they? whispered Mowbray to Penfold.

"There's a first time for everything I suppose" replied Penfold drily.

"That's murder!"

"With this lot anything might happen. We never saw Thompson-Brown again. did we?"

"And you shall be witness" continued the Abbot, cranking up the menace, "to how such evil is to be removed, nay, expunged, from the bodies of those who are traitors to this school, indeed to the nation. And now, Grace."

Heads bowed as the familiar words were sung. Henry, however, kept silent, his face tense, his mind miles away. He knew he had to act, somehow, to save his friend Ambrose, the boy who had stood by him for so long. This was to be a public humiliation from which Ambrose might never recover. He'd seen the terrible thrashing poor Hook and his friends had received and this, from what the Abbot had just said, was going to be worse, far far worse. He somehow had to stop them, delay them, frustrate them.

A thought came into his mind, a wild one, a crazy one, but the more he thought about it the more he realised that it was the only option he had. Henry had

had a relatively good term despite the loss of Royston and the ongoing war with Miss Tremble. He was unaware of the plots and scheming of the seniors, though he had gathered that something was afoot from the few times that Ambrose had taken him down to the Carps' house for secret meals. He was accordingly quite mystified by the euphoria created by the receipt of the telegram. He was good at games, had made many friends and fortunately had had nothing to do with Brother Secundus, whom he saw as a brutal enforcer of Miss Tremble's directives. She, rather than he, was the target of his hatred, for she had done, and was doing, everything possible to make him as miserable as possible. His resentment was fuelled by her refusal to allow him to see his mother, who had clearly come all the way to the school to break the news about the death of his father.

He wondered what life would be like without a father at home again, if he was ever to be freed from what seemed to be his endless confinement to boarding school. Ambrose had been a tower of strength and had given him confidence in himself, though at his age he was too young to appreciate it; he did not absorb his metamorphosis from timid new boy to cunning, crafty and fearless junior.

Unknown to Henry, Bennett too had brought forward his plans. This was the perfect opportunity for the ultimate conflagration he had always craved. He would finalise his plans that night. Ward, thinking the unthinkable but mindful that he was too young to be hanged for murder, brooded upon another plan and kept his silence .

★ ★ ★ ★ ★

"Who's that man with Leno?" the Abbot demanded of Miss Tapscott as the teaching staff were leaving the room.

"I've no idea sir" declared Miss Tapscott. "I'll ask him. Leno!"

The Italian came running over "Si, Missa Tapscott? What is for Leno?"

"Who is that new man who was serving today? We haven't hired anyone new as far as I know."

"No, Missa Tapscott. E's Alberto. Romano, e 'ave to take Rosie to hospital. She 'urt real bad. She 'ave accident. Cut bad. Alberto is friend. E staying here."

"Another Italian? From the war?" asked the Abbot.

"No, sir. Alberto 'e is Spanish. 'E too fight in war with army but in Espain. 'E very good with knife. 'E fight for good people against Franco. 'E says 'e looking for traitors.

"Traitors?" asked the Abbot

"People 'e says let Franco win. They kill 'is

family." "Well he won't find anyone here. Didn't you take a gun off some Spaniard a while back, Leno?"

"Yes sir. 'E too say something about seeking revenge but I tell 'im 'e is lyin' bastard."

"Thank you, Leno." the Abbot turned away, lost in thought, and wandered from the room.

"What happened to Rosie?" asked Miss Tapscott.

"She 'ave bad attack. From someone with glass. Romano take 'er to Branchester 'ospital real quick."

"Oh I am so sorry to hear about this. I am surprised Miss Tremble was not able to help."

"Missa Tremble, she no wanna know."

THIRTY-ONE

A sense of urgency now engulfed the Lower Fifth. Where had the Abbot put the escapers? All the usual places were sought out.

"Bennett says he's ready and thinks tomorrow would be an excellent time to put the plan into action, especially if we are all in the memorial hall. He has found a much better place to start the conflagration and he is pretty sure it will succeed." said Elmden enthusiastically.

"Any idea where?" asked Pychley.

"Somewhere next to the Abbot's bedroom to begin with. Leno says it's at the back of the building. There's a lot of combustible material in a storage place just above it. Bennett has already soaked part of it with petrol. He has got the candles primed. He plans to disappear after prayers and before the "execution". He thinks it will take about ten minutes to light them all, by which time we will all be in memorial hall, including all the monks" continued Elmden.

"Do we have any idea where Kite and Primus have hidden Carmichael, Ambrose and Dhering?" asked Bentley.

"Still no news. There must be a secret second bedroom or something in the Abbot's part" said Elmden.

"Or the dungeons, right under the school? We've heard that there has always been something secret about the bit where the Abbot lives. Tertius once referred to it, in a history lesson, but he did not elaborate" declared Ward.

"So Tertius knows. Carps?" asked Bentley.

Ward shook his head. "Never heard of it."

"Primus could be keeping secret Nazis there!" beamed Elmden.

"Or more likely a whole lot of stolen money" suggested Pychley.

"That's Campbell's speciality" declared Davenport, intervening.

"Who's this new man, Alberto?" asked Elmden.

"Friend of Leno and Romano's. Spanish. Fought in the Civil War" said Bentley.

"What's he doing here?" continued Elmden. " I mean right out in this miserable part of the world. Spaniards work in hotels and restaurants in places like London. Did Romano know?"

"Said Alberto was looking for a Captain Forks or some name like that. He's also after Rosie which has upset them. They say he's good with a knife!" replied Ward.

"Golly. Kite! How do we get him to kill her?" suggested Pychley

"We have to find the prisoners first" Ward reminded them sternly. "We have to do everything we can to frustrate the plans of the Abbot and Secundus. You know they intend to flog Carmichael as well. We must get an anonymous note to the Abbot about Rosie and Secundus."

"Oldham tried that, to rescue Carmichael. His note fell on the chapel floor and Secundus missed it."

"I'll have another go" said Davenport. "I'll use an old typewriter that's in the geography room."

Davenport did as he said he would. Secundus looked at it briefly, scowled at the seniors and crumpled it into a ball and put it in his pocket. He clearly didn't give a damn.

★ ★ ★ ★ ★

In London, Commander Selincourt collected up a sheaf of papers and placed them in a large portfolio. He walked over to the office of his superior, knocked on the door, entered and saluted.

"I've ordered the car for six thirty tomorrow morning, sir. Driver Denise will be taking us down to Horkinge. I have had our people get in touch with the local constabulary to ensure that no one tries to make a run for it from the school premises."

"Excellent work, Chips. I congratulate you on your efforts. Tell me about the contact, the person they are using at the school. Mrs Walpole's sister mentioned a man called Upton. Any news?"

"Yes sir. As a matter of fact it was RCS, the Signals people, who confirmed the name. What is more, he worked with a man called Parker, who is very much under the microscope with MI5. Rabid Marxist, sheltering under the left wing elements of the present government. Upton and Parker worked together towards the end of the war. Parker lives in a dingy basement flat not a quarter of a mile from here in Woburn Square. MI5 have had him under observation for a number of months, but they've no record of anyone by the name of Upton having come to see him."

"Could have slipped the net?"

"Not impossible. What is strange, sir, is that the transmissions from the school seem to have stopped. Now we don't know whether this is because something has happened their end or because Parker, who we are convinced is the source of the confidential leak, has rumbled us and stopped sending any more tapes to his contact at the school."

"And?"

"We sent a phoney, a trap to draw in the Ruskies. Secret rocket testing off the Northumberland coast and all that sort of stuff, but they don't seem to have reacted. Strange."

"The contact at the school - any news?"

"Not from Mrs Walpole's sister. The local constabulary however have been pretty busy. Seems several boys have absconded after the headmaster declared that he had cancelled their Easter holidays and one of the monks working there is wanted on a number of charges for theft in the Home Counties. There was also a death recently. One of the monks was said to have had a heart attack. Last year they had a suicide; one of the boys hanged in the lavatories."

"Charming. What a place! Excellent detective work though, Chips."

* * * * *

In his dormitory that night, Henry slept well. He had neither worry, fear nor guilt. He knew exactly what he had to do and how he had to do it; it was the timing that was critical.

Thirty yards away, in the South Dormitory, Bennett too slept soundly; his plans were complete and everything was ready.

* * * * *

In London, the Hinghams made final preparations for the drive to Saint Eusebius. Food was prepared for Mr

Binks, extra clothing chosen and the old family MG saloon cleaned, oiled and fuelled for the long journey to the school.

* * * * *

The following day dawned bright, breezy and surprisingly warm. Henry winced as Miss Tremble forced open his buttocks and examined his backside. He loathed this daily ritual, which she seemed to take particular pleasure in executing.

"May I wear my sweater, matron? I am feeling very cold and I think I've got a temperature" he asked. She pushed him down the line towards the cold showers and turned her attention to Turnbull, who was next, shivering in the queue in the washroom.

"Feebleness will get you nowhere, Hingham , but if you must, you must. Yes, put on your sweater, but it's got to come off at games."

This was what Henry had wanted, for it gave him the extra cover he needed; his shirt alone would not have been sufficient. He had had a relatively good term, despite the loss of the battle with Miss Tremble over Royston. He had survived the cold and made many friends. He was unaware of the plots and activities of the seniors and was accordingly somewhat mystified by their overt jubilation on receipt of the telegram announcing that someone had won the St Leger, whatever that was.

With holidays now cancelled and a return to London and home ever harder to contemplate, Henry was eternally grateful to the seniors, especially Ambrose, who had taken him under their wing, supported him when his mother and Uncle Gilbert had called and had introduced him to the wonderful food provided by Mr and Mrs Carps. Ambrose had been a tower of strength and had given him confidence in himself, helping him to lose his sense of fear and subjugation. Larkin, a good friend, still remained permanently miserable and repressed. Henry saw the challenge and knew what he would have to do. Now he started working out, mentally and without divulging his plans to anyone, how he would achieve it. Not far away, in another dormitory Ward was thinking out his strategy, his timing and his specific objectives.

★ ★ ★ ★ ★

Upton was threatened on one side with exposure as a spy by the devious and cunning Parker, and on the other by Rosie, whose lies and falsehoods could lead him to a fearful beating from Brother Secundus. He was in no mood for confrontation with anyone, including the boys in his charge. Accordingly, when Henry declared in

Geography, the first class of the morning before prayers, that he was not feeling well, he was allowed to disappear to the lavatories in the changing rooms. He was lucky, for had he been in one of the other classes he would have been refused outright and told to put up with pain in accordance with the doctrine of the school.

Henry dashed out of the changing rooms and shot round to the back of the school, to the area he knew so well from his attempts to save Royston. Then he made his way across the grounds to the gatehouse lodge, using the route Secundus had taken to stop him reaching his parents. He knew Carps would still be at work repairing the roof and that Mrs Carps would almost certainly have taken the dogs out for exercise.

His mission achieved, he returned to the class quicker than he had expected and came back into the room clutching his stomach. Miss Tremble, on the telephone to the police, had seen the figure of a small boy dart by, but could not identify him; quietly she cursed, frustrated at not being able to give chase as the Horkinge constabulary pressed for more details of who had run away.

Carps continued with the major work of repairing the roof of Brother Secundus' house yet again. There was no sign of the recaptured escapers. No one had been able to ascertain where the Abbot might have hidden them, and no food was being sent anywhere unusual, according to the three men in the kitchen.

The Lower Fifth were becoming desperate; only Bennett, they hoped, could save the day. There were now only four hours to go. The punishments, the Abbot had decreed, would be administered after chapel that morning, just before the lunch break.

★ ★ ★ ★ ★

With heavy hearts and morale at a very low ebb, the boys trooped into the Memorial Hall, as was customary, with the juniors at the front of the assembled company, the more easily placed to witness the punishment. Mr Ainsley, somewhere out of sight in his windowless room, had already begun his rendition of the usual music, as the boys, with their hymn sheets, filed into their allotted places. It was just before eleven in the morning.

Bennett looked at his watch and nudged Pilcher. "Any second now!" he whispered. He feared that the noise from the organ would muffle the sound of the first explosions. Quietly he smiled. Yes, he had heard something in the distance. He was pretty sure the first of his incendiaries had gone off.

To one side of the stage, like cattle for a ritual slaughter, stood the three condemned boys. No one knew where Carmichael and the escapers had been kept; all were shivering and shaking with fear. Not only were they in the traditional black sackcloth, but each wore a sign round his neck that said in large letters: "I am a traitor. I must be punished before God and my school".

The Abbot himself approached the stage and repeated his oration of the previous day.

"Those who have betrayed you in their quest for self-indulgence must now submit to the ultimate punishment and be cast into outer darkness. They must be driven, cleansed, from within your ranks. No longer will they darken the doorways of our noble school. Long may Saint Eusebius survive and serve our noble country. Long may you too who stand before me carry the flag of freedom and lead, obey and serve your King and Country. God save the King!"

The Abbot, having completed his condemnation of the doomed boys, climbed down from the stage to the rendition of the National Anthem. He walked solemnly through the ranks of the assembled boys and, without looking back, nor taking his usual place, raised his right arm as a signal for the Chief Disciplinarian to begin. To the surprise of the four monks at the back of the hall, he did not stop to watch the punishment but continued straight out of the building into the quadrangle beyond.

Upton felt nauseous; it was the second time in as many weeks that he had been made to watch this barbaric ritual. Tertius watched impassively. What was awful, Upton realised, was that in the absence of the

Abbot, the severity of the punishment would be determined by Secundus and him alone. His heart went out to the boys to be punished.

Miss Tremble, a cruel smile on her face, mounted the stage and stood behind the whipping block, hands on hips, legs ready to hold down the head of the first unfortunate to be called forth. Secundus, swishing a new, long and particularly vicious switch which he had prepared early that morning, noted the Abbot's signal.

"Ambrose!" he roared above the National Anthem. "Ambrose, come forward!"

Ambrose, shaking with fear, shuffled forward, turned and mounted the whipping block.

It was then that Henry made his move. He had ensured that he was standing on the end of the row, closest to the aisle.

"Don't do anything silly or they'll beat you too!" whispered Turnbull, trying to restrain him. Henry moved quickly to the steps before the stage. Putting his hand inside his sweater, he shouted "Stop! Stop this at once!"

There was a moment of stunned silence. The singing stopped; no one had ever done anything like this before.

"How dare you challenge us, you insolent worm!" bellowed Secundus.

"Let Ambrose go!" shouted Henry again. He was absolutely without fear; this was now a war.

Miss Tremble, holding Ambrose's head locked firmly between her thighs, shouted "We'll flog you next, you filthy scum. Just you wait!"

In a flash Henry pulled out the object he had been concealing beneath his sweater. It was one of Carps' pistols. He raised it and aimed it very carefully at the matron. "Let Ambrose go!" he repeated.

Everyone craned forward to try and see what was happening. Campbell and Jenkins, aware that something was wrong, slipped silently from the hall. Only the organist played on vacuously in his windowless box.

"Drop that at once!" barked Secundus, his eyes blazing with rage.

Henry had never fired a gun of any sort and his sole experience was playing with toy pistols. Murder was not on his mind, merely to liberate Ambrose from the sadistic pleasures of the two school executioners. He pulled the trigger, the pistol jumped, and the bullet destined for the matron hit the garish memorial window, which shattered with a mighty crack. Secundus, fatefully for him, turned to see what had happened behind him. Ward, older, much more experienced, immediately saw the danger that Henry, in seeking his revenge upon Kite, might hit and possibly kill Ambrose by mistake if he fired another shot. He grabbed his .410, which he had surreptitiously smuggled into the memorial hall and hidden where he had chosen to stand, and ran down to the front row. He seized the pistol from Henry before he could fire a second shot and passed it quickly to Oldham, who was just behind him.

Levelling the shotgun at the monk, Ward opened fire as Secundus ran to grab it from him. Secundus, wounded just below the groin, lost his balance and fell heavily onto the stage. Miss Tremble, releasing Ambrose from between her mighty thighs, ran to assist Secundus, but Ward caught her squarely in the backside with the shotgun's second barrel. Roaring with pain and anger, Miss Tremble quickly scrambled back on to her feet, seemingly only peppered by the shot. But then Oldham raised his pistol and fired a second bullet directly at her. At the report a bloody, oozing hole appeared in the middle of Miss Tremble's forehead and she fell back flat on to the stage, her mouth gaping in silent shock as life and consciousness ebbed away.

There was a moment's horrified silence. Then a cry rose up of "Kill! Kill! Kill!" from the boys in middle school. "The assegais!" shouted Oldham. Melchett, Chiswell and Bourne led the mob onto the stage and prised away the six weapons from their rusty mountings.

On the floor, the Chief Disciplinarian continued to writhe and thrash in agony. Ward shot him again, straight in the stomach and Secundus gasped in shock and pain and slumped to the floor, bright blood pumping on to the boards. As the other boys started to stab with the assegais Secundus began roaring like a wounded Cape buffalo. He fought in vain to get to his feet, his boots skidding on the rivulets of his own dark, sticky blood.

The twin threads of terror and fear which for so long had maintained discipline at Saint Eusebius abruptly snapped. Anarchy broke out among the boys, all eager for sweet revenge. They stabbed and slashed with the assegais. One boy rammed the point of his weapon brutally into Secundus' backside, right between his buttocks. Upton and Tertius now pushed their way through the throng to try to escape the mayhem and blood lust of their charges.

Tertius was in tears. As he reached the door, Leno appeared.

"Meester Tertius, school 'e is on fire! I call nine nine nine. Meester Abbot 'e nowhere to be seen!" He ran off, no doubt to try and save whatever possessions that he had.

Great clouds of smoke could now be seen wafting across the inner quadrangle. Bennett and a group of friends watched in silent admiration. "There should be another two incendiaries to go if the fire spreads as I intended it" he told the others. "They should go off when the fire reaches the third window on the left."

Upton and Brother Tertius slumped down on a little bench outside the Memorial Hall. They both knew that there was nothing they could do to control the boys, wild savage beasts as they had now become.

Tertius took out a handkerchief and wiped his eyes. "I never realised there was so much hatred in their hearts" he sobbed. "After all that we did for them, looking after them and educating them."

"They have nothing against you, George" said Upton. "Rest assured of that." Upton had broken school rules by calling Tertius by his Christian name; not that it mattered now.

"You think so? You really think so?" Tertius looked up, dabbing his sad, spaniel eyes.

"Of course! You taught them properly, you never hit them or did anything like that. Look at your colleagues! What a bunch of scoundrels, perverts and sadists they are. I'm sure Miss Tremble had a secret too, she was always so awful to everyone. What happened to the Abbot, by the way?"

"He told Leno earlier this morning that he had to go to Branchester, to see the diocese and the bank about the school's financial problems. So unfortunate; I hope he'll be back soon."

The sound of fire engines could now be heard coming up the drive.

★ ★ ★ ★ ★

Colonel Hingham put his foot down hard on the accelerator of the old MG saloon. They had reached the last long straight stretch of the road across the Fens before entering the twisting lanes which took over near the coast. It was a warm, sunny, late spring day, and the whole countryside was coming alive once again after the gloom of winter.

"Do we have a time, or are we just taking pot luck?" he asked.

"I have a confession to make" declared Veronica. "I called the school yesterday, and that frightful matron answered the phone. She told me in her usual charmless manner that the school was not closing for the Easter holidays as they were in quarantine for measles. None of the boys, including Henry, was to be allowed home. We should have received her letter, she added with some sarcasm, informing us of this and that extra fees were now required to cover the Easter weeks."

"A ruse to get more money out of us?"

"That's what Gilbert said. I'm afraid I gave her some of her own medicine. I told her we had decided to remove Henry forthwith as a direct result of her appalling treatment of the boys."

"What did she say to that?"

"Oh some rubbish about their legal position and guardianship of the boys being made on a contractual basis."

"You mentioned what Gilbert had found out about her? The real Miss Tremble?"

"I thought we'd announce that when we get to the school."

"Hello, hello, what's this?" A black Wolseley police car had suddenly appeared behind them and roared past them at speed.

"Oh, God. Here's another one! Something must be going on."

He pulled over to allow the second police car to pass; this time it was ringing its bell. "I expect they've had a tip off. Probably some murderer lurking in the Fens. Good place to hide out here if you're wanted by the law!"

Veronica let out a little laugh. "It wouldn't half be funny if they were heading for Saint Eusebius to arrest that South African brute I told you about. He's the sadist who does the beatings, according to Henry's last letter."

"Could be a Nazi. There are supposed to be lots of them around. Oh, no. What now?"

A dark blue Humber saloon with Navy number plates had caught up with them. It hung on their tail for a moment, then shot past at the first opportunity.

"Good driver, woman!" observed Richard. "They look a pretty serious lot. Two big fellows in uniform with lots of scrambled egg and a civilian, another woman, up beside the driver. Either they've found some deserters or maybe some Russians have come ashore seeking asylum."

★ ★ ★ ★ ★

The boys, their thirst for blood sated, had run from the memorial hall to watch the growing conflagration. Only Ward and Oldham, realising the need to get the pistol cleaned and back to Carps' house and his shotgun hidden before the police arrived, took the other route from behind the kitchens. Laurie rushed over to look at the fire engines. Harwood ran by, waving what looked like a dead cat. It was reddish brown. As he passed them he threw it into the air with glee and caught it again.

"Look, Kite's scalp!" he called. "I pulled it off. Yippee!" He threw it at the others, horrified until they realised it was a hairpiece. Kite had been wearing a wig all along.

At that moment the two police cars swept into the inner quadrangle. Burly constables jumped out and ran past them into the memorial hall.

"Everyone safe?" asked a young one, stopping by the two monks. Upton shook his head.

"I dread to think what your colleagues will find in the hall, constable" he said. "The boys just went crazy. I can't explain."

The constable ran in to join his colleagues. The hall

was empty now save for the two corpses lying on the stage. Someone had pulled up Secundus' habit and thrust a second assegai posthumously into his rectum. From his little windowless room, Mr Ainsworth was still playing his repertoire on the organ; no one had told him to stop.

"Someone tell that idiot to stop playing!" shouted the sergeant. "And evacuate the building." He looked at the bodies and shook his head. "Who would have believed that mere boys could have done this!"

He turned to one of his subordinates. "you'd better get the detective inspector over here as quickly as possible. Who's responsible for this place?"

"An abbot sir, but we can't locate him. There are two other monks outside, shall I get them?"

"No. Seal this place and make sure no one comes in. I'll have a word."

"Our dear Abbot has left us just at our moment of c-c-crisis" stammered Brother Tertius as the police officer took out his notes. "I have only Brother Upton left with me. The other masters have deserted us and fled."

"And they are?"

"Brothers Campbell and Jenkins."

"We apprehended one of them, sir" interjected the detective constable. "He was hiding in the woods. He had a suitcase full of silver with him."

As he spoke the large blue Humber with navy registration roared into the yard and screeched to a stop beside them.

THIRTY-TWO

Richard and Veronica Hingham reached the main entrance to the school five minutes later. Their car turned the corner into the drive and started up beside the old ruined towers. As they climbed the bank and came out from the trees they could see that the main school building was on fire; great flames shot fifty feet or more into the air and a huge column of whitish-grey smoke rose slowly into the sky.

A policeman was running down the drive towards them; he signalled to them to pull off onto the grass. Henry's father wound down his window.

"There's been an accident sir" the officer explained. "We think the fire was caused by an electrical fault, but we're investigating." "No one hurt I hope, officer, the boys all safe?"

"Yes sir. Two of the teaching staff are not too well, but otherwise there are no casualties."

"Thank God for that. We're the Hinghams. We've come to collect our son."

"You'll find two of the monks talking to our officers, sir, just through the gates. Please keep to the side of the drive, we have more fire engines on the way."

"Oh, I do hope Henry is safe!" cried Veronica, as they both jumped out of the car. "Where on earth do we start?"

No one seemed to be in charge, but the boys appeared deliriously happy. There were shrieks of mirth, everyone pointing where the fire was strongest. Other parents started to arrive. Miss Tapscott was trying to give advice and directions in the mayhem. Richard and Veronica were watching, not sure what to do next, when Richard felt a huge hand on his shoulder. He whirled round to see Lord Ward, Ward's father. They had been at school together.

"Good god Padraic, how are you?" said Richard, surveying his old friend. Lord Ward's clothes had seen better days.

"Well, well, well, quite something eh? And there's still no clear idea of how it started ."

"Started what? The source of the fire?"

"Oh, no. I had a look inside the building before the Navy kicked me out. Two dead. One of them's a big monk, a frightful bruiser by the looks of things, apparently known as the Chief Disciplinarian. The other's that Tremble creature, the matron. Shot in the backside and the head. The boys apparently finished them off with the assegais from the war memorial. My boy is boasting that he shot the brutes himself, but he has always been a bit of a romantic."

"What are the Navy doing here?"

Padraic pointed to the towers. "Someone's been transmitting secrets to the Soviets. MI5 have been aware, but it took them some time to track down this place."

"Both those people were frauds" said Veronica "we checked them out in London."

Padraic Ward expounded on the situation "They're after a man called Upton, one of the monks. He's been detained. I was talking to one of the naval officers, the big fellow over there" he said, pointing at the large naval officer who was bending over the corpse of Miss Tremble with one of the policemen. "The so-called Brother Secundus is apparently a man called Praetorius Duplessis, someone whom the police have been after for years. He was one of Mosley's thugs – he killed a man. He was found guilty and should have been hanged in Wandsworth in 1940 but he broke out during an air raid, no one quite knows how, and then simply vanished."

"What about that awful matron?" asked Veronica "We know she was a fake because my brother had the name checked out. The real Nurse Tremble was killed at Singapore."

"Yes. That's even more interesting" he continued. "The boys pulled her wig off. The evidence has not yet been corroborated, but the intelligence people have a theory that she might be a long wanted Soviet spy, very senior in the NKVD who had spent time in Spain in the civil war. Her real name was Tatiana Borashnikova, born in Odessa in 1893. She assisted in the murder of Trotsky in Mexico and in assassinating a number of white Russian aristocratic refugees in London in the nineteen twenties and thirties. She was sentenced to death but was sprung by the Russians and went to fight Franco. When Spain fell she simply vanished. Everyone assumed she had returned to the Soviets and had probably been purged. The only anomaly is that, if she were a Soviet sleeper, why would she have suddenly become active only after the new monk started work? Given her past, and that she had a criminal record in this country, it is odd she risked blowing her cover," he mused, adding, "The Royal Navy's intelligence people have slapped a "D" notice on the whole affair. You won't find anything in the national press. They're dictating something innocuous to the local papers; unfortunate fire, two casualties, school had to be closed, that sort of thing."

"Does anyone have a clue where the Abbot is? Is he going to reappear to sort out this mess?"

"I asked that too. No, no one does. The school's got financial problems, so I've heard. There's said to be some legal business in the wind - lawsuit, that sort of thing.

"You don't think the Abbot's done a runner? What with the school's debts? He must have known who

Tremble and the South African were. What's to become of the boys? Where will they go?"

"Miss Tapscott, the housekeeper, is ringing round. It looks as if the Seaview Grange Hotel in Horkinge, that awful pile on the front, might be able to take them for a night or two until a train is organised for the London boys. There's only one old monk left of the teaching staff; he's helping."

As he spoke a Black Maria appeared. To roars of delight from the boys Campbell and Jenkins were transferred to it, handcuffed and scowling. They were driven off in haste.

* * * * *

A fireman emerged from the door that led to the stairs to Miss Tremble's room carrying a large heavy bag. He dropped it down in front of the two Naval officers. Commander Selincourt stepped forward to open it.

"What's in it Chips?"

"Just what we were expecting sir. Tapes, masses of them. When we have analysed we think they'll show that the Tremble woman was the key link in sending these signals to the Soviets. Mrs Walpole is arranging for a despatch rider to be here in half an hour to take them back to London."

"And the monk? Brother Upton?" asked Captain Sands.

"Confesses to being made to set up the structure by Parker, but says he had no idea what the content was. Parker had apparently been planning a general strike with the mining unions."

"Keep him detained at Horkinge. The security people are sending someone up to interview him tomorrow.

THIRTY-THREE

As Joyce and Ted Edmonds watched the boys trooping into their hotel carrying what meagre possessions they had rescued from the fire, they felt Christmas had come early. The income from the boys' board and lodging would be enough to repaint the front of the hotel before the summer season.

An air of excitement at their pending liberation, hung in the air as the boys tucked into hot lamb stew, mashed potatoes and boiled cabbage; they ate as if they hadn't been fed for weeks. Nobody bothered with grace.

"Tell us where they put you" one of the boys asked Ambrose.

"There's a dungeon under Primus' rooms. It was very cold and damp. No one fed us. We only had the Abbot's cat for company when it came down looking for mice." he replied.

"There was something strange though" added Carmichael, now dressed in new bandages for his many unhealed wounds. "We found all sorts of strange things, crates and boxes, all with markings in some foreign language."

"In Spanish, I thought " interjected Dhering. "It looked rather like Latin."

"And there were symbols too, with the hammer and sickle on some of the boxes."

"Wow! Perhaps Primus was a Russian spy after all!"

"And Upton was sent by our people to catch him out?"

"You three were lucky to escape your flogging" said Harding

"We have Hingham to thank for that" added Bentley

"Hingham and Bennett. The fire worked wonders."

"Shame my poison didn't get them sooner" muttered Williams-Jones with a sigh. "It could have saved us all a lot of trouble."

★ ★ ★ ★ ★

Miss Tapscott made her way wearily back to Herga. It was almost eight at night and she had had a very long day, discussing finances with the bank, arranging the pay off for the Italians and the extension of the Marshalls' employment; they would now work for the bank as managers of the site. She had left Brother Tertius with the boys at the hotel; it was the second night after the conflagration and a heavy smell of burning wood still hung over the former school. Tomorrow the school train and the parents with cars would take the boys home.

She wondered what had happened to poor Brother Upton, who seemed to be having a hard time with the security people for some reason. She hoped that it was nothing serious, as he had always seemed such a nice man.

Miss Tapscott, despite her tiredness, was nevertheless in an upbeat mood. Captain Sands had given Lottie a very good bottle of wine, a Puligny Montrachet, for all her work in bringing the Parker plot its demise. She had insisted on opening it and sharing it with her sister before returning that day with Captain Sands to London. She had also brought some very good news; there was a job becoming available in an office in London, not far from Berkeley Square, where the present incumbent was leaving to have a baby. Lottie wouldn't elaborate on the work involved, but she said the office engaged a number of highly intelligent single men who might be fun to know.

This news had stimulated Miss Tapscott, yet made her rather melancholic when she thought of the good times that she had had with her fiancé before the war. He had been so amusing and, she was embarrassed to think about it, so good in bed; his big hairy chest pressing down on her breasts, pushing her legs back, all the fun of secret illicit premarital sex, especially in other peoples' houses.

There was a small amount of wine left in the bottle

and, uncorking it, she gave herself a generous glass before turning on the radio. She was the only occupant now of Herga, but somehow it didn't worry her. She lay back on the bed and pondered what the future might bring.

Brother Upton returned to Herga a little after eleven that night. The police car had dropped him at the school gates and he had been forced to walk the long way up the drive; unlike the boys and Brother Secundus he had no knowledge of the short cut through the woods. He let himself quietly into Herga, passing Miss Tapscott's room as he climbed the stairs. He heard the sound of her radio, but Brother Tertius's room was clearly unoccupied. He felt completely drained, unshaved and filthy still wearing his monk's garment.

Climbing into a hot bath, he ruminated on the day's events. The whole time he had been in custody in Horkinge police station he had had only the foul language of his former fellow monks Campbell and Jenkins for company. It was the thin-faced man, known as the "colonel", who had stressed him most. He had no idea who this man was nor what he represented, but he was a very clever interrogator, probably a barrister by training. There seemed to be an obsession among the security people that a cadre of homosexual left wingers were working with Soviet intelligence and passing state secrets to those who were now the de facto enemies of the country.

Over and over again the thin-faced man had tried to trick Upton into exposing a deeper relationship with Parker, and to admit that he was in fact a committed homosexual himself, which was why he had chosen to obtain work in a boys' preparatory school infested with like-minded teachers, and that he and the matron Miss Tremble were working in collusion.

Unknown to Upton, Brother Tertius had been interviewed by the security team at the Seaview Grange Hotel and had in fact disclosed Upton's earlier confession to him of his hatred and fear of Parker and the blackmailing that he was being subjected to. There never was any relationship with Miss Tremble as far as Tertius could see, particularly in Upton's fear that Miss Tremble would bring about Upton being beaten by Secundus as he had so brutally done to their former colleague Everett.

Suddenly, without explanation, Upton had been told that he was free to go, that he would be taken back to the school and that, as he had done nothing wrong, he would not be charged with any offence. Lying back in the bath, almost asleep, he realised that the fear that had haunted him ever since he had come to the school had now left him. A dark cloud had been blown away. He was not a homosexual, and he would never be tempted by Brother Tertius again. He could now look forward to a much easier life in the south, where Margolis & Tring had pointed to many opportunities in Kent, Sussex and even London.

An unexpected cry of distress woke him from his reverie. It was a woman calling for help, and that could only mean one thing; someone was attacking Miss Tapscott. Maybe Campbell had somehow escaped from custody. Leaping from the bath and quickly drying himself with the tiny towel the school had provided, he rushed down the stairs to Miss Tapscott's room. The cries continued, and he rushed into her room expecting an imminent fight with the intruder, who ever he was.

Miss Tapscott, in a rather flimsy white nightdress, was crouching on her bed shaking with fright. Seizing Upton's arm, she pointed to the corner of the room, where a tiny little grey mouse was endeavouring to find its way to freedom.

"Oh, Charles" she gasped "Thank God you're back. Please get rid of it! It must have come from Brother Jenkins' room next door. He was always leaving food around."

Upton guessed that the mouse had probably gone behind a heavy chest of drawers, and he started to move it away from the wall. As he did so the mouse vanished, as he suspected it would. As he lifted the piece back into position, his tiny towel came loose and fell on the floor. He was now overcome with embarrassment at being stark naked in the housekeeper's bedroom. At least the regime at St Eusebius had toned his physique, a fact which Miss Tapscott could not help noticing.

"It's gone. Pity we didn't have the Abbot's cat!" he said, winding the towel round his torso very tightly so that it wouldn't come loose again.

Miss Tapscott had other ideas. She jumped off the bed, seized Upton's head in both hands and planted a long and vigorous kiss on his lips, forcing her tongue into his mouth. Then her hand reached down to undo the towel. As it fell to the floor, she stood back, hooked her slim fingers around the hem of her nightdress and drew it quickly over her head. Upton gazed in mingled shock and wonder at her naked form.

She seized him under the arms and fell back, drawing him on top of her on the bed.

"Now Mr Schoolmaster, it's time for someone else to give the lessons, don't you think?" she whispered. Then she rolled him onto his back and straddled him with a confidence and skill born of years of experience and a hunger imposed by six years of wartime abstinence. Upton knew that resistance was useless; not that he had the slightest intention of offering any.

Much later, soaked in sweat and locked in each others' arms, they slept soundly in the confines of Miss Tapscott's narrow bed. Neither of them heard the vehicle that came up to the ruins at three in the morning, stayed for two hours and then left as quietly as it had come. Only the Marshalls' dogs, aroused and barking, broke the silence, but they were ignored; the occupants of the cottage had more important things on their mind, if indeed they were awake at all.

★ ★ ★ ★ ★ ★

A clear blue sky and a warm wind from the south heralded the day of departure. Spring was in the air as the boys stood lined up along the platform looking expectantly towards the distant cutting from which the London train would emerge.

"Anyone own this rabbit?" shouted the stationmaster, holding up a sad and worn-looking little white creature.

"That's your rabbit, Turnbull? Surely it is" said one of the boys. He tugged Turnbull's sleeve and drew his attention to the stationmaster's offering. In the distance a whistle could be heard. Everyone picked up their bags.

"Yes, that's my rabbit" replied Turnbull. "He fell under the train when we arrived. They wouldn't let me pick him up."

"Well, don't you want him back? Now's your chance!" The train appeared round the corner, squealing brakes heralding its arrival. Turnbull shook his head and turned to watch it. "He can keep him. I've grown out of rabbits. I don't suppose Hingham would have wanted his bear back either."

"He shot its murderer!"

"I'm not about to do the same, Philpot. Remember Bentley, Williams-Jones and Mowbray, how they teased us on the train about our teddies? They were right, you know. The spirit of Saint Eusebius and all that. We've grown up."

"In a funny sort of way I shall miss Saint Eusebius. It was exciting, at least at the end. I don't know where my parents will send me now. Doubt if it will be as interesting."

"Me too. I think I'm being sent to somewhere in Sussex."

"It's an Atlantic!" shouted Laurie jumping up and down with excitement as the engine clanked past into the station. "Very rare!"

No one paid him any attention. The train stopped with a jolt, steam hissing from beneath the carriages; doors were flung open, everyone scrambled for a seat.

"We would have been swished next term, Turnbull. You realise that?"

"I wouldn't have minded. Everyone said it earns you respect to be swished."

Whistles sounded and slowly the train pulled out. Rude gestures and vulgar comments poured from open, grimy windows. Tertius watched silently as his former charges disappeared down the line. He turned and walked back through the station office, where Turnbull's rabbit now lay stuffed into a wastepaper basket. He walked out into the yard, where Carps waited to take him back to the school. There was still no news of the Abbot, Carps said, but the insurers had sent some people to look at the damage. It was clear that the school had been utterly destroyed and would never open its doors again.

Carps felt bitter. He had helped them in their hour of need and now, as he had predicted, they had nearly ruined them. He and Mrs Carps had nowhere to go, no job prospects, although Lord Ward was working on getting them a job as assistant to an agent somewhere in North Yorkshire with a fellow Brigade officer they had known in the war. He had, after all, found him the job as a gift for saving his life at the crossing of the Rhine. Regimental loyalties still ran deep after the agonies of battle had been overcome. They were not about to be discarded.

* * * * *

In the comfort of his father's car, Henry watched the flat countryside roll by with mixed emotions. He couldn't believe that Kite had lied to him so maliciously about his father, and he was pleased that he had had the courage to see her off for destroying Royston, for all the awful examinations of his bottom, for her locking him up and denying him his mother's letters. He chuckled to himself thinking how he and Ambrose had defeated her, how the school had outwitted the awful monks.

He wondered how the fire had started. He knew he would miss his friends, seniors like Ambrose who had seen him through the first awful weeks of term in the endless struggle against deprivation and discomfort. They had spent the night at Horkinge and Henry had stayed with his friends for the last time at the Seaview Grange Hotel. Henry's eyes were on the road, but his mind was miles away. He wondered how the others would be faring on the train. He would miss them; Turnbull, Philpot and the rest of them.

"We could always stop in Royston again, darling, and buy another teddy if you want?" his mother suggested optimistically from the back seat of the car.

"That's kind, Mummy, very kind. I did treasure Royston and he gave me great support in the weeks before Kite got rid of him but I've grown out of teddies now."

"Kite, you called her?" said his father. "What a funny name. I wonder who shot her. They said it was the South African monk."

The car bumped over a level crossing and turned left for London. Clearly they didn't know. Henry kept his silence. Now they never would.

POSTSCRIPT

A ray of sunlight fell upon the Vicomtesse de Beaugrande-Charente as she sat in a tall high-backed chair by the window of her enormous apartment in Buenos Aires. She lived in Recoleto, one of the smartest residential areas of the city, in a Belle Epoque late nineteenth-century building with three porters on permanent duty by the door. Her golden hair, with just a touch of grey, was rolled back and perfectly in place. Her dress, for it was high summer in January, was made of silk, almost certainly from one of the great houses, Dior most probably. On her hands and on her lapel glittered jewellery, Belle Epoque, discreet but very valuable. A diamond brooch on her lapel glinted and sparkled as she moved her arms. She had about her that aura of a very rich woman which at times can be so intimidating; she exuded superiority.

It certainly seemed so for Oldham, who had finally managed to track her down. He felt a twinge of nervousness. They had warned him at the clinic which the Vicomtesse owned, the Clinica Atletico, that she could be overbearing, cold and haughty, characteristics which derived from experience, maturity and of course her wealth; in some respects she was akin to those great French and Italian actresses who, having played steamy roles in their younger days, now adopted the air of the Grande Dame, the mistress to the great and powerful.

"I am at a slight loss as to why you wish to see me, Mr Oldham" she began. "You are not another journalist, I hope?" She spoke formally, coldly, with the slightly lilting accent of the Anglo-Argentine. "As you may know it is not in my habit to give interviews. Furthermore, as I have stated before, I am not prepared to discuss any matters relating to my family."

It was an inauspicious start. Oldham had rehearsed over a hundred times what he would say if he finally managed to meet this woman, but now words failed him. He scratched his head. The last time he had seen her she had been a young girl of twenty-two, stark naked and engaged in activities of a very intimate nature; over half a century had now elapsed. Where had she been, and how had she come to have so much money and such a title?

At that moment the aged butler who had shown him into the room reappeared with a note, which he handed to his employer.

"What's this, Colbert?" she said, taking the letter and a small knife from the silver salver.

"It came from the clinic, madam. I understand

Signor Roberto wanted your opinion." Poor Colbert was ancient, bent over with arthritis and balding. He wore the standard white dinner jacket of a manservant in Argentina. His shoes were immaculate, black and highly polished.

"He knows very well I am not disposed to discuss the business by correspondence or on the telephone. He must arrange to come and see me" replied the Vicomtesse, speaking in the *Porteño* Spanish of Buenos Aires.

The aged butler had turned to leave when the Vicomtesse issued a further instruction. "Bring us a bottle of the Veuve Clicquot and two glasses, would you Colbert?"

"Of course madam. Immediately."

Oldham watched as he tottered off, and wondered where he had come from and how he came to be working for this woman.

"You would like a drink, Mr Oldham, I assume?" she asked still extremely formally. It was not obvious how the conversation was going to proceed.

Oldham nodded. "I always enjoy my visits to Buenos Aires" he declared, settling back into one of the Louis XV chairs. "It is so delightfully European. Like Paris or Barcelona perhaps. It has style, unlike my last call in São Paulo."

"Yes" the Vicomtesse sighed "Latin America has many variants, many faces. Personally I like it here but somewhere like Costa Rica might be just as nice if one were to but know it. The Brazilians are badly served by their Portuguese inheritance. Rio, of course, is something else. My late husband, the Vicomte, couldn't leave the place alone." Quietly she added "You see he was gay. He found everything there he wanted and indeed much more. Personally I have never been attracted to sexual irregularities of any kind; they are so degrading. I trust you agree with me, Mr Oldham?"

Oldham, nearly choking, nodded in agreement. What hypocrisy! For one awful moment he wondered, after all his research and the information from the agent, if he had stumbled upon the wrong woman. But those brilliant blue eyes were unmistakeable. This cultured, glamorous woman had once been Rosie Robinson, the sex-crazed tart at St Eusebius. How fifty years could change a person

Colbert tottered back across the Persian carpet carrying a large salver with the champagne and glasses, which rattled nervously as he placed the tray on a small antique table. It was clear that Rosie had developed a liking for fine living. Remarkably, she still had her shapely figure, if slightly fuller than it had once appeared.

"But you, Mr Oldham?" she asked him, handing him a glass, "You have been most diligent in your search to find me. Please tell me why I am of such interest to you?"

It was the moment that Oldham had been dreading. How would she react to being reminded of her past? Would she take umbrage? Refuse to acknowledge who she had been before this remarkable makeover? It was a risk he had to take.

The last time he had seen her had been under very different circumstances; she had been stark naked, straddled over the body of the odious Brother Secundus. It was unlikely that she would wish to be reminded of her earlier life. He was comforted by the thought that while he, Ward and the others knew what she got up to, there was no reason to suppose that she had any idea that the boys knew about her private life; that the roof of the cottage caved in while she was in congress with Brother Secundus was the result of another boy attempting to flee the school not of voyeurs of her sex life.

Oldham knew He would have to choose his words carefully.

"For many years my business has been bringing me to Argentina, in times both good and bad" he answered, fixing his eyes on her face for any hint of displeasure, of impending change of mood. "On one of these visits our agent told me of a meeting he had once had with the writer Sebastian Pilcher. This man recounted the story of an Englishman, a clergyman, who had come to Patagonia with a young woman many years ago to escape some sort of persecution, though he knew not what. It struck a chord, for in my youth I was sent to a school in England owned and run by an abbot. One day this abbot disappeared without trace. He was said to have fled to Argentina, but I have no idea who this woman was who was said to have been with him, if indeed I, or rather we, are talking about the same person."

"So? You think this abbot of yours might have come to Buenos Aires?" she asked rather aloofly.

"That was the rumour, Vicomtesse, but then thousands of people came to this country in the years after World War Two." Oldham wondered furiously what he was going to say if she simply denied her past. Fortunately Colbert chose to make a further entry at that moment, shuffling across the carpet with a large envelope.

"They said you should see this at once, madam" he said. "It has come from the lawyers.

"Are you a lawyer, Mr Oldham? Perhaps you can help?" She handed Oldham the contents of the envelope, after glancing them it briefly. "I really find all these people so tiresome. It is I suppose the price of fame, or in my case, misfortune!"

Possibly this unexpected intrusion might be fortuitous; it might break the ice. She took a sip of champagne and sighed. There did not seem to be much evidence of misfortune in the way she was living now.

Oldham withdrew the contents of the envelope and ran his eye quickly over the contents. As a commodity broker he was used to scanning contracts with complex documentation. This was pretty simple by contrast; a claim against the clinic, and against her family as owners, from the family and relatives of the late senator and former state governor, Juan Valdes de Navarro; he had apparently died while having treatment at the clinic.

"He was fat, ridiculously overweight. It is no responsibility of ours that he should have suffered a heart attack while undergoing therapy" she said.

"Therapy?"

She shrugged her shoulders. "You know what I mean. We can all be grown up about this. You think they have a case?"

It was the break Oldham wanted. She could see that he had tried to help her, maybe she might return the favour, give a bit of information as to whether or not she was the former Rosie Robinson.

"I'm not a lawyer, Vicomtesse. I wouldn't know. I mean I don't know enough about Argentine law to make a comment" he replied.

The Vicomtesse seemed lost in thought; she drummed her fingers on the table beside her chair. Oldham guessed that silence was probably the best course of action. He waited to see what would happen next. At that moment Colbert returned and , picking up the bottle with unsteady hands, refilled the glasses. It seemed to break the ice, for suddenly she spoke, quietly, looking out of the window rather than addressing herself to Oldham, as if to seek solace, to relieve her herself of some onerous matter that was taxing her mind.

"My husband was a banker, very prominent in France. He was in what they call the private banking business and had access to many secrets. He had many interests in Switzerland, America, South Africa. He was close to the Cabinet in France, especially the finance ministry and Quai D'Orsay. He had many secrets. After his death.."

"He died unexpectedly?" interjected Oldham. He was surprised that she would divulge such an intimate, private confidentiality so soon. Maybe it was the effect of the champagne.

"Oh yes. He was murdered; by two rent boys, in a hotel room in Rouen" she sighed.

It was an extraordinary admission, delivered so casually. "I was forced to leave France and return to Argentina. I was granted half of the estate in France and all assets that were outside Europe."

"It sounds a good deal!"

She smiled wryly. "If only! It unleashed the Peronista wolves; greed, blackmail and extortion. This business with the clinic is just another example of their endless, relentless pursuit of taking from the rich.

However" she continued, flashing her bright blue eyes, "you came to see me about an abbot who lived in Patagonia?"

"Yes, as I was saying before you were interrupted, I had heard that you might have known of him, been with him at some time? He was the headmaster of my school in England, but I could well be wrong! He may well have married someone in England or out here. No one ever mentioned what age the lady was" he smiled.

There was a long pause, Then, unexpectedly, she got up from her chair and, still carrying her glass of champagne, walked over to a large bookcase which filled the entire far wall of the room. Oldham watched intrigued as she did so, her hips moving langorously; she had developed a Latin style of deportment probably derived from the many years she had spent living in France and Argentina.

She took a book from the shelf and walked back to where they were sitting.

"I think you will find this to be of interest in your search for the Abbot of whom you spoke" she said, passing the book to Oldham. "It covers the period of the great conflict in Spain and is an account of those who fought in it."

It was an expensively bound hardback publication, in Spanish, titled *La Historia de un Padre Perseguido*, 'the story of a hunted priest'. But what caught Oldham's eye was the name of the author; Rosalie Beaugrande Charente.

"You yourself wrote this?" Oldham looked up from the pages.

"Most certainly" the Vicomtesse smiled. "You know a little about the Spanish Civil War?"

"Only from the works of people like Hemingway. A terrible conflict, the gateway to the Second World War."

"People here in Argentina have no interest. I had to arrange publication myself. Some copies have sold in France and in Spain now that Franco has gone. I am always looking for new outlets. We must not just let history fade like a morning mist, can we?"

"Indeed we cannot" said Oldham, shooting her a direct look. "The Abbot appears here? You can help me?"

"Most certainly" she declared. "And your people were correct in directing you to me. I am the person you should see. The Abbot who controlled your school, Mr Oldham, was a very fine man, an idealist, a liberal who wanted to see justice for all men." She replenished her glass from the bottle which Colbert had left on the table, "You little boys probably did not know of his participation in the Spanish civil war?"

Oldham shook his head. There had indeed been Spaniards lurking in the grounds in 1947 and the mysterious crates in the vaults, but no one made a connection with the abbot.

"He fought so bravely for the Republicans. He was wounded at the terrible battle of Teruel and was rescued by some other woman to whom he said he owed his life; I never heard the name. You probably noticed that he had a limp?"

"We did. No one ventured to ask why. Frankly we were rather scared of him and of the other awful monk who beat us all the time."

The Vicomtesse continued without reacting this comment. "As the Spanish war worsened, the Abbot realised that not only would the Republicans lose but that the Russians had really taken over the fight against Franco. The Russians were executing his colleagues from the International Brigade. He found himself trapped, so he told me, between the two factions, but then he had some good fortune. You know what it was?" Oldham shook his head. "One day he was charged with transporting the wages for the Soviet commissars in a van. It was just before the fall of Barcelona." She smiled, as if recalling what the Abbot must have told her. "Instead he drove the van straight across the border into France. After hiding up in the mountains, he and a Spanish shepherd split the proceeds fifty fifty. That was how he came to buy your school."

She held up the glass to the light before continuing; for Oldham it was riveting.

"My father had been brought up by the Jesuits when

he lived in Spain as a child. He adored the country, the Spanish language and its culture. He was a great believer in democracy. He had many enemies though in Spain and in Russia."

"Your father and the Abbot fought together in Spain? How wonderful. I hope he survived too."

"Oh no, Mr Oldham." She turned and looked him squarely in the face with her brilliant bright blue eyes "You misunderstand me completely. The Abbot *was* my father. I suppose you boys at the school never realised this."

★ ★ ★ ★ ★

"The Abbot was her father!" Lieutenant General Anthony Ambrose stared at Harry Oldham in amazement. "However did you manage to find her, let alone hear such an incredible story?"

"It wasn't easy by any means" declared Oldham, looking at the assembled company. There were seven of them, from the final days of Saint Eusebius, whom Ambrose had managed to invite to the reunion. They were seated at a large round table in the Cavalry and Guards Club in Piccadilly, London, guests of the general, to mark the fiftieth anniversary of the demise of the school. Around the table, in addition to Harry Oldham, were seated Dr Wynn Williams-Jones, consultant anaesthetist at St Thomas', The Rev Christopher Melchett, Vicar of St Mathew's Petworth, Judge Richard Harding, recently promoted to the High Court, Professor Lionel Bennett of University College London and John Steatham, now a successful insurance underwriter at Lloyds of London.

"It was an incredible story" continued Oldham. "The Abbot fled to South America with her and they lived in Buenos Aires for a while. When things got tough for the foreigners with the Peronistas, they sought refuge in the wilder parts of Patagonia, well away from their tormentors. Rosie, no stranger to sex as we all know, and probably still in her late twenties, got pregnant by a local rancher. Life got progressively harder for the three of them. One day out riding the Abbot fell off his horse, broke his back and died of septicaemia. In desperation, seeking work, Rosie and her little boy moved to Buenos Aires, where she got herself employed as a secretary."

"Did she become a tart?"

"Good heavens no, nothing so demeaning. She was much more adventurous! She became the mistress of the number two at the French Embassy. He insisted on taking Rosie and her boy to Paris when he was transferred home. He tired of her, of course, but not before she had had a chance to mix with the great and the good."

"Don't tell me that's how she met the Viscount. I hope she improved her English!" joked Mowbray.

"The viscount was gay. I'll come to that. No. Have any of you heard of what is called a *maison clos* in France?"

"Some sort of private club, like a bordello" said Williams-Jones. "Only the best and most sophisticated girls for the most exclusive clientele; very private, very carefully vetted I believe. Very French."

"She got herself a job in one of them. That was how she met the Viscount's brother."

"After what you and Johnny Davenport saw her doing to Secundus, Harry, I should think she was well qualified!" laughed Bennett.

"The Viscount's family had a problem. He was a candidate for the Interior Ministry, but he was gay and had to be seen to be normal, straight and married for the French electorate. So this was the deal they put to Rosie; she would become the Vicomtesse, attend all the society functions and so on and get a huge fee which would pay for the boy's education, but she had to give up her so-called day job, or profession, so to speak."

"The French always handle affairs of the flesh with such aplomb. Being Catholic of course helps" declared Melchett. "Weekly confessions and a large payment to the clergy along with their privacy laws protect the most outlandish scoundrels. Look at Mitterand, Chirac,

Giscard and their ministers."

"I bet she screwed around though!" enjoined the Lieutenant General.

"That was maybe why the family shoved her back to Argentina when the scandal broke about the rent boys who murdered her husband in a threesome in Rouen."

"What does she actually do now, Harry?"

"Well, not a lot obviously, but one must never envy the rich. Everyone, not least her son, seems determined to get their hands on her money. She told me she was thinking of giving up the whole idea of living in Buenos Aires and was looking for a flat in Monte Carlo."

"I often wonder what happened to old Ward" said Bennett.

"You clearly don't read your *Daily Mail*" laughed Steatham "He's Lord Doneraile now, ascended to the earldom when his uncle was killed out hunting. His father had died much earlier, not unexpectedly, of drink. Very naughty boy; his latest wife, his third or fourth I believe, is reported to have slit the crotches of all his trousers, including his Savile Row suits, and passed round his cases of fine claret to the deserving poor in Ireland."

★ ★ ★ ★ ★ ★

The dinner had gone well; good food, excellent wine

and most convivial company. They all knew that they would probably never meet again.

There was of course one man no one had mentioned; Henry Hingham. Without him, their lives could all have taken very different courses. Henry it had been who had raised the flag of rebellion, so to speak, who had been imbued at an early age with that spirit of courage and loyalty that the Abbot was so dedicated in instilling in his pupils. Henry had done well in a military career, then vanished, as far as anyone knew; probably into one of the many branches of the Secret Service.

Thanking Ambrose for his hospitality, the men made their way slowly down the grand staircase of the club. "Taxi to Kings Cross anyone?" asked Harding hopefully.

"I'm on. Yes please," replied Bennett.

"Me too" said Steatham, "oh dear. I nearly forgot my briefcase." He walked across to the porter's booth, where there were a number of cases, and picked one up.

"Careful sir" warned George, the night porter. "I think you'll find that that one belongs to Brigadier Hingham. Yours is the next one to it, sir."

"Brigadier Hingham? Would that be Brigadier Henry Hingham by any chance?"

"I am not really at liberty to say, sir, but I have not heard of there being another gentleman of that surname and rank, certainly at this club."

It was raining hard again and there was no sign of a taxi as the wind continued unabated; across the park the lights of Buckingham Palace could be discerned among the leafless trees. Then, as luck would have it, a cab pulled over and disgorged some people right in front of the club.

With some difficulty, for none of them were exactly slim in their advancing years, they all squeezed into the taxi. It pulled out into Piccadilly and was quickly swallowed up in the traffic.

END